Stars and Stripes

S.N. Moor

Contents

Hey Dad

Here is your one page in every book that you can read. I feel like the girl who cried wolf with these. I keep saying I'm going to write a book you can read and then I don't. Super awkward. I know. I have readers itching to get their hands on the next book, and I'm a born people pleaser. I know! It sucks, but it's also so wonderful! The notes I get make my people pleasing heart so happy. I'd share those with you, but some of them are NSFD (not safe for dad's). Ha! I guess this book is a NSFD. I will have to create a new category for that! Any whoozle, I will quickly summarize this book for you.

It's summertime and Everlee and her friends decide to head to the beach for a beach getaway. Yay beach getaway! She's there with her brother and best friend and then her brother... Ugh! He accidentally invites their mother, but he doesn't think it's a big deal because there's no way she would come to the beach without their father... but does she? Well, you will never know! Just kidding. If you ask me, I will tell you. I won't do you that dirty. Haha.

As always, thanks for your support, even on the NSFD books!

XO

This book is dedicated to all those girls who want to be a mermaid just so they can get fucked under the sea.

Introduction

<u>Stars and Stripes</u> is the fourth book in the series. It's highly recommended you read Cupid's Contract, Bunnies and Bowties, and Rainbows and Unicorns first. If you haven't read those yet, stop here, because there are spoilers below (the title links will take you to the books).

In **<u>Cupid's Contract</u>**, Everlee meets her four delicious men who give her the time of her life and the confidence she lost after dickface, Rich, destroys her. The only problem is the men make her agree to only sleep with them two times before they part ways. By the end of the arrangement, Everlee gets attached but doesn't know how the men feel, so she honors the agreement against her own desires and leaves. She's scared of getting hurt again.

<u>Bunnies and Bowties</u>, picks up two months later. She's been absolutely miserable, and unbeknownst to her, so have the men. Lizzy, being the amazing BFF she is, gets her back out on the scene, but she runs into her men and things are as hot as ever. She wants to talk with them about a future, but she's already committed to visiting her family for Easter. We get to meet her eccentric brother, Beckett, and her mother and father. Her mother is hellbent on a marriage and grandkids for Everlee and uses every opportunity to remind her, going as far as setting her up on a date with a lawyer.

Everlee does her part but is missing her men desperately. The church her family attends is hosting a birthday party for one of their members and during the celebration Everlee comes face to face with her men (while on her date). They were all in foster care together a few towns over from Everlee growing up. Small world. As you can imagine, fireworks ensue, and Beckett picks up on all the sexual tension between them all and calls out she's in a poly relationship. Our favorite fivesome is formed and it is HOT! HOT! HOT!

Rainbows and Unicorns picks up soon after Bunnies ends. This one centers around Memorial Day and Pride Month. Sammie, a woman from the men's past enters the picture with a proposition for them that is hard to refuse. Because of personal reasons, Sammie has to go back to Texas, but offers to sell Allure back to the guys. Allure was their first successful business, a sex club, that gave them the funds to open Vixen and Bo's. Scared of how Everlee will react, they are hesitant to tell her, but when they do, she shocks them when she's excited about it. Sammie sets up a night where our fave five can visit Allure and experience Eden and Infernus (hello fave wood scene), two other areas of the club she added. While at Allure, Knox and Everlee participate in a Shibari demonstration that is... ahem... hot AF and we learn that Knox's nickname in the SEALs was Knots. In the end, they all decide to buy the business, Everlee included, so she's now an official owner of a sex club with the boys. Things continue to progress with the relationship and by the end of the book everyone says they love one another with hints of something more developing between Emmett and Jax. Lizzy is still in wedding planning mode so who knows what she'll decide about her wedding, and we also finally get to meet Betty's husband.

EVERLEE - STARS AND STRIPES

The insistent banging on the door grows louder.

"Evy baby, let me in!"

"You don't get to call me that Lizzy," I say, leaning across the sink to apply my fun new blue eyeliner.

"Why the fuck not? Knox does, and you melt into an enormous pile of goo." Her muffled voice sounds like her lips are pressed against the door and I wouldn't be surprised if she asks me to build a snowman with her next breath.

"That's his name for me, not yours."

"You don't want to know what my name is for you."

"Lizzy!"

"Fuck! Call me Seraphina and let me in."

"Are we back to Seraphina?" I tie the bow between my breasts before giving my girls an encouraging lift.

She bangs open-handed on the door, causing her ring to make a tick noise. "Let me in," she whines.

"I'm almost done."

"Huzzah! We're running late."

"Is there a reason we have to be there at a certain time? You don't have anything planned, do you?" A small trickle of panic tingles across my skin. There's no reason she would, but you never know with her.

"God no. I told you. The only thing I'm planning is my wedding. Well, and our vaycay."

Our vacation.

We leave tomorrow and head down south to a beach house for the week. I don't know how the boys swung it, but they're taking the entire week off. Loveuz is pretty self-sustainable with the management Jax has in place, Low is going to manage Vixen, Sammie is still in town and agreed to watch Allure, and Emmett is trusting his baby in the hands of a few head chefs. He's worked diligently over the last two weeks to make sure that plans and schedules are locked down in place. It helps that all the businesses are closed Monday and Tuesday for the holiday and Vixen is also closed the Wednesday after. The employees are super appreciative the guys are giving them three paid days off for the holiday.

Oh fuck!

My stomach drops when I realize my luggage is in the bedroom, unsupervised with Lizzy. Shit! Shit! Shit! Shit! Shit!

I give my ass a quick clench, to make sure the boy's gift and request is still tucked away nicely.

Yes. When I got home from work today, there was a note with a little box and a bouquet of roses and lilies waiting on my kitchen counter. Excited, I opened the box to find a shiny new butt-plug. The instructions, hand written by Knox, said to turn it on and plug 'er in. That was then scratched out and I can tell Jax took over, saying the same thing only more eloquently. I chuckled, because I could just picture Jax telling Knox to shut the fuck up or move out of the way. Those two make me laugh so much. Knox is so playful and loves to rib Jax, and Jax gives him the reaction he wants every time.

I love it.

I love them.

My boys.

Leaning over the sink, I check my mascara one last time, then tuck a loose strand of hair up in one of the many bobby-pins I have scattered through my hair. This afternoon I got a wild hair up my ass to do these super cute curls. And they are. Super cute. But fuck if it didn't take two damn hours. I kept telling myself I was almost done and only had a few minutes left.

I did that for one hundred and thirteen minutes.

Go me!

Sighing, I check for any other loose hairs, turn around in the mirror, check out my ass, then walk to the door. With my hand still on the lock, the handle twists and the door pushes open.

"It's about damn time."

I have this horrible tendency to hear words and break into song. Case in point... "In a minute, I might need a sentimental man or woman–"

She joins me and we both sing, "To pump me up."

Thanks, Lizzo! Such a catchy song that will now be stuck in my head all night.

The only difference in our mini performance is I curl my hand into a microphone and Lizzy curls her hand into a penis and begins jacking it. I swear she's like a teenage boy.

Once we stop our impromptu singing, she grabs me by the shoulders and looks me up and down. "Shut the back door, you dirty whore. I love it!"

"Thanks." Shut the back door has become her new favorite saying. It was shut the front door, but she feels like that's too PG for me since I'm a *dirty little fucker* and because I like ass play so much now. "Do you think it's ok?"

She grabs her chest. "I think it's wonderful. Your fantastic four will..." she bounces her shoulders from side to side thinking about how the guys will react. "Testy two will not like it. Tasty two will love it."

Testy two. The name she's given to Callum and Jax.

Tasty two. The name she's given to Knox and Emmett.

I nibble on my bottom lip. "You're probably right."

"Oh honey badger, I know I'm right. Those two are going to lose their shit, then drag you into their office and fuck you. So I suppose it's a win-win for you."

Lizzy's new favorite game is to dress me in outfits she thinks will set the guys off to see how long it takes before they drag me into their office. She even sets a timer. So far the record is twenty-two minutes, and that was on Rainbows and Unicorns night.

Tonight is probably going to beat that... not that I have made it into a game... because who would do that?

This girl.

This girl would do that.

I mean really, in a way it's their fault for getting so damn worked up about it and then turning me on with their 'touch her and you die' vibes. I've read about it in books and it makes my pussy tingle a little, but to experience it in real life times two. Holy shitballs batman. Paging Dr. Orgasm to Aisle fuck me.

To be fair, I'm not wearing anything overly skimpy. I'm wearing thigh high white stockings with lace tops, a pair of high-waisted dark blue short shorts that make my ass look incredible with three golden star buttons down the front, and a blue and white striped shirt that is really no more than a bra with some capped sleeves with a red bow in the middle tying the top together. Very sexy sailor patriotic vibe going on. It's close to the Fourth of July and it's a Stars and Stripes party soooo...

"What shoes are you going to wear?"

Excitement pulsing through me, I race over to my closet to show her what I bought. Rifling through the shoe boxes, I find the right one, pulling it out of the stack and bring it to the bed. "These!" I pop the lid off dramatically.

"Yes!" she growls, reaching in to lift out the red six inch heel. "Can I bang you? Damn. You're definitely going to end up in the office tonight." She laughs and I blush.

Seeing my luggage open on the bed reminds me of why I opened the door. The whole impromptu singing and Lizzy's reaction made me forget. I swear she's like a tornado. Whisking in and making you forget things, then she disappears, and you feel discombobulated and wondering what in the hell you were doing before her. My eyes scan the room, looking for any hint of foul-play from the queen bee, but all seems to be normal. When I get home tonight, or better, tomorrow morning, I'll have to double check my suitcase, because there's no doubt in my mind that something will be there I didn't place.

We leave tomorrow at two in the afternoon. Commercial. Ugh! Apparently, Michael Dufrey had to go back to wherever it was he and Brady just came home from so his plane isn't available. I don't know why Brady didn't go back, and I didn't ask. He seems to be ok, although we don't talk a ton. He keeps to himself, talking only to Jax and Knox, really, but even then, I haven't seen them really chatting with him this time.

Brady is getting the week to himself while we're gone, so he can relax and do whatever he wants. I don't know what that would be because he's like a black hole to me. However, even though we've said probably less than fifty words to each other, I trust him with my life.

It's weird.

To feel that level of a connection with someone you barely know.

"Are you ready?" Lizzy asks, standing in front of the mirror on the back of my door, lifting her boobs out of her top to perk them up.

"I am. Are you?"

"Yes, but let's get a quick selfie first!" She moves to the dresser and sets up her phone without waiting for an answer, then runs to stand beside me, looping her arm around me. "I set it up for three photos."

The light on her phone flashes, so we quickly pop our hip out and smile.

"Silly face!" She shouts, so we quickly change poses before the flash snaps. She waits a beat and when the lights starting flashing again, preparing for the last photo, she yells, "Motorboat!"

Before I know what's going on, she jumps in front of me and buries her face in my chest just as the flash pops off. I'm equal parts shocked and dying with laughter. "What the fuck, Liz?"

"I couldn't help it." She laughs the entire walk over to her phone. She grabs it and quickly flips through the photos. "Oh my God. Look!" She runs over and shoves the phone in my face.

Tears are running down my cheeks within seconds of seeing the pictures. Lizzy's ass is stuck out, while my eyes are wide with shock, looking down at her with my hands in mid-air hovering just behind her head.

"Definitely a keeper!"

"You need to delete that."

"Not going to happen." She chuckles, emailing it to herself. "This bitch is getting printed. Poster size, here I come."

"No, you aren't!"

She laughs, but doesn't speak.

"Lizzy?"

"No, of course I'm not going to get a poster print of me motorboating you. Could you imagine?" She has that sly look in her eye that says she's ninety percent kidding and ten percent serious if she can justify a use for it. "Perhaps I'll hang it beside the picture of Knox in the leopard print banana hammock."

"Jax would lose his shit."

"I know." She giggles, placing her hand over her mouth, before walking back over to the mirror to make sure her make-up isn't messed up. She pats her lips a little, then twists and looks at her butt in the mirror before slapping it.

"You had to get that one last smack in?"

"It just looks so good."

I roll my eyes and shake my head, smiling at her. "You're too much."

"Quite possibly, but you love me." She walks across the room and loops her arm in mine. She grabs my phone off the top of the dresser and hands it to me and we head out of the back door to a waiting Brady.

He looks as handsome as ever, dressed in his dark suit with his tan skin that makes his green eyes pop with a shadow of a beard. Wherever he went, he must have been outside because he came back ten shades darker and with a beard. I wouldn't have recognized him at first because he looked so different. In fact, when he first got back, he nearly scared the shit out of me because I thought someone was breaking into the guy's house.

"Looking very nice ladies," he says, twisting the button on his suit before opening the door of the black Audi.

"Thank you, Brady!" Lizzy returns with an overly dramatic gesture before sliding in first.

A smile plays on his lips for a second before he closes the door and walks around.

It's not that far to the club, and I told Jax we could walk, but he insisted Brady bring us. I refused to show them or tell them what I was going to wear, so I think he's being overly cautious. Several times, the guys tried to not-so-subtly warn against wearing anything too provocative, which I then kind-ly told them to go fuck themselves. I have my limits I won't cross, but I swear they'd have an issue if I wore a potato sack.

Once Brady walks around and climbs into the car, Lizzy peppers him with questions about his plans for the week while we're gone. If he's seeing anyone, if he's going out, what movies he's going to binge. They were all met with simple answers and by the time she got to the tenth question, I put my hand over her mouth to stop her.

She's excited for the trip, but sometimes her excitement turns her into a talkative little chinchilla. It used to get her in trouble at school because she would just rattle on forever and not shut up. Eighth grade graduation won her the certificate of most talkative, which she, of course, then stood in front of the school and gave an acceptance speech.

For six and a half minutes.

The principal had to gently walk her off stage and she was still talking as she moved her down the stairs, garnering laughs from the audience, which only validated her craziness then.

When we pull up to the side entrance of Vixen a few minutes later, Brady turns around, slinging his arm over the back of the seat. "Callum said he'll be waiting for you at your booth."

"Thank you, Brady."

We have a permanent booth in the VIP section now, after Rainbows and Unicorns night. Lizzy convinced them to add a numbered plaque to it and three guesses what number she picked and the first two don't count.

Yes. Affixed to the table is a small golden plaque with the number sixty-nine on it. It's the only table in the entire club with a number plate on it that is always reserved, so it's not super weird.

Since Rainbows and Unicorn party and my partial ownership in Allure, the guys have given me a key to Vixen that allows access at the side door, as well as the office. Lizzy, of course, thinks it's because they want me waiting for them spread eagle on the couch, or perhaps on my knees with my hands tied behind my back, but I think it's a gesture of inclusivity. They've all told me they love me and it's been pure bliss since then. Jax has even said it a few more times and is getting better about it. Even though he doesn't say it as much, he shows it.

Because of the side entrance key, Lizzy now thinks she's the cat's pajamas. So of course, she exits the car, pretending paparazzi are lined up ready to take her picture, protecting her eyes from the hordes of flashing bulbs.

The only flashing bulb is the street light that flickers because the city has yet to replace it.

She pauses at the door with her hand on the handle, glancing at her watch. "Ten. No, twelve minutes. I really think this outfit is going to have you in that office pre-tty quick-ly."

"You wouldn't try to make it happen, would you?"

She places a hand on my shoulder and tilts her head to the side. "Ev. Do you really think I'd do that?"

"One thousand times, yes." I swear, she's made it her mission to get me in their office on my back or on my knees every time we come here. She's like the best friend who likes to spend your money when you go out shopping, only with her, she likes to see how many dicks she can get stuffed in me. It's not a horrible thing... but, damn. I could understand why my pussy pleasure was her mission after Rich and I broke up, but now... I think it's just a game to see how far she can push the guys, mostly Jax. They seem to have this love-hate kind of relationship. They like each other, but constantly make digs or try to piss the other one off. It's usually Jax making the digs, because Lizzy is purposefully trying to get a rise out of him, but they both give as much as they get and Knox eggs it on. He thinks it's hysterical.

"Ready?" she asks before turning the handle.

With my stomach twisting in equal parts excitement and nerves, I nod.

"Let's go, bro!"

EVERLEE - DROWN ME

THE THUMPING MUSIC FEELS like home as it pulses through my body causing my skin to tingle with excitement.

"Home, sweet home," Lizzy sighs, holding her arms in the air.

We're in a dark hallway, with only one door to the right, painted in black and easy to miss aside from the illuminated keypad. Emmett showed me that room last week, but I don't remember much because my eyes were rolled into the back of my head. There were shelves. I do remember those, because he tied my wrists to the top shelf and then went down on me.

Heaven.

We decide to pass the set of back stairs that go to the second floor and do a quick sweep of the main floor to see who's working the bar. It had been Low for the last month or so, but I know she's hoping to get VIP tonight. I've said nothing to the guys about it, because I try to keep their work and our personal lives separate at the house.

Lizzy pushes her way through the crowd at the bar and looks down it before she turns back to me. "I don't see her."

I pump my brows. "Maybe she got VIP tonight."

"What can I get you both?" A man asks, sauntering over flashing a bright smile. He has tattoos on both his arms and a piercing through his eyebrow and has those boyish good looks with his blonde, spiked, hair. I think his name is Thomas, but he's only been here a few weeks, along with two others down at the other end of the bar.

With the upcoming vacation, the purchase of Allure, and the extra day they plan on adding to the week after Fourth of July week, they have stocked up on staff to make it a smooth transition. The club has absolutely been killing it lately, and Lizzy was right. The socials are going crazy over them and they have even allowed her to help manage it, since they have little interest and they know Lizzy will crush it. She's doing it in exchange for a free bar tab, which I told them was dangerous, but she's been surprisingly responsible.

The guys have all but faux-fired Emmett from working here, because between Bo's, Allure, and Vixen, he was running himself ragged. Low has stepped up and was recently promoted to bar manager. This was a big step for the guys, but I think they're starting to look at more long-term plans, which is nice, plus they've been working a ton and we were hardly seeing each other. Which may have been their plan all along, because as a result I've practically been living at their house, so while it isn't official... I've moved in. Most all of my stuff is over there except for a few items. The outfit tonight was pretty much the only clothing at my house, because I didn't trust Snoop McSnoops Knox not to find it.

Lizzy hands me a lemon drop martini with a sugar rim. Since Emmett has introduced me to Old Fashioned's, these sugar rimmed drinks are almost too sweet, but I won't tell Lizzy that. She still loves them, and I love her. So...

But I will have to switch to the Old Fashioned when we get upstairs with Emmett- it's his last official night bartending and even now he's really just supposed to be supervising. Fortunately, he's been teaching Low his recipe, since it's my favorite. I still haven't been able to sway Lizzy to the dark side, but it's ok. More for me.

The chilly edge of the martini glass hits my lips at the same time I feel a prickling on the back of my neck. I tip the glass up and savor the drink, before swallowing it and turning around to find those delicious fierce blue eyes staring at me from upstairs. His face is taut and his jaw is clenched.

He's not happy.

I wiggle my fingers at him in a flirtatious wave, and he returns my gesture with an unblinking glare. Oh, he's really pissed, which means I hit the mark. If he didn't want me testing him like this, then he should really work on that look, because goddamn, he's looking so fuckable right now. Where is Knox when I need him? He's my cheerleader when Jax and Callum are trying to control me.

Callum points at me, then points at the floor beside him, with staccato-like movements. When I don't move, his eyes widen and his teeth slip over his lip, causing a tingle to move up my spine through my nipples. The devil on my shoulder urges me to keep pressing because fuck... I need him to dominate me, but I will not go gentle into this great fuck. I blink slowly and hold my glass up, cheersing him before taking another sip. The drink nearly flies out of my mouth when the vibration in my ass catches me off guard.

That fucker.

I'd completely forgot about the butt plug.

The vibration stops and I look up at him, and again, he points at me to come up to him.

Excitement fans the flames within as I cautiously take another sip of my drink and turn to look at Lizzy and lean over to whisper to her. "Callum isn't a fan of the outfit."

She holds my shoulder. "Oh, he loves the outfit, just not with everyone else-" She stops talking and looks over my shoulder before pulling her face.

I slowly turn around and Callum is standing there with fire in his eyes. "Hello, love," I say, patting his chest.

"Everlee," he grumbles quietly. "What are you wearing?"

"You like?"

He continues to glare at me, his nostrils flaring with that look in his eyes.

Hunger.

Lust.

Dominance.

"I'm going to go upstairs," Lizzy says slowly, backing away.

"The fuck you will," I snap. "We're going to dance." I didn't want to dance before, but his look makes me want to push him until he breaks. Because, fuck. When he does... my stomach clenches. She tenses when I grab her hand and walk past Callum to land on the dance floor.

"Girl. I can feel his lasers on my back and I'm not liking this feeling."

"Ignore him."

"Have you met him? He's pretty fucking impossible to ignore on a good day and right now..."

A shadow descends around us, and I turn around expecting to find Callum, but find Knox.

Asshole.

Callum, not Knox.

He knows Knox is my weakness and has a way of getting me to do almost anything they want. I mean to be fair, in the end I want it too, but I want to want it when I want it, not when they want it. Is that too much to ask?

"Evy baby," he says in a low and sultry tone as his fingers trail down my arm, causing a wave of goosebumps. I've noticed ever since Jax all but claimed me on the floor at the Rainbows and Unicorns party, they have all been a little more open with their affection towards me in public. Or maybe it's been since the deal with Allure went through. We've seen several other poly groups there, so maybe they're realizing that it isn't as taboo as they thought? I mean, it's still pretty wild, but... I don't know.

I suck in my breath. "Knoxxy baby." These have been the pet names we've used since Easter. He would occasionally use Ali, but Evy baby was when he wanted to get his way. I don't know why, but it makes me nearly melt.

"I would really love it if you came upstairs with me."

"Would you now?"

He bobbles his head from side to side, like he's not quite sure of what he wants. Which doesn't surprise me since he rarely does Callum's bidding when he's trying to dominate me. A wicked smile curls on his lips. "Yes, I would, but obviously you have to make me work for it." His eyebrows pulse. "You can't just give in." A smile curls on his lips. There he is. My lovebug.

"Obviously." I reach my hand behind me and wrap it around Lizzy's neck and begin to rock my hips from side to side.

"Ev?" Lizzy asks cautiously.

"All good," I mumble.

Her breath stutters in her chest. "Shitballs. They're like vultures... watching."

When I follow her gaze, I see all my men watching me. Callum, several feet behind Knox, and Emmett and Jax on the upper level, hands with a death grip on the railing. Emmett is looking delicious, wearing a tight black t-shirt with the Vixen logo on it and Jax, as usual, is dressed in a suit that fits his body like a glove. A perfect fucking glove I want to peel off.

"Let them watch." My hand tightens on her neck while I snake my body down hers. "We'll give them a show."

"Fuck it," she moans, running her fingers around my stomach when I stand back up and I can't help but smile.

A techno version of the star-spangled banner plays, pumping bass into the room as we continue to dance. None of my guys moving. Her watch flashes from the movement, and I see her timer ticking up second by second. Nine minutes and counting.

Turning to face her and running my body down hers, I catch her worried gaze over my shoulder. A second later, I feel a set of hands on my hips and recognize them almost immediately as Knox's. Lizzy steps back and dances by herself for a moment, while Knox's cheek presses to mine. "Evy baby. Have you made your point yet?"

I snake my fingers behind his neck, holding his head in place.

"Ev," he groans, the lust dancing in his voice as his fingers grip into my hip.

"Knoxxy baby," I moan out, pressing my ass against his hips, swaying them from side to side. His cock is hardening, angled up in his slim-fit dark blue cotton twill pants.

"Fuck, Everlee. You're playing dirty."

"Am I?" I whisper back. "See, I think you are."

He chokes out a laugh. "How so?"

"We talked about this outfit and you asked me if I thought you should wear it. I told you no. And well... you're wearing it."

"It's patriotic. The pants are blue and my shirt-"

"Your shirt fits your body like a glove, hugging it in all the right places, and shows off your beautiful tattoos and biceps. When I saw you," I turn my head to the side so my lips are brushing his cheek, "You made me so wet."

He blows out a warm breath on my lips, fighting the urge to kiss me in public as we continue to rock and grind to the dance music, nearly fucking in the middle of the room with our clothes on, because one, if not both of us, will orgasm if we don't stop dancing this sexy tango.

He growls out a sound. "You better be glad we aren't at Allure, because if we were, I'd be shoving my hands in those tight little pants of yours and I'd finger fuck you until you came around them and then I'd make you suck it off."

A whimper pulses out of my chest. I was not prepared for him to dirty talk back to me. He's my happy, jovial guy, not this.

He spins me around in his arms, pressing both of his hands against the lower part of my back and brings me to him, placing his leg between mine so his thigh is rubbing on my... I sigh. "You asshole."

"I've been known to be one. Only exercising that part of me when it's needed, of course."

"Of course." And apparently right now seemed like that time. I'm so wet there has to be a huge fucking spot on my shorts to the point it looks like I've pissed myself.

He leans over, his cheek pressed to the side of mine again. "Are you wet for me?"

"Why don't you find out?"

He chuckles softly.

"Why don't you tell me?"

His thigh shifts in such a way that a quiet moan escapes from my lips. Thank God the dance floor is packed, so no one can tell I'm about to come apart.

My hand snakes up the inside of his red and white striped shirt, the ripples of his abs acting as a playground for my fingers, "I'm so wet right now, that even being a SEAL, and being able to hold your breath underwater for over two minutes, I'd drown you with my arousal."

He stops moving and pushes back to look at me, his eyes dark with need and want.

"Yep. Fuck this. Drown me."

KNOX - PLAY WITH FIRE AND YOU'LL GET BURNED

THE WORDS BARELY ESCAPE my lips before I grab her hand and lead her off the dance floor. We need to go, like now, before I fuck her right here and I'm so fucking close.

Callum asked me to work my magic to get her to behave and come upstairs with him to the VIP section so they could keep an eye on her. Although it's more like keep her ass planted on a seat so no one can look at her, but fuck that. She's a work of art and needs to be shared. That's where Callum and Jax differ from Emmett and me. I don't know why they keep trying to control her, because if they haven't learned yet, she will not listen. She's going to stick her foot in the ground and not budge, and I fucking love it.

I love her.

Ugh! So much so I want to shout it from the fucking rooftop!

I love Everlee McKinley. God help me!

She came to play tonight, knowing exactly what she was doing when she picked this outfit. It's not super risky, but fuck, she looks delicious in it. Her boobs are... there are no words. Just an angel's song, singing their praise. They're delicious and I just want to stick my face in between them and motorboat the fuck out of them. Even while we were dancing on the floor, rather, fucking with clothes on, they were just bouncing there happily looking up at me. I just want to rub my hands over them, squeeze them, suck them, bite them. So perfect.

And then those shorts.

My cock twitched before I even said one word to her. Girl knows how to show off her perfect ass and I swear they're so short I could probably slip my cock in the side and fuck her because I know there is no way she's wearing underwear. One it's Everlee, but two, there's not a single line over that smooth ass and for good measure I rubbed my hand across it, which was a bad flipping idea since it made me uncomfortably hard. These pants were already tight to begin with, but add my cock getting hard and trying to press its way up between the waistband and we have a guillotine situation. Does she not care for my cock, because I'm pretty sure my pants are about to strangle it to death.

I should have been better prepared for this situation because I knew... I knew! She wasn't going to just say, *Ok Knoxxy baby, let's go upstairs where I will stay in the booth all night and be a good girl.*

No. Everlee is only a good girl when she's either fucking or sucking our cocks. If she's not doing either of those things, then she's being her delicious, bratty self.

My hand grips hers tighter and I ignore the slight chuckle from her lips as I weave her through the crowd on the dance floor to the dark hall where we first laid eyes on one another. I should have known then, between the fire in her eyes and the condition of the douchecanoe that tried to take more than she was willing to give, that she was going to be trouble.

My Ali.

My Evy baby.

The keypad on the door at the end of the hall blinks green after I swipe my card. I push the door open and before it even clicks locked, I lift her in my arms and carry her across the floor. She instinctively wraps her legs around my waist, hooking her ankles behind. I know she's not even thinking about it, or trying to do anything, but it turns me on even more because I can feel her hot pussy pressed against me.

And I know she's so fucking wet, too. I can almost taste her arousal in the air.

I toss her on the couch and nearly rip off her shorts and untie the bow on her shirt, letting the thin fabric fall down to either side.

My fist moves to my mouth as I clamp down on my knuckles to prevent... I don't know, perhaps a groan, as if that would prevent me from blowing my load in my pants right now.

Perfect. Goddamn piece of art.

"So fucking beautiful," I mumble, leaning over, grabbing the outside of each of her perfect breasts placing my lips on them. I'd die a happy man if I was suffocated by these morsels, these peaks of love. Their size, their fullness, and her dark pink nipples are perfect in every way and they're currently asking to be sucked on, so I do the only thing a gentleman would do in this situation. I bend down and suck her right breast into my mouth, letting my tongue flick across her nipple until it feels like I'm about to chop my dick off.

Bolting upright and hopping off the couch, I drop both her breasts and undo the button on my pants and try to pull them down. Freaking amateur hour here. Why in the hell did I wear fucking slim-fit pants tonight? Yes, they look fucking amazing on me and part of me knew Everlee didn't want me to wear them tonight, because when I asked her, I saw that look in her eyes and heard the whimper in her throat. These pants made her hot. But I should have known. I should have known she was going to wear something like she did and that I'd want to get my dick inside of her pronto. I have no self-control with her and here I am, now, trying to peel these pants off of me and it's like trying to peel the skin off a kiwi.

She sits up on the couch and moves my fidgeting hands out of the way and drags them down. Her eyes twinkle with that sexy little look as a grin curls along her lips as she stares at my cock. My come is already beaded and glistening at the tip because she's so freaking irresistible.

Her eyes cut up to look at me, while her tongue swipes across her bottom lip before she sucks it into her mouth. Her sexiness has me immobilized in a trance.

She grabs my cock with her right hand, and her thumb rubs across the tip, wiping my arousal away before she sucks it off her thumb. A satisfied murmur vibrates in her chest.

I fucking love this chick with every fiber of my being.

My legs get weak and my head lolls from side to side as my eyes roll into the back of my head. Before I can look back down, I feel her warm mouth wrapped around my cock, her tongue running along the underside. My hands move down to grab the side of her head, but they freeze in mid-air. Her hair looks fantastic tonight. I can tell she worked hard on it and I don't want to mess it up.

Jax or Callum would have said screw it and would have just ran their fingers through it, but that's why I'm better than them, even though I'd never say that to their face.

See. Fucking gentleman.

He says, getting sucked off by her.

My chest clinches. Why in the hell am I thinking about them right now? She is licking and sucking on my cock like the queen she is.

"Evy baby," I pant out.

She slides off my cock and looks up at me. "Yes, Knoxxy baby."

"Your mouth. It's like a goddamn wet dream." I reach down and grab her breasts, the palms of my hands pressing on her nipples while the tips of my fingers grab the underside and squeeze. "And these breasts. I want to fuck them."

"Then do it." She runs her tongue around my length, getting it slick with her saliva, then sits forward on the edge of the couch and spreads her legs wide so I can move between them.

She wraps her hand around the base of my cock and guides it to her chest and notches it between her breasts and I let out a moan.

"Fuck them," she commands, grabbing the outside of her breasts and squeezes them around my shaft.

A hiss escapes between my teeth. Her breasts are so soft around my cock as I slide it up and down slowly, savoring the feel. She runs her fingers from the tip down the length of my shaft, making it slick with arousal.

Oh, fuck.

I thrust my hips repeatedly, driving up between her breasts as she uses her palms to press them in while her fingers play on the top side of my cock. After a few thrusts, she bends her head down and sticks out her tongue, licking the arousal that's seeping out of my tip like the good girl she is.

"Your breasts feel so good." I grind down, thrusting faster.

"So does your cock." She drops her breasts, grabs my cock, and sucks me into her mouth hard and fast.

The back of her throat clenches around me, causing a tingle to shoot up my spine. I'm so close to exploding. "Ev. I'm about to come."

She moans her consent, her mouth and her hand equally working my cock. She's not taking me as deep, because that usually triggers her gag reflex and causes tears to stream down her face.

The door buzzes behind me and I turn, expecting to find Callum, but Emmett walks in.

Her eyes quickly dart to him, then back to me, never stopping. She knows I'm close, and she's not slowing down. Our perfect girl.

"You were supposed to get her upstairs, not fuck her down here."

"I'm not fucking her."

"You're going to."

I look down at her, then back at him. "Am I?"

"You're sure as shit not going to let her suck you off, then just leave."

"You're right. You're going to fuck her."

"I came–"

"Already?" I tease.

That must have got Ev, because she's pulling off my cock, wiping her chin with a smile on her face.

Emmett lowers his head. "I came," he pauses, then continues, "down here to tell you to hurry it up."

"Perfect. You're fucking her. She needs your big daddy pierced dick." She takes my cock back in her mouth and I have to fight the urge to grab her head and fuck her face. "After you watch me feed her my cock and fill her with my come."

His eyes haven't left my cock or her mouth since he walked into the room and judging by the growing bulge in his pants, he wants in on this action. "Oh, God E. She feels so fucking good, wrapped around my cock. Her mouth is so hot... and wet."

"Knox," he warns, rubbing his hand over his pants.

I let out a groan. "Ev."

Her hand slips around and grabs my balls.

"Fuck!"

She gives them a tug and I can't hold back anymore. My orgasm lifts me on my toes and I explode in her mouth. There was still so much I wanted to say. I had this whole monologue planned I was going to lay out on E because I know how much he likes to watch and listen to the words and the sounds. Perhaps we can add a sex-sounds sound machine room at Allure.

She drains every last ounce from my cock, then pulls back and licks her lips.

"I love you," I say, cupping her cheeks and pressing my lips to hers before she can respond. I love her. Love her with every breath inside of me. Love her with every fiber of my being. My love for her is all-consuming and not simply because she is fucking wonderful and sucks my cock like a world class champion, but... she never asks for more than I can give.

My tongue swipes over her lips, remnants of me still there. I lean into the kiss, driving her backwards onto the couch, wishing to God I could fit my cock in her tight little pussy, but I can't, because it's only semi-hard. Why did I let her blow me? I wanted to taste her, be drowned by her, and she fucking flipped the script.

I blame my pants. They are the cause for this detour. Had I been able to get them off with ease, she wouldn't have helped and then my cock wouldn't have flopped in her face and then her little cock sucking monster inside of her wouldn't have come out to play.

There.

Pants fault. Not mine.

I'm not a selfish asshole.

Maybe a little, but I can fix it.

I will.

With her laying back on the couch, my cock is floating just above her pussy, and goddamn it is wet. My hips thrust, pressing the tip against her clit, and we both moan out.

I need to taste her.

I need her on my lips.

My kisses move off her lips and make the trail along her jawline to her neck, just behind her ear to her collarbone, over each glorious mound of love. I suck her nipples just enough until her back arches, then I continue working down past her stomach, kissing each hip, then pause over her clit.

My warm breath floats across her needy little cunt, causing her to wiggle.

I love torturing her as much as she loves torturing the guys. That look in her eyes.

That need.

My head drops down just a little more, and she's already moaning and I'm drooling.

Her arousal is perched on the edge of her pussy, inviting me in for a taste.

"Do you want me to taste you?" My eyes look up to see her panting, with her hard nipples framing her face.

"Fucking eat me Knox, and stop playing," she growls out.

I chuckle, wanting to keep playing, but... fuck that. I dive in and bury my face in her glistening pussy.

She cries out. Her thighs lock in place and her hands clamp around my head at the same time her back arches off the couch. "Yes!"

When I lick up her arousal from base to clit, I suck it into my mouth and her legs fall to the side, relaxed, giving me more access. Emmett shifts around me so he can have a better view with his thick, pierced cock in his hand, pumping it slowly. He won't unload. He's just teasing himself, for when he fucks her because he wants this pussy as much as we all do.

"I love you too, Knoxxy baby," she moans out.

Her words set a fire under me and I straight up devour her pussy. God, I love it. Her, the taste of her, the moans she makes. I would live on my knees at her pussy for the rest of time if I could.

My need consumes me, and I moan out.

"Knox," Emmett calls, but I don't look.

He's getting closer and I know what he wants. He wants a taste too, because he may be the only one who loves her pussy more than me. After pressing my tongue inside of her a few more times, I force myself to pull off her, just as her walls start to quiver and her hands clamp tighter.

Am I an ass for edging her for E?

Yes. But she'll thank me later when she's riding that orgasm into the clouds. E will take her there. He has the magic cock and the magic mouth.

"Do you want to taste her, E?"

"You know I fucking do," he growls back with hunger in his eyes.

Raising up on my knees, my hands glide down her leg, while I watch E stroke his cock, his arousal glistening at the tip and his pants abandoned by the door.

I press my lips to the inside of Ev's knee. "When you're done in here, for fuck's sake, please go upstairs." My words come out as a plea.

She nibbles on her bottom lip with a grin on her face. "Did you use sex on me to get your way?"

"Wasn't the plan, but fuck... you... and that outfit." I sigh and shake my head.

"Ok. I'll let you win this one time." She smiles and her eyes are twinkling with love and happiness.

When I jump off the couch, E takes my spot, settling in between her legs, but waits. I slip my pants on, press my lips to her forehead and whisper another I love you. She grabs my hand and brings my knuckles to her mouth and I'm fairly certain she would have said it back, but E was tired of waiting. Her back arches, her hand clenches around mine, and her lips fall open. I'm immobilized, wanting to stay and swallow her impending moans.

I pull my hand out of hers and place her hand on her breast, like I'm molding play-doh. She grabs, squeezing her perfect breasts, and I'm torn.

Fuck.

Leave Knox.

Walk out of the door.

But *her breast*, the devil on my shoulder, sings.

Fuuucckk.

My feet slowly guide me away, just as another moan threatens to bring me back.

I reach the door, hand on the handle. Looking over my shoulder one last time, her hands are wrapped in E's hair and she's holding him to her pussy, riding his face.

It's ok. We leave for the beach tomorrow for a week and I plan to fuck her and eat her until she has no more come left to give.

EMMETT - OH MY FUCKBALLS

THE DOOR CLICKS BEHIND me, and I don't have to turn around to know we're alone in here. Just me, my girl, and her pussy.

Watching her with Knox earlier was driving me crazy, not because I don't enjoy sharing. Because I do. Watching her with the guys lights my body on fire, but fuck, I wanted in there. I wanted her moans to be because of me.

Wasting no time, I swipe my tongue up her hot, wet center, causing her ass to grind down into the couch and her hands to clamp into my hair. Her response to me, to us, is addicting. Like a drug. She is a drug, and we are all hooked on her.

My cock is leaking, eager to feel the warm hug of her pussy like two friends who haven't seen each other in a long time... or since last night. I moan and hum against her clit and she returns with her own.

"Emmett," she moans out. "I want to feel your cock inside of me. I need it."

"You will, but first you need to come around my tongue, then you can come around my cock." I spear my tongue into her, licking and tasting, before I slip in two fingers.

"Ooh." She presses up on her elbows and stares down at me. "E, I really need your cock."

"I really need you to come."

She's stubborn, but so am I.

I work my fingers, pumping them in and out of her while my tongue presses and flicks along her swollen clit. "Come for me, baby. Come all over me. I want to drink you up." I press my tongue down and curl my fingers and she comes. So fucking hard, strangling my fingers and squirting into my mouth.

She lurches off the couch, hands clasped around my head, holding me to her pussy, as she shatters into a thousand delicious pieces. I pull my fingers out, grip her ass, and lift her off the couch to my face, serving her pussy to me like it's a piece of watermelon and I'm in a contest to win first place.

Not slowing down, I continue to lick and suck, swallowing her down until she collapses with bones made of rubber onto the couch. There's nothing better than her orgasm, the way she takes it, the way she moans, the way her pussy quivers like it's feeling too much. And her look. The one in her eyes as she's coming. It's like they're unfocused and her mind is somewhere else. An out-of-body experience and then she comes crashing back down a second later with so many emotions and feelings her body doesn't know what to do. Doesn't know how to process. So it just makes these noises as her body seizes into this tiny little ball.

I climb up her body, my dripping cock sliding against her wet pussy, as her satiated gaze falls onto my face.

"Hey beautiful," I say, brushing the few strands of hair off her face before taking her lips in a soft kiss. She moans, pressing her body against me, tilting her chin up, eager for more. The fact her release is still on my tongue and she's lapping it up is so fucking hot.

My cock presses at her entrance and she greedily shifts her hips to take me, but I shift up and she lets out a frustrated growl, causing me to laugh.

"Eager beaver."

She presses her head back into the couch, staring at me, shocked.

I kiss just to the left of her lips, then on the other side.

"I need your cock, Emmett. I need to feel it inside of me."

"I know what you need, Trouble. I always know what you need."

Fighting the urge to sink my cock into her, I sit back, creating distance between us, and she scrambles to sit up.

"What are you doing?" she pants, worried. "If I wasn't clear. I need your cock," she says each word slowly and clearly.

I smile at her. "So then take it." I motion for her to sit on my lap and ride me and a smile spreads across her lips.

"Thank you, daddy," she teases.

I chuckle, shaking my head. "So we're clear buttercup. I'm not your daddy, so don't call me that, because the things I want to do to you…" I simply sigh, because I need time to formulate the list. "I want to feel your wet, tight pussy sinking onto my cock, until it presses so far inside of you that you can feel it in your throat. I want you to ride it so fucking hard with your tits in my mouth and my finger up your perfectly tight ass, making you moan my name. I want you to strangle my cock with your pussy and then come all over it. And then I want to fill you with my come. I want it to drip out of you all night."

She looks at me, eyes wide, and throws her leg over my lap. "Fuck me." Her hands loop around the back of my head and I shake my head slowly from side to side.

"Not tonight, baby. You're driving."

A smile curls on her lips. She lowers, so my cock is pressed right at her entrance, then stops, teasing me.

I link my fingers and place them behind my head and watch her, not playing her game.

Her brows quirk up, waiting.

"I'm not working tonight. It's my last night officially, and Low is running everything, so I'm fine to wait here and feel your arousal slowly seeping out of you onto my cock."

"Asshole."

"I do love them. Yours especially." I wink.

She huffs, then sinks down, taking my cock in her tight little pussy and we both moan out.

Oh my fuckballs.

EVERLEE - HERE A TOOT, THERE A TOOT, EVERYWHERE A TOOT TOOT

THERE IS NOTHING BETTER than that first thrust in, as my body stretches around him, feeling every delicious ripple of his Jacob's ladder piercing. My head falls back as I sink all the way down his thick shaft, taking him to the hilt.

My head swings back up like it's being pulled by an invisible rope so I can watch him. He's nibbling on his bottom lip and I just want to suck it out of his mouth. His shirt is still on or else I'd be playing with his nipple ring right now. I know how much he loves it when I flick and suck it.

I grind my pussy on him, then pull up, sinking back down again. "You're so fucking big."

He brushes the hair off my shoulder and just stares at me, completely enraptured.

Wanting more friction, I start to bounce on his cock, but I'm not getting the speed I want, rather need.

"Do you want some help, love?"

"Yes," I nearly plead out.

He lifts me off of him with ease, sitting me on the couch and climbs off. "Flip around. Hands on the back. I'm going to fuck your pussy so hard."

"Please." I almost add daddy to the end as a joke, but I don't want to risk him leaving me wet and wanting as a punishment.

He presses his cock at my entrances and punches it in.

"Oh my fucking God!" I cry out as my back arches up.

His fingers dig into my hips, holding me in place as he drags his cock out, savoring the feeling before punching in again, reaching new depths. "Take my cock."

"Yes, please."

He thrusts in several times, getting faster and faster. Another wave is building inside, threatening to be bigger, louder, and stronger than the last.

I'm wearing this outfit every damn time.

"You feel so good. I love sinking my cock into you. It feels like home."

"It is your home. I'm your home."

"I know." His thrusts pick up speed, getting faster and deeper.

He releases my right hip and a second later I feel a slap on my ass, the sting quickly muted by the sensations and feelings in my greedy little kumquat. That's what I've been calling her since that one sexcapade with Jax and me a few weeks ago with the fruit bowl in the kitchen.

His hand returns to my side as he fucks me with everything he has. He feels so good, working his cock and those rings, rubbing them along all the right areas inside of me. He brings me back onto his cock several more times and then his right hand slides to the front between my legs, where he plays with my clit.

"Oh, goddamn E." My arms are weak and they slide off the back of the couch. I fall forward, head at the crease, doing a fucked up version of the downward dog.

"Ev?"

"Don't stop," I pant out. "Arms are just tired."

"You sure?"

My boneless arms flop behind me, reaching to grab his ass and bring it in to me. Once he moves again, they fall like the limp noodles they are.

"I'm about to come."

I press my hands into the couch, pressing back into him, and feel his cock explode in my pussy, triggering my own release. My legs turn to jelly and I stumble briefly, but not too far, since his cock is currently spearing me.

He lifts me up, wrapping his arms around my waist and spins us around and sits down. His cock presses inside of me as we sit and the loudest fucking pussy fart escapes. But not just like a regular fart, quick and over. No, this mother fucking fart plays a whole fucking symphony then comes back for a flipping encore. A little pfft pfft on the end like the little engine that could.

"Oh, my... shit. I'm." Fucking speechless. That's what I am. I'm probably an inferno on his lap because my body is flushing all sorts of red, looking like a fucking neon red glow stick.

Fuck me.

I'm terrified to move, unsure of what's going to come out.

"Are you done?" There's a hint of humor in his voice, but I'm still too mortified to look at him.

I have to leave them.

There's no way I can stay now.

Will he- they, because there's no doubt this will be shared, be able to look at me again without fear of a symphonic reprisal?

"I."

His hand slides up to my cheek, and he turns my head to face him. "Are you embarrassed?"

"Are you shitting me right now?"

His brow furrows. "You are. Babe. You don't need to be. That could happen to any of us."

"You don't have a vagina that's like a fucking Hoover vacuum sucking up all the air in the room, then blowing it out on a cock."

He laughs. "No. I don't have a vagina, but... it's normal."

"It's normal to play Beethoven's 5th symphony on your cock."

"Well, that is a first, technically."

Mortified, I turn back around.

"It is normal. The way you were bent over at the end... taking my cock." He gooches my side a bit.

"No amount of dirty sex talk can make this better."

He wiggles and another small toot escapes. "Fucking Christ. Is my vagina a bagpipe right now, storing up all the air? Am I going to be walking around on the dance floor tooting? Here a toot, there a toot, everywhere a toot toot?"

He grabs my hips and rocks me around from side to side, back and forth. "Look at that. You can call my cock the toot be gone."

I roll my eyes, still slumped over on his cock, head in my hands.

After a moment, he plants a kiss on my neck and hooks the fallen piece of hair up into the Bobby-pin. Shit! I'm pretty sure that downward doggy fucked up my hair.

"Damn it."

"What's wrong, love?" He lifts me from his cock and we both stand.

I keep waiting for another little pussy fart to present itself, but it doesn't.

"Babe. Seriously. Please stop worrying. If I'm being honest. I kind of liked the way it felt."

My eyes tilt up to rest on his.

"Seriously, I kind of want you to do it again."

A smile spreads across my face as my chest swells with love for this man. Here he is trying to make me feel comfortable...

"You're a kinky fucker, so I can't tell if you're being serious or not."

He laughs, pulling me into his arms. "You'll never know." He presses his lips to my forehead. "I love you, Trouble."

"I love you, too."

"And I love your pussy farts."

"Shit!" I swat at his chest and he lets out another infectious laugh and I can't help but smile.

EVERLEE - THIS IS WHAT BEST FRIENDS ARE FOR

I'M SITTING IN OUR VIP booth twenty minutes later. That's how long I take to clean myself up and get myself to leave the privacy of my embarrassment filled room. Emmett, being the amazing guy he is, tries to stay around and offer words of encouragement, but they don't help. I think if it was just a little one or a little pew pew pew or something, then it would have been fine, but it wasn't.

It was like a tuba inserted itself into my vagina. It was so long... and flappy sounding.

Total mortification.

Lizzy puts her hand on my arm. "What's wrong, chickpea?"

I shake my head because I can't talk about it.

"Do you want to go dance?" she asks with a hopeful tone in her voice.

When I don't answer, she slides out of the booth on the opposite side. I think she's gone downstairs wanting to get as far away from this pity party as possible, but a few minutes later she is back with four of Emmett's red, white, and blue shots. Layered perfection, but not very strong. It's a layer of grenadine, blue Curaçao and a cream-based vodka he found. Even though he's no longer bartending after tonight, he's still on retainer to make the special drinks that everyone has come to expect and love.

"Four?" I laugh.

"Two for you, and two for me."

When I tip back the first shot and let it slide down, I don't get the usual burn that makes me grimace. Not super strong, so I'll probably need another thirty before the end of the night, but it's sweet.

"So what happened? You were looking all hot and bothered, then Knox nearly fucked you in the middle of the floor, then tore across the room with you trailing. I imagine you were having sex when Emmett walked in. Knox was out a few minutes later, looking lighter in his step, and then you were in there for a while with Emmett."

"Were you stalking the door or something?"

"God, no. Well, maybe. Fuck. I was dancing my little heart away and then Jax came over with his super broody self and was telling me to keep an eye on you... like duh. And I was about to head upstairs and talk to Low, but then I was like, oh no... Ev will be out soon... and then I kept saying it and kept saying it... seriously, what happened?"

"Nothing."

"Listen here sassafras. Don't piss down my back and tell me it's raining. Something happened and I can't fix it if you don't tell me."

A smile quirks on my lips. She hasn't said that stupid ass saying in years.

"There's a smile. You know I'm a dog with a bone and we don't keep things from each other. I will find out."

"I queefed all over Emmett's cock."

Lizzy slumps to the table like a limp noodle in an overly dramatic fashion. "That's what has you all worked up? Jesus fuck." She hands me my other shot and hers. "Here. I thought it was something serious."

"It is. I've never done that before."

"Are you serious?" Her face falls in shock.

"Yes. I'm being serious. You have?"

"A lot of times during yoga. My pussy sucks air in downward dog like my lungs suck air after running a marathon."

"Liz, stop."

"I'm not lying. The first time it happened, I was embarrassed, but a few other women did it. Now, I'm not ashamed to say that I rather enjoy it. It feels freeing, liberating."

"You're shitting me."

"I shit you not. A little pussy flutter is like its way of saying," her voice notches up an octave or two, "thanks for working me out today. I really enjoyed seeing the sun instead of the dirt."

I wipe my hands over my face. "You're not serious."

"What about my face says I'm kidding? I'd invite you to my yoga class, but I'm pretty sure your guys keep you more stretched out than my class would."

"Liz, it was all over his cock, and sooo long and loud."

"I say better to queef on a cock than on their tongue."

"Is that what you say?" I laugh.

Admittedly, she's helping. Like she always does. I don't know how much of her story is true, but it doesn't matter at this point. I've mostly moved on from it. I just won't be able to have sex with Emmett ever again.

Ok. Like tonight. Who am I kidding? I'm pretty sure I couldn't say goodbye to his cock if my life depended on it. Boy knows how to work it and his Jacob's Ladder.

"So?" She clasps her hands together.

"Have you talked to Low? How is she doing?"

"She's good. Excited for the opportunity to manage, but a little nervous about running this place on her own. She'll have tomorrow and Sunday and then Thursday, Friday of next week. Four days. She said Emmett and the guys have been super helpful, walking her through everything she needs to know and do and says they're only a phone call away."

"I think Callum is actually going to stay here tomorrow, then fly down Sunday. He doesn't want to overload her."

"She's managed a bar before," Lizzy defends, then adjusts her tone. "Granted, not one like this, but still. She can do it. I think her nerves are getting the best of her."

"He trusts her or else he wouldn't even consider leaving her. I think he's planning to talk to her about it tonight to see how comfortable she is."

"Are you excited about our trip?"

"Yes. I'm looking forward to it."

"Will said he and Beckett should get there tomorrow around noon. They're going to do all the grocery shopping for us."

"Sweet. It's all coming together beautifully." Callum has already paid for the house in whole for the week and allowed Beckett and Will to buy the groceries and Lizzy to order the two rental cars. She apparently rented a suburban and an open top Jeep, *because it's beachy*, and with Will and Beckett driving down, we should have enough space. "And Will? So you're really taking this whole 'Will and me against the McKinley's' thing seriously."

"When am I not serious?"

"Always. You are never serious. I think if you were, hell would literally freeze over."

"I'm serious about you and your pussy health."

"That is true. You're oddly serious about that."

She grabs my arm, hugging it into hers, and rests her head on my shoulder. "Now that you aren't throwing a pity party, do you want to go dance the night away?"

I lean my head on hers in a comforting gesture. "Sure."

We stand from the table and before I can take two steps, I feel a hand snake around my waist and pull me in tight, my ass hitting their hips. "You want to take your hands off me?" I command through set teeth, then stop when I turn to see Jax.

"Hello love. Where are you going?" he asks in a cool voice.

"You know it's not healthy to be all up in her pussy?" Lizzy snaps.

"You are, so why not me? In fact, I rather enjoy being all up in her pussy." He sounds funny using her words because they sound so foreign on his tongue.

My hand rests on his, my fingers slipping in between his. "What are you doing?"

"I came to dance with you up here, since that's where it seems like you're going."

"We were going to the main floor. More people," Lizzy says. She's extra feisty tonight for some reason.

"I think up here is fine."

"I think we have different definitions of fine." She quirks up her eyebrow with sass.

Jax lets out a low hum. "Fine. We'll go to the main floor. Where is Tony at tonight?"

Her eyes narrow at him, no doubt wondering what angle he's taking. "He's at home, trying to wrap up some stuff before next week."

"Yes. Our vaycay," Jax quips.

"Did you just say vaycay?" I lean to the side and ask him because he still hasn't let me go as we walk towards the stairs.

"It's going to be totes faboosh," he says deadpan.

"For the love of Ev's pussy, please stop. I can't take it," Lizzy groans.

"Welcome to the party," Jax volleys back.

She cuts her eyes at him, then smiles. "Jax. I know you like me. Somewhere in that chest of yours is a heart that beats for me."

"Nope." He squeezes my hand, then releases it when we reach the stairs. I reach back for it as I descend, missing our connection and general display of affection. He's been getting more open about showing it in public. Ever since the Rainbows and Unicorns party when he told my co-worker we were together. Which will make it super awkward when we have another function and he may or may not be the one I take. Although I suppose people don't have a clipboard following me around, noting who I bring to what.

Then again, who knows if I will stay there. I've been helping with the business side of Allure for the last couple of weeks and have really been enjoying it. If I left and worked at Allure full time, there would be no more reports, no more selling ideas and stories to execs. Just coming up with ideas and selling them to the guys. Sexy ideas to help drive the business forward.

Because Sammie is still in town wrapping up home and business items, she told the guys she'd stay on to run Allure while we're on vacation. She volunteered, but the guys plan to pay her since she's doing them a huge favor. I'm fine with them paying her, but I don't think she sees it as working. The more I've worked with her the last two weeks, she really does love that place. She's going to have a hard time letting it go.

When we get downstairs, the music is pumping, and I feel Jax move in closer.

"Should you be seen dancing down here with a patron?"

"I'm a partial owner of this club, so I can dance with whoever I want to whenever I want." Both of his hands slip around to the front of my hips and he pulls me back into him as his lips brush against my ear. "And you aren't a patron. You're my girlfriend. Although that sounds too trivial for what you mean to me."

I'm dead.

Put a fuck in me, I'm done. His words make my stomach tighten, my pussy clench, and my knees buckle. I breathe a few times, in through my nose and out of my mouth. Maintain your cool Everlee. Ignoring the last part of his sentence, I press, "Whoever? Is there someone else you want to dance with?" I step away from him and turn, pressing my back against Lizzy.

He grabs my arm and pulls me into a spin, ending with his leg pressed between my legs, reminiscent of earlier this evening when Knox and I basically had sex through our clothes. He leans down, pressing his forehead against mine, his bowed lips only millimeters away, asking to be kissed. With his breath slow and controlled, and his hands cupping my ass, he whispers, "There's no other woman in this world I want to dance with. You are it for me. My one and only."

Tilting my chin up, I take his lips in a slow and sultry kiss. He hesitates for a second before he returns it, opening his mouth and moving his hand from my ass to the back of my head, holding me to him, swallowing me in. A flush flashes across my skin. This man and his kisses.

"People are watching," Lizzy whispers beside us.

I pull off his lips and look at him. His pupils are blown. "I'm going to dance with Lizzy now before I take you in a room and fuck your face."

He laughs and shrugs his shoulder. "That's fine. I'm pretty sure no man is going to come over here and try to dance with you now."

"Jax."

A wicked smile crosses his lips. "Love you, boo." He winks, then quickly glances at Lizzy and turns away.

"The audacity of that man!" She huffs, staring after him. "Nobody calls you boo, but me."

I laugh, closing the distance between us. "I love you, you know that?"

"You don't look at me like you look at them."

"It's a different kind of love."

She grabs my hand and spins me around like Jax did, pulling me in. "See, I got the moves too."

"Will you stop? I never pegged you for the jealous girlfriend type."

"Sorry. I stopped listening after peg."

EVERLEE-LIGHT 'EM UP!

"PLEASE STEP FORWARD," THE female TSA agent says, waving me forward into the large tube.

"Shit," Emmett curses behind me under his breath.

"Hands up, feet apart, and don't move." The agent sounds like a robot, thrilled with her job. Ignoring the simple request, only for a moment, I take a quick peek at Emmett, trying to figure out what he forgot and see Knox jumping up and down behind him like a kid in a candy store.

"Please step out." The second agent looks at the screen behind me and waves me through, then I realize why Knox is so happy.

"Please step through."

Emmett sighs, holding his arms up and the little body image on the screen lights up on his chest and between his legs.

"Please step over here," the agent guides him.

"Light 'em up up up," Knox sings.

"Shut up!" Emmett snaps back, only semi-irritated.

The rest of the guys walk through and we get our luggage and wait on Emmett. Callum had a good talk with Low this morning and decided he would just take our same flight instead of changing it. It made the most sense, since we already had a seat for him.

A man walks up to Emmett, who spreads his legs and holds his arms out while the man pats him down. Rubbing each arm from armpit to his waist and up and down his shorts to his crotch, where the man twitches a bit.

Yea. He has a big fucking cock.

Emmett's eyes fall on mine like he knows exactly what I'm thinking and just smirks.

Knox perches his chin on my shoulder. "Do you think he likes it?"

"Shut the fuck up." Jax shoves him off my shoulder.

A moment later, we all have our luggage and we're walking towards our gate. Why is it always the last one? Every time. Doesn't matter where I'm flying to, I'm always at the last gate.

Quickly glancing around, I try to find Lizzy, but don't see her. She said she was running a few minutes late when she texted this morning, which isn't shocking. She's always been the type to show up as we're boarding.

I couldn't do it. Nope. I'm the person who's at the airport an hour early. I hate running in general and running through the airport gives me the heebie-jeebies.

"We have some time to kill," Callum says. "Want to grab a drink?"

My lips pull to the side with guilt for making them be here so early, but in addition to running in the airport, I also hate being late for a flight.

"Please," Emmett groans.

"You didn't like being felt up?" Knox teases.

"Drinks on me," I offer.

"I knew you were turning into a little exhibitionist, but here? Really?" Knox teases.

I stare at him for a second with a furrowed brow until I realize what he's talking about. "On me. I get it."

We walk into a restaurant and pull up a seat at the bar. The bartender, a spunky little red head named Dahlia, hands us a drink menu.

"You all want food, too?"

"No, thanks," Emmett answers.

Dahlia flicks her chin up with a flirtatious grin, and I take in a deep breath to calm my nerves.

I've been getting less patient lately when we're out in public and ladies think they can just hit on my men. I guess to be fair, it's not normal for a girl to be with four guys at the same time, and the way we act in public probably leads people to believe we're just friends. But come on!

I'm going to have to have a talk with the boys. We need to figure out how to act in public, because I don't like the whole friends thing. I want to stake my claim! Let the world know they're mine and fuck their judgmental stares.

We order our drinks and Callum pays for the tab. We argue briefly about who's going to pay, but Emmett wraps his arms around my waist and transplants me to the corner booth where we sit and enjoy our drinks. Dahlia looks at us a few times, then gives me a slight nod of approval, reading the situation. I don't know why, but her nod does something to me. I feel like I'm soaring.

The screen behind the check-in stand says we have fourteen minutes left before boarding begins, and Tony and Lizzy still haven't showed up yet.

"Man. I'd hate if Liz misses the flight," Jax quips.

I smack his arm playfully and go back to reading my fairy-tale smut. "The fact you're calling her Liz and not Lizzy tells me you'd miss her."

"Would I though?" His eyes cut towards me with that sultry, sexy stare.

"Never fret, my darlings! The queen has arrived," Lizzy shouts from across the airport with her arms spread wide, pillow around her neck, fuzzy pink slippers on her feet and a pair of noise canceling headphones on her head. Tony is pulling both of their carry-ons a few steps behind her.

"Yay," Jax says deadpan.

I look over at him and smile, placing my hand on his thigh. He grabs it, interlacing his fingers in mine and squeezes, then looks up to Lizzy. "Noise canceling headphones. Good call. I should have brought mine."

Her gaze narrows at him, knowing that he was making a dig at how loud she is.

"I figured I'd need them as much as you all fuck."

My eyes bulge out of my head and I do a quick survey to see if anyone heard. Fortunately, it's not a huge flight with a lot of people and of those people, they have their heads buried in their phones.

"Lizzy."

"Oh, shush." She bats her hand at me. "It's the truth."

"What took you so long to get here?" Emmett says, trying to change the topic.

"I had to get a pat down." Tony's gaze shifts quickly between all the guys.

"Why?" I ask cautiously.

A large smile spreads across her face. "Nip nip inspired me."

"Oh geez."

"Who?" Knox asks, confused. Jax and Callum have moved on from the conversation.

Emmett moves to her side, wrapping his arm around her shoulders. "Go on. Tell me how I've inspired you."

"You know about nip nip?" She looks at him, shocked.

"Of course he does," I say, turning to her. "We don't keep things from one another, unlike you, apparently."

"Oh stop. I was going to tell you last night, but you were... ahem... busy."

Ignoring her, I press. "Why did you get your nipple pierced right before vacation?"

"I wasn't thinking about that..."

"Obviously."

"We were at-" she stops talking and looks at the guys, then continues slowly, "out. And I was on that post..." she looks at the guys again, then continues, "*out* high. Found a piercing shop, went in and got 'er done."

She was talking about Allure, but was following the rules in front of the guys.

"You know you aren't supposed to get in the pool or ocean now, right? Not until it's healed," Emmett says, removing his arm from her shoulder.

"Shut the back door!"

He cocks his head, staring at her. I love how he doesn't question it, or her, rather accepts it. His face hasn't gotten the memo though, because it's still twisted.

I place my hand on his forearm. "She thinks we're a bunch of ass loving heathens, so she says back door because of..." I roll my hands in the air to finish the rest of my sentence.

"Makes sense."

"You get me," she says, patting him on the chest.

BOARDING FOR GROUP ONE, the voice calls over the loud-speaker.

We're group two, so we break from our conversation and grab our bags. Poor Tony finally just got his breath back from lugging their two suitcases across the airport.

"What seat are you?" I ask Lizzy.

She flips up the app on her phone and lets out a groan. "23F, and Tony is 23E. What about you?"

"16E."

"Middle seat? You had the middle seat." She grabs my arm. "Please tell me your guys are beside you in D and F. I'd actually like to get to Charleston without them having to divert because your guys are losing their shit. For guys that like to share-"

NOW BOARDING GROUPS ONE AND TWO.

"That's us. What group are you?"

"Five. But you can say we're traveling together and I think they'll let us on."

We get in line and make our way up to the stand, scan our boarding passes, then head down the gangway. Lizzy and Tony are in tow behind us.

"Vacation here we come!" Lizzy shouts, shifting her bag on her shoulder.

"Yay," Jax moans up ahead.

"I hope you aren't sitting beside grump-butt."

"Grump-butt can hear you," Jax responds.

"Good. Then maybe he will turn that frown upside down."

Knox hangs back and grabs my hand and brings it to his lips. "I, for one, am very excited. This is the first family vacation we've ever taken together, which seems crazy. I mean, we've gone away for a quick weekend here or there, but this." He kisses my hand again and continues to bounce down the gangway, throwing his arm over Jax's shoulder.

We take our seats and I'm nestled in between Jax at the window and Emmett on the aisle. I didn't know who settled where because this morning they were randomly drawing the seats to see who would sit next to me and who got the seats across from us. When Knox booked the flight, he had bought all six seats in the row, so there was an empty space in the middle. He apparently got the window seat and Callum got the aisle. Seems to fit their personality. Knox, always the eager beaver, wanting to look outside while Callum needs to be on the aisle, always in control and ready to move.

I grab my logic puzzle book from my carryon bag and begin working the puzzles while the rest of the people fill in their seats. The flight wasn't sold out, which is baffling to me. South Carolina beaches on Fourth of July? No better place to be.

When we were younger, we would take day trips to the beach, setting up chairs and umbrellas and just play on the ocean all day and then watch the fireworks at the neighboring resorts and parks at either end of the beach. It was great.

I hope we get to do that this year. I'd love to just dig my feet into the cool sand and lean back on my guys and watch the fireworks show their vibrant display off in the distance, and possibly catch a sea turtle or two come up on the beach to lay their eggs.

One year, Beckett and I were walking on the beach in the early morning and saw a turtle flipped over on its back. We waved several other people down who were running or riding a bike and flipped it over to help it get back into the ocean. It was one of the greatest feelings I think I've ever experienced. To know that we helped save that turtle's life. Because of that moment, I became obsessed with turtles, to the point, I promised myself that when I get my first tattoo, it will be of a turtle.

Maybe while we're here this week, we'll see flags on the beach where the turtle patrol has marked nests. It should be about time for some of the earlier eggs to be hatching, so maybe we will get to see some baby turtles making their way to the beach if we do an early morning walk.

This is going to be such a great week! I can feel it!

EMMETT – SOMETIMES YOU NEED TO HULK OUT

THAT WAS FUCKING EMBARRASSING. I haven't traveled on a commercial plane since I got my piercings and as soon as Ev walked in, I realized what I was going to have to go through. And freaking Knox. As soon as he realized it too, he started jumping around like a freaking kangaroo in a cage and singing Light 'em up.

Asshole.

He's been so excited about this trip. Probably more excited than all of us combined, including Ev and Lizzy. He's always wanted to do family trips like this, but we never found the time or would always forget to plan until it was too late. Part of me wonders if he had anything to do with this trip, or if it really was just Lizzy and Ev.

Whatever the reason, I don't really care. I'm just excited to get away with our girl for a week. No work. No commitments. Just rest, relaxation, and sex. Lots of sex.

Jax is staring out of the window and Everlee has her head in some book with words and boxes. I watch her for a while, read and place X's and O's within the boxes, wondering if it's some sort of single person Tic Tac Toe.

"It's a logic puzzle," she says, looking up at me. I don't speak, so she continues, "You have these clues and you have to solve who did what, where, and when. There are only green, blue, red, and yellow socks. If Thomas has red, then no one else can have them." She points at the O for Thomas and red sock and the X's for everyone else. "You just keep going through them until you have the answers. This one is an easier one because it's at the front of the book. Do you want to try?"

"No, but I'll watch you."

"Creeper," Jax mumbles quietly.

I reach across Ev and pinch his nipple. "What's your deal?"

He looks at me, his eyes setting on my face, staring at me for a moment. "Nothing."

"Something. If you're going to be a grump the entire trip, then I'm going to throw your ass into the ocean."

"Good luck." He notches his head with a playful dare.

A flight attendant comes on the speaker and walks us through the safety procedures as the plane backs out of the gate.

"Here we go," Everlee whispers, placing her book in the back pocket of the seat in front of her. She lifts the arm rests between us and grabs our hands and places them on her leg.

Is she nervous about flying? I try to replay the memory of us flying back at Easter, but the only thing I can remember is being in her with Jax's cock rubbing against mine. This flight is going to be torture compared to that one, but perhaps once we get to the house, she'll want to take us both. I catch Jax's eyes and wonder if he's thinking the same thing.

I squeeze Ev's leg, curling my hand around the inside of her thigh, my pinky just inches from her little honey pot, and my dick twitches at the thought. Control yourself, E!

Jax mirrors my movements and his knuckles brush along mine. I wait for him to move them, but he doesn't and I can't help but wonder if it's on accident or on purpose. I shouldn't be thinking about him at all like that. I've gone years, like almost all of them, not thinking about him in any other light than a friend, but I swear. Ever since Everlee...

Fuck. She loves taking our cocks together, and it has almost become like a drug to me. Pleasing her because I love her so incredibly much it scares me, while at the same time, absolutely loving the feel of Jax's cock rubbing against mine. When we've done it before, we would just thrust in together, but I swear, lately... it's like he moves against me on purpose so he can feel my cock too. I know he likes my piercings even if he hasn't said anything, because he's changed. His moans when he feels his cock rubbing along mine.

My thoughts are going to get me in trouble, so I close my eyes and take a deep breath, pressing my head against the headrest. The growing bulge in my pants is making me uncomfortable.

Ev leans over and whispers, "Are you getting hard because you're thinking of me, because you're thinking of Jax, or because you're thinking of both of us?" Even though the cabin is loud from the rush of the wind outside as we accelerate for takeoff, I hear her words perfectly.

She's been asking me these questions lately, because she sees, feels, things shifting. Or maybe that's just my wishful thinking. Wishful? I don't know if that's the right word. Jax isn't gay, and I'm not sure if he's even bi. He's never talked about another man, liking cock or anything else, but I know he likes mine. Ev has seen it and she hasn't gotten upset, rather the opposite. I feel like in her own way she's trying to encourage this connection between us. I get the feeling it turns her on. One of the many reasons I love her.

She brings her legs closer together, so Jax and my fingers are interlocked by our knuckles. I wait for him to move them, but he doesn't. He just keeps his focus out of the window.

Ev lays her head on my shoulder, then kisses my neck and whispers again, "You're getting harder. I wish I could pull your cock out right here and suck you in so deep. I want to feel your piercings against my tongue then have your come fill my pussy."

Eyes wide, pupils blown, breath shallow, I turn to look at Everlee. "When we get to the house, your ass is mine."

"Promises, promises."

"Oh baby." My free hand slides to her cheek and I guide her chin up so our lips meet. As the airplane angles into the sky, I press my tongue in and kiss her. I kiss the fuck out of her until her legs are squeezing together.

I slide my pinky out, hooking it right under the hem of her shorts, and swipe it over her underwear. She groans into my mouth. Loving her response and unable to stop myself, I move my hand up her leg further and slip two fingers under her panties.

Shit. She's so fucking wet.

Pulling away from our kiss, I stare into her love drunk eyes. This girl, I sigh.

This must catch Jax's attention because he looks over at me, then down at my hands and smiles. He bends down and grabs the blanket rolled into the side of Ev's book bag and unfolds it on her lap. She looks between the both of us with a mixture of apprehension and excitement. I need that blanket over my lap because I have a raging boner right now that will not get any better.

Fuck it. I would walk around this earth with a raging boner for the rest of my life just to see her orgasm.

Jax slips his hand into the top of her pants, while I twist my arm and run my entire hand under her shorts and insert my index and middle finger into her warm and waiting, wet pussy. They sink in, smooth like butter, causing her back to arch.

Jax leans over and presses his lips to her neck. He swipes his tongue against her skin before his teeth gently bite, then suck it in. My cock twitches, watching him suck on her, nearly making me explode in my pants. Her head falls to the side giving him more access while his finger dips in between mine, pressing into her for only a second to get her arousal on his fingers to spread over her clit. Her hips slowly grind on my fingers as she bites down on her bottom lip to prevent her moan from escaping.

I turn my head, so my lips are right by her ear. "Are you going to be our good girl and fuck my finger until you come?"

She cuts her eyes at me with a fuck you look, causing me to stifle a laugh.

"I'll take that as a yes."

She sucks in a breath and pinches her eyes closed at the same time her pussy strangles my fingers. Oh, she's close. Jax must sense it too because I can feel his finger moving faster and faster on her clit, so I push my fingers in as far as I can go and curl them, hitting her g-spot. Her hands clamp onto our thighs and I can tell she's stopped breathing. Holding it, trying to focus on voice control, so she doesn't moan out.

I lean over to her. "Kiss me."

Without hesitation, she turns and kisses me, pressing her tongue in while she grinds down on my fingers. Her legs tense and she pulls away from our kiss and bites down on her knuckles. A small squeak escapes at the same time her pussy tightens around my fingers.

Using my free hand, I turn her face to look at me. The best thing in the world is watching her come, barely beating out the taste of her when she does.

When I gently press my lips on hers, I pull out my fingers. She looks at me with her hooded gaze, watching me bring my fingers to my mouth and suck her off of them. She mouths I love you, then looks just to my right and her eyes widen with a mixture of looks.

I follow her gaze and nearly pass the fuck out. Staring wide-eyed, sucking on a pacifier, is a one-ish year old on their mother's lap, eyes locked on us.

"Fuck," I whisper under my breath.

Everlee smacks my arm like the kid can one, either hear me, or two, read my lips. And would that be worse than what they just saw? The blanket shifts as Jax pulls his hand out, following our gaze, and lets out a low chuckle. Clearly, he's not as concerned about damaging the child as much as I am.

When I turn to my left, Knox and Callum are staring at us in disbelief. I smile, shrug my shoulders, then stick my fingers back in my mouth. Knox's eyes squint to narrow slits as he silently thrusts his fists in the air and Callum just stares at us, before perking his brow up, then glancing at my massive boner that is threatening to rip a hole in my pants. I thought it would be a good idea to wear my Fair Harbor bathing suit as shorts, because it's light, comfortable, and I'd be ready to go as soon as we get to the house, but now I'm regretting it. The inner liner feels like a vice grip on my cock.

Torn between trying to have blue balls or go to the bathroom to relieve myself, I glance down the aisle behind me. Seven rows. Row 23.

Fuck.

A moment later, an over eager hand is in the air waving at me.

Lizzy.

How and why in the fuck does she have to be on the same damn row as the bathroom? Who picks that row? I know she had to because there are several sets of open seats all over this damn plane, but no. She had to pick that row, like she knew something was going to happen on the plane and wanted to catch us.

Ugh. She has like Everlee pussy vision or some shit.

Rubbing my hand over my face, I calm down. I don't think she sat on that row to catch us, it just FUCKING SUCKS!

I flip my hand in the air, waving back.

"Is everything ok?" Jax asks, leaning across Everlee. I don't miss the fact he has a smirk on his face and currently has his hand between her legs, teasing her. He's playing with fire, because she has no qualms, playing right back.

But I guess mister window seat doesn't care if he has a cock working his way up his chest, does he?

I puff out of my mouth three times and move to stand at the same time the flight attendants start pushing the snack and beverage cart down the aisle.

"For fuck's sake."

Jax takes the balled up blanket on Everlee's lap and lays it over mine. "You look cold."

"Thanks, ass."

He lets out a low chuckle with that delicious fucking grin he has, and our eyes lock.

I need to look away, but I can't.

Everlee, being the angel, fucking angel, fucking kinky ass pro-love angel she is, takes each of our hands and makes Jax and I grab hands before she puts her hand over both of ours.

Jax fights her at first, but then intertwines his fingers with mine.

Not. Helping. The. Raging. Boner.

Why is he letting her do this?

His hands feel rough and calloused, although mine probably don't feel any better. When I look in his direction, I see him looking out of the window again, while Everlee rubs circles onto the back of our hands.

The cart is a few rows behind us, so I slip my hand out of Jax and Everlee's and rub them on my pants, urging my boner to go down.

Callum crooks his finger at me and leans across the aisle. "I've watched you suffer long enough. Think of something disgusting or flex your muscles. Thigh muscles, arm muscles, all the above... flexing your muscles will help you get rid of your boner. It will send your blood to those muscles."

Oh, thank God. I flex my thigh muscles and arms for good measure, looking like I'm trying to hulk out and don't feel anything happening. Glancing back over at Callum to see if he was just bullshitting me, I see him watching me, but not laughing. He didn't say how long this would take.

Oh wait.

Something is happening.

Oh happy day. It's going down.

Praise Jesus!

"Would you like some cookies, crackers or something to drink?" The attendant asks, with a chuckle in her voice. "I've never seen someone so happy for a snack before."

I look at the cart. Oh, she thought...

"He really loves those little cookies. Always raves about them," Jax says, reaching over Everlee to pat me on the leg. The leg that is still flexed for good measure. Don't need my cock to be like a reinflatable tire right now with Barbie standing here.

I'm not being rude. Her name says Barbie.

"Cookie please, with water."

"Same," Everlee and Jax say in unison.

We pull our trays down and enjoy our refreshments while I let the flex out of my thigh before I get a charley horse.

Because that would happen.

EVERLEE - LET THE VAY-CAY-CION BEGIN

"ENJOYABLE FLIGHT?" KNOX ASKS, walking up from behind me on the gangway.

"Shut the fuck up."

His eyes grow wide and his hand goes to his chest. "You've been sitting with Jax for too long. His..." he has no words, but waves his hand around my body, "has rubbed off on you."

"I didn't really mean it," I say, slipping my hand in his. "I just love to see your reaction."

"You do that a lot, you know?"

"What?"

"Do things to see our reaction."

"Are you talking about the fact I refuse to wear a potato sack to Vixen?"

"A little."

"Well, you should trust I'm not going to wear anything too crazy and that I only have eyes for you. Why would I ever leave? You all have broken me for all future relationships. No *one* cock could satisfy me ever again. Well, I mean one cock can, as long as it's one of y'all's."

"Fuck with the y'all again. We just stepped off the plane," Jax mumbles just behind me.

"I think it's in the air." I turn around, smiling at him.

"Hello vay-cay-she-on!" Lizzy screams, walking into the airport from the plane, still looking as goofy as ever with all of her items strung around her neck and on her head, this time without the pink fuzzy slippers. Did she pack another pair of shoes?

That's a dumb question. She obviously did.

"I just got off the phone with Will. They were able to get in a few hours early, so they're there waiting on us. Said the house is gorge and the private pool is amazing and has one of those infinity edges. They are going gaga balls over the place."

"Yay," Jax chides.

Lizzy deepens her voice, imitating Jax. "Oh my God, girl. You did such an amazing job setting this up and planning all of this with our love, Everlee. I'm so excited for all the adventures that are ahead of us this week with my boo and her best friend that is totes amazing."

I can't help but smile, watching them together. They have a weird relationship. I know Jax has an affection for her, even if he constantly pretends he can't stand her.

Lizzy scrunches her nose and looks around at the signs, then points up ahead. "This way, entourage."

"Fuck. We have her for a week," Jax grumbles beside me.

I grab his hand and kiss his knuckles. "We're going to have so much fun."

"I can't wait. I'll be in the ocean if you can't find me. Away from her."

"Are you sure it's not because you simply just love the water?"

He cuts his eyes at me with a smirk on his lips. "Go." He nods his head. "Please help her so we don't go blindly wondering around this airport for the next thirty minutes." He pats me on the butt, causing me to squeal.

I run up ahead, with my luggage trailing behind me. "Need help?"

"Did grump send you up here?"

"Maybe I just wanted to talk to my boo on our first cou—hmm. It's not a couple's vacation. What would you call this?"

She puckers her lips. "I don't know. Group vacation sounds too... blah."

"Right?"

"Here we are." Liz points to the sign that says car rentals.

Twenty minutes later, we're all stuffed in the cars. We put all the luggage in the suburban, and Lizzy, Tony, Knox and I decide to take the Jeep. Lizzy said I could sit in the front with Knox. Something about wanting to be chauffeured around.

Her and Tony were here just a few weeks ago looking at wedding venues and they still haven't made a decision. Last we spoke about it, she was going to have it near us, but when she came home, she fell in love with the southern charm. At the rate she's going, she'll be getting married at the courthouse.

I take in a deep breath. Aside from the smell, it feels good to be back home. The sun warming my skin, and the wind blowing through my hair. This is going to be such a wonderful week, I can't wait. What could go wrong with my brother and his boyfriend, my best friend and her boyfriend and all my guys? Holy shit. I just realized that's a lot of cocks in one house. Wow! Ok.

Lizzy taps me on the shoulder, so I run my fingers through my hair and fist it tightly in my hand and turn to look at her. Yes. I forgot a fucking hair tie.

"Are you excited?" she asks, beaming. She's sitting in the middle of the Jeep, snuggled into Tony, whose arm is wrapped around her with her beautiful dark hair wrapped tightly on top of her head.

"Very."

She smiles. "Me too. It's going to be so fun!" She slips a hair tie off of her wrist. "Here. You can use this."

"I could have used it ten minutes ago."

"I know, but you needed to learn a lesson of preparedness."

I shake my head, smiling. "You better be lucky I love you."

She makes her fingers into a heart and holds it in front of her chest. "Let's go!!" she yells.

Knox presses the accelerator and we tear off down the two-lane stretch of road, hands raised up, letting the wind whip around us.

"Jack! I can fly!" Lizzy belts from behind me.

The entire Jeep bursts into laughter.

I glance over at Knox, with his shaggy sandy blonde locks whipping in the air, left hand balanced on top of the steering wheel, right hand resting on my leg, and a smile on his face. He's wearing loose fitting khaki shorts with a very beachy button up, full of beach balls and palm trees on it. A stark contrast from the tattoos jutting out around his neck and arms.

Emotion swells in my chest and I squeeze his leg. He looks over at me, with his bright white teeth showing. "I love you."

He smiles, squeezing my leg. "I love you," he says, winking at me.

"How cute are you two?" Lizzy asks, leaning forward.

I reach across my body and plant my hand on her forehead, pushing her back. "No less cute than you two."

She shakes her shoulder and tosses her legs over Tony's and curls under his chin.

EVERLEE - THE SAND CASTLE

FORTY MINUTES LATER WE'RE at the house, and the online pictures don't do this beauty justice. We pull onto the semi-private turnaround drive, which is flanked with palm trees and ferns on either side. Sitting just behind it is a beautiful two-story white, hardy planked house with black trim around the roofline and windows, with stained wooden accents above the double entry door. Just behind the house, hints of the ocean crash on the white sandy beaches welcoming us to our home for the next week. A brick pathway separates the house from the drive, with large black cast iron lamps spread evenly in between. It's like this house was plucked right out of Southern Living or a Coastal Homes magazine.

The driveway is wide. It can probably hold four rows of cars, two wide. When Knox pulls to a stop behind Beckett's car, he honks the horn twice.

"What was that for?" I ask, hopping out of the Jeep.

"I didn't know if they were inside boning or something. I didn't want you to walk in on them. Not the best way to start a vacation."

"For literally one person. One person in the entire group wouldn't want to see that. I would venture the rest of us dirty fucks don't fall into that category," Lizzy chimes in, poking her head back up in the front again.

"Lizzy!" I smack her arm.

"I'm Seraphina this week."

"I'll wear that name out, too. Fuck."

"Like those boys are going to wear out your ass?" She spanks the air in front of her.

"Lizzy!" Beckett calls, stepping out of the house.

"Beck!" She clamors out of the Jeep, dropping her stuff and full on runs into his arms, jumping on him.

"I used to be greeted like that. Then I put a ring on it... and now I'm lucky if I get a hand wave," Tony teases.

"You lie like a rug," I say, lightly punching him in the arm. "She is always on you like white on rice."

"Yea. Stage five clinger, that one." We laugh as we walk to the back of the other car to grab the luggage Callum and Jax are offloading onto the ground.

Lizzy and Beck join us a second later. "Need help?" Beckett offers.

"I think we're all good here," Jax says, shaking Beckett's hand. "How's the house?"

Beckett shakes his head, blowing out a breath. "Wow. Simply, wow. I don't know if I'll ever be able to go to the beach again in anything less than this house. It's stunning. The back wall is floor to ceiling glass panels that look out at the ocean and accordion fold to open the whole back side up. The kitchen and living room are huge. There's a game room upstairs with a pool table, darts, and a shuffleboard table. Pool in the back is an infinity, with a built-in ledge on the far side so you can just chill and look out at the ocean. I tell you... this place is fire!"

"Well, let's go then, bro!" Knox says, hopping up and down.

Beckett laughs and looks at Lizzy. "Thanks for getting them to let us in early. We were able to get all the groceries and get them put up. We have a ton of food, so don't freak out when it looks like we have a mini grocery store in the kitchen.

But someone was very particular about the food items they requested."

Everyone in the group turns to Emmett.

"What?" he bats his hand in the air. "You won't have the same look on your face when I'm stuffing your bellies. You'll be moaning out my name."

"Like Ev? Oh Emmett. I love when you stuff me," Lizzy teases, moving her body like one of those air things outside of car dealerships. What in the hell do you call those things? They look like bright colored worms dancing in the wind.

"Lizzy!" Beckett and I shout at the same time.

"Liz is out, Seraphina is in."

"This again?" Beckett asks, looking at me.

"This again?" Lizzy mocks, smooshing Beck's cheeks together.

"I told her I was going to wear out that name too with all the inappropriate shit she says."

"It's only a problem for you when you're in front of your guys. I bring my whole self to all situations. You're the fucker that changes," she snaps back, face full of sass.

"I get this for an entire week. I'm so excited," Jax says deadpan.

"Jaxxy poo," Lizzy says, walking over to him with open arms.

He holds his arm out, pressing his palm against her forehead, stiff arming her.

"I have a week to woo you."

"You'll need more than that, darling."

"You've just called me darling. Step one complete. Call each other pet names."

"Fuckin' hell," he groans, dropping his arm and walking towards the house.

Will is waiting for us at the door with his shirt off and bathing suit on, looking like he just got out of the pool.

"How is it?" I ask, giving him a quick hug before walking inside.

"Amazing. I heard Beck out here, so I won't repeat what he said. But amazing. We took a walk on the beach after we got all the groceries unloaded, then were in the pool when you all arrived."

"Hope it's still–"

I cut Lizzy off. "Lizzy. Do you want to go pick out a room?"

"Oh," Will chimes in, holding a finger up so we all turn to look at him. "Beck and I took the room down here, and then we figured Tony and Liz will take the room to the left of the stairs on the second floor. It has its own bathroom, then down the hall to the right of the stairs are the other rooms. We figured you all would want to pick out one or several. The one at the very end is the main room with an enormous bathroom and walk-in shower."

"Could this get any better? I don't have to go grocery shopping, or put up all the food. I basically have my room assigned and have my own little wing..." Lizzy jumps up and down, squealing. "Tony and I are going to put our things down and relax. We'll be down in an hour or so." She winks over her shoulder as she drags Tony upstairs.

"My bingo card didn't have you having sex first! Totally thought that was going to be Everlee," Beckett yells after her.

"That's your first mistake of the day, boo boo brother!" She yells from upstairs.

"Do you really have a BINGO card?" Knox pops into the conversation.

Beckett looks at him and then at me with a sly grin on his face. We used to do BINGO cards when we were growing up and taking long road trips, but we haven't done one of those in a while. "Maybe..."

"Did you?" I hit his chest, the palm of my hand catching his peck just right, causing the perfect sting. "Shit, sorry."

"Fuck. Be. Aggressive. B-E aggressive, why don't you?" he cheers.

"Sorry. You know I get slappy when I get happy."

Knox nods in agreement. "True story. I flinch now anytime I tell someone good news... or bad news... or any news at all, really." He flinches. "See."

Looping my arm around his waist, I pull him in for a hug. "I'm sorry."

He turns, brushing his lips on my ear and whispers, "It's ok. I like it." He tilts his head down and kisses on the side of my neck.

Beckett checks the time on his watch. "Sweet! Mark out a spot for Everlee is kissed within ten minutes of being here."

"I want to see the BINGO card. I know you have one."

"I made some for all of us. Well, teams. It's Everlee and her men, Will and I, and Lizzy and T man."

"T man?"

"Yea. We came up with little names for one another when he was here a few weeks ago."

"I see."

"Cool dude. He's great for Liz."

"He is."

"Well, enough chitty chatty. I say, you and me put our bags in the room, let the guys sort it out while you and I head out to the beach," Knox coos.

"Tide is starting to come back in. I printed off the schedule and posted it on the fridge in the kitchen. You all just struck me as taking morning bike rides on the beach kind of people. Unfortunately, they don't have a bike built for five. Assholes." Beckett chuckles. "High tide is around seven thirty tonight, so don't get caught."

"That will give us a couple of hours. And if we get stuck, we'll just swim back."

"Says the SEAL. Is your ass going to let me perch up on your back to swim us both home?"

He loops his arm around my waist, dips me backward, and holds his face inches from mine. "Love, you can perch anywhere you want on me and ride me whenever you want." He kisses my nose, then pulls me back up to standing.

"Shit. I really wish I had my BINGO card handy."

"It shouldn't start until after dinner... or at least until everyone else knows about it."

"Where's the fun in that, sis?"

"Sis." Knox oohs, clasping his hands together under his chin.

"Let's go. I just need to change and I'll be ready. Give me ten?"

"Seconds? You got it. I'll be outside on the deck waiting."

KNOX - SEX ON THE BEACH

MAN, I LOVE THE smell of the ocean air and the way it feels on my skin. The heat of the sun coupled with the constant breeze blowing through my hair makes me feel relaxed and at ease. It's like being here just breathes life back into me.

Turning my ear to the wind, I hear seagulls ha-ha-ha in the distance and see them circling in a flock around a poor unsuspecting child, no doubt carrying a piece of bread or something around on the beach.

"Are you going for a walk?" Will asks, climbing into the pool, taking a seat on the bench looking out at the ocean.

"Yea. Ev and I."

"Hint... walk in the direction that is against the wind, that way when you turn around it will be at your back. Trust me. We went on a run earlier and made the mistake of running with the wind on the first leg. Ran ten miles quick. Probably would have broken a record had we been keeping time, but running back." He points at the hot tub. "It's why I've been alternating between the pool and the hot tub. I'm so sore. I didn't think we were going to make it for a bit. All that to say... walk against the wind so when you're tired and on your way back, it will help to push you along instead of fighting against you."

"Thanks man."

"You ready, babe?" Ev asks, bouncing out of the house in nothing but a triangle top string bikini.

Fuck me.

I swear to God if she runs and those perky little breasts of hers join in, I'm dead. I have no self-control with her. It's impossible. When I look behind her, Jax and Callum are standing with their arms crossed with smug looks on their face.

Emmett is still going through all the groceries with Beckett. The menu for tonight is lasagna. Liz and Everlee planned every detail down to the dinners and the lunches for the week. They were talking about going out to dinner for a couple of nights, but trying to get a reservation for a party this large proved troublesome and Emmett, fortunately, loves to cook.

Trying to help, Lizzy and Ev took Tuesday. Taco Tuesday. And also took Thursday. It's breakfast for dinner. They said they didn't want everyone to get used to five star dining every night.

Ev loops her arm in mine and looks at me.

"Yes. I'm ready."

"Thank goodness. I needed to get out of the kitchen. Beckett and Emmett are talking about the different kinds of pasta."

"Did we get the wrong one?" Will turns to climb out of the pool. "It's my fault. We stood there looking like the biggest idiots with two full carts of food staring at all the pasta options. Then we had to figure out how to get all the boxes in the cart without them falling off. We have so much damn food. When we checked out, I'm fairly certain our cashier thought she was being punked. And then near the end, the manager of the store walked over to watch her and I assume to make sure we were going to actually buy all the groceries."

"I just peeked in the fridge and some of the cabinets and wow."

"If it was on your list, we bought it," Will says, towel drying himself off before he walks inside. "I'll go see if they need any help. Enjoy your walk or whatever it is you two are doing."

Ev pulls her arm out of mine and starts jogging across the deck and across the walkway over the sand plants. I don't know what they're called, but they look spiky. When we get to the end a minute later, we slip out of our shoes and leave them at the edge of the steps on the sand. As soon as my feet hit the warm white sand, a wave of peace washes over me.

"Let's go bro!" Ev yells, jogging away, then turning around.

Fuck. Her breasts are bouncing up and down in that little triangle top, threatening a nip slip each time, and fuck am I hopeful.

"Come here!" I run after her.

She squeals and turns and runs towards the ocean, trying to throw her hair up in a messy bun as she does. She runs along the edge of the water, glancing over her shoulder at me a few times.

Within seconds, I reach her and lift her into my arms, spinning around. "You can't outrun me."

"Knox," she peeps with a modicum of concern.

"Yea?" I put her down, and she turns to look at me and fucking hell. A nip slip.

Quickly looking around, I realize no one is close enough to see, but they are close enough that I can't motorboat her right here.

"You are a temptation I can't fight against." My hand moves up and cups her breast.

"Knox," she whispers out, nearly moaning.

"I'm helping you fix your top."

"Does your cock know that?"

"Ignore him."

"It's kind of fucking hard to." She nibbles on her bottom lip.

"You need to stop that." Every time she does that, it drives me wild. Makes me want to suck it out of her mouth.

"He says, as he's cupping her breast, teasing her with his gigantic cock," she says with that level of sass that drives me wild.

"I love your breasts."

"I love your cock."

"I love you, Everlee." Well, shit. That just happened. We were all fun and flirty and then emotions just took over. Time to double down. "Everything about you. The way you are, the way you look, the way you make me feel. You are... ugh. Men you were with in the past are fucking idiots for letting you go, but thank God they did because they led you to us. To this."

Her eyes are glassy, but she's not crying. "Knox." She cups my cheek. "I love you guys so much it scares me. You're all so different and so perfect. I love you too." She pulls my hand off her breast, then grabs it and starts walking down the beach.

"Let's take it slow, if you don't mind?" I ask, nodding towards my crotch.

She lets out a soft chuckle and nods.

We turn down the beach and walk into the wind like Will suggested, hand in hand. Just us, the ocean, and our thoughts. After a few minutes, I bring her hand to my mouth and give it a light kiss.

"What was that for?"

"Just because." I give her hand another quick kiss, then let our combined hands fall between us.

The seagulls I heard earlier are just ahead, following a toddler around as he wobbles on the sand, plopping beside a set of sand toys with a cup of goldfish.

"This is nice," she says, swinging my arm back and forth.

"The beach?"

"Well, yes, but not just that. Being on vacation with you all, away from everyone and everything. Away from work. This is going to be such a great week. I really don't think anything can ruin it."

"Don't say that. You'll jinx us."

She laughs. "What could go wrong?"

"A lot of things I'm not going to name. I'm not going to put that out in the universe."

She scrunches her nose at me.

"What? Don't look at me like that." I drop her hand and wrap it around her hip, pulling her closer to me. My hand slips just under the string of her bathing suit and she does a little stutter step and looks at me, causing me to laugh. "What?"

"Your hand is awful close to the string."

"This string?" I ask, pinching it between my index finger and thumb.

"Knox. If you pull that string, I will punch you in your cock."

"You'd do that?"

"Yes. Let go of my string."

Lips puckered, I shake my head. "I didn't know how jumpy you'd be about me simply holding your string."

"Knox," she threatens. "There are people around, kids."

"Are there?" I look around and don't see anyone. We seem to be in the undeveloped part of the island because there are no homes, hotels, or public access points.

She quickly looks around and sees I'm right. "Shit."

I throw my head back, laughing.

"Knox. I will still cock punch you."

"I don't think you will."

"Do you want to risk not being able to walk home?"

"I like to live on the edge."

She shakes her head and tries to take a calming breath.

"I don't know why you're so concerned. I thought you liked people to watch."

She smacks my arm and I flinch and unfortunately, the string goes with me, pulling and unraveling. I drop it, freaking out. "Shit!"

"Knox!" She quickly grabs the back and front of her bathing suit and hoists it back together and quickly ties it. And as promised, or warned... not really sure which, she takes a swing at my cock.

"Ev! I didn't mean to! It was an accident!"

"So is me hitting your cock!"

I dart down the beach with her running after me and shout over my shoulder, "It doesn't feel like an accident when you're chasing me down with your fist in the air!"

"Get back here Knox!"

"No! I'm looking out for our future sexual gratification. If I have a banged up... wrong choice of words, bruised cock, then I won't be able to pleasure you later."

"Who says you do!" She yells back, still running after me, waving her fist in the air.

I stop dead in my tracks. "What did you say?"

She slows to a stop several feet behind me. "You heard me." Her tone is defiant, but her body language is quickly reassessing the situation.

"I don't please you?" I take a step towards her and her pupils dilate quickly as she realizes she's no longer the one in control and the hunter is becoming the prey.

"Knox," she whispers, taking a step backward. "I was only kidding."

"Were you? It didn't feel like it."

"Knox." She takes another few steps backwards, eyes locked on me, then turns and bolts towards the ocean.

"You are so in trouble now!" I sprint after her as she draws closer to the water. Wrong place for her to run. Water gives me energy, gives me life. In another life, I had to be a fish, a seal, or some other kind of water creature, because I love it.

"Knox!"

"When I get ahold of you, which I will very soon. There will be no accidents. I will rip your bathing suit off your body and fuck you in the sand, giving you so much pleasure it will blow your fucking mind. I won't be the one who will have trouble walking back to the house. That's for sure." My cock is getting harder with each step I take at the thought of catching her and taking her right here. I don't give a shit who sees us.

She's right in front of me. An arms reach away. I quickly glance around. Still alone. It's getting late and most people have gone inside to get ready for dinner. Just me and my girl.

I reach out and grab at her, catching the string on the back of her bikini top and pull.

"Damn it, Knox!" Her hands fly up to her chest as she clutches the top of her bathing suit.

"That's one."

With her focused on her top, she loses significant speed. I grab the string that I had earlier on the right side of her hip and pull.

"I swear to God, Knox!" She grabs the right side of her bikini with her right hand.

I grab her right wrist and spin her around, quickly passing her wrist to my left hand, crashing our bodies to one another. "Don't swear to God, swear to me."

She puffs out a breath, her breathing erratic.

"Now, what was it you were saying earlier? About me pleasing you?"

"I was kidding." She tries to push away from me, but my grip only tightens.

Again, I glance around and see we're alone for a while, the next closest people only dots moving on the horizon.

"Hmmm," I groan out, pushing her closer to the surf with my hips, the water brushing along the tops of our feet.

"Knox."

"Shh." Leaning in, I press my lips to hers, silencing her with my kiss.

She whimpers into the kiss.

"Now, I'm not going to pleasure you." I slowly drag my right hand up her bare leg.

She shifts slightly into my touch, causing the little bit of resistance her bikini had on the left side of her hip to release and fall.

She looks down and then back up at me, not moving.

I can't help but smile, because I know her better than she knows herself. For all the showboating she does about not wanting to be exposed, I know it lights her on fire. Makes her hot. Although, for as much as I say I don't care who sees, I very much care. I don't want to share her with strangers.

I don't want visions of her delicious body dancing around in their heads while they jack themselves off. She is mine. Ours. But not theirs.

I slowly drop to my knees in front of her. "Do you want me to pleasure you?" I blow a warm breath on her clit. Her hands drop to my head and I know she's fighting with herself to press her pussy to my mouth and ride my face.

"Yes."

I lean in painfully slow, cupping both of her ass cheeks with my hands and run my tongue up her wet middle. Her taste is like heaven. God, I love it.

Her hips roll slowly into my mouth, savoring the first lick.

"Hmm. If only I did… pleasure you, that is." I move to stand back up.

She presses her hands on my head, forcing me back down. "Knox." Her voice is low. "You are not a quitter. You hear me? You get back down there and finish what you've started." She reminds me of a coach giving a motivational speech during a sporting event.

I drop back to my knees, looking up at her, completely enraptured by her beauty and everything else about her. The wind is blowing her half-fallen hair backwards, and the sun glows on her skin. "I feel like I should say yes, coach."

"Atta boy." She winks playfully at me, then grabs my head, bringing it to her pussy. "Now seriously. Finish what you started." She throws her leg over my shoulder.

"Goddamn Ev. Your little meetings with Sammie are starting to show."

"Just wait until my strap on comes in the mail and I take you from the back."

I don't know if she's kidding and I don't ask. The only one of us who's been taken from the back is Emmett, from Jax, but that's because they have their thing. Their understanding whatever that is. I know Emmett has come out as bi, but he's never done anything with us, or even asked. He loves the girls, but occasionally he does like to fuck while being fucked.

Why am I thinking about Emmett right now?

I need to be thinking about Ev and pleasuring her so much she never thinks of joking about that ever again. Running my fingers up her leg, I split her pussy open with my index and middle finger, giving me access to her clit. I suck it into my mouth and let her moans feed my energy. She arches, thrusting her hips into my face, as she rocks on my tongue.

Her moans, her thrusts, the way she pushes me back down and throws her leg over my shoulder... all of it is making me feral. I lose all control and devour her pussy. I need to hear her moan. I need to watch her moan. Fuck. I need her to come in my mouth.

"Damn Knox. I can barely stand." She's grabbing onto my head and holding on for dear life.

Grabbing her ass and holding her to my face, I drag us, so we fall to the ground. My head is at the water's edge, but I don't care. I'm going to drown one way or another today. Either from her pussy or from the ocean. Hopefully, it's not the latter.

To my point earlier, that would likely ruin the week.

She hovers over me, pausing as her eyes flicker from the ocean back to me.

"I don't care. Fuck my face and come down my throat."

She glances up one more time, then lowers her delicious pussy on my face. Moans dance around us and she grinds down, letting my tongue spear her. I pull it out and suck on her clit, snaking two fingers up between her pussy and my mouth and sink them inside of her, feeling for that special spot that makes her moan.

"Fuck, Knox," she moans my name. "I'm about to..."

Her pussy quivers and she doesn't need to finish. I press my fingers and suck on her clit and she explodes around me.

"Shit. Shit. Shit. Ooooohh."

She freezes, but I don't stop. Licking and sucking every ounce of her I can.

"Knox. You have to stop."

She tries to push off me, but I lock my arms over her legs and around her hips, holding her in place.

"Knox. Please. It's too much." She presses harder and I release her, immediately pushing her back onto the beach.

I pull off my pants and toss them to the side, lining my cock up at her entrance. "Are you pleasured, my darling?"

She looks at me and I can see it in her eyes. She wants to press, to play, to take this to the next level, but the other part of her is hesitant. "Very."

"Good girl."

She smiles at the words before she gasps, arching her back into the sand as my cock presses in.

My eyes nearly roll into the back of my head because nothing beats the first thrust in. The way her tight, wet pussy hugs my cock. It's heaven. "You feel so good."

EVERLEE – POSEIDON'S FURY

Knox's words nearly send me over the edge and he's just pressed in. That feeling when he sinks in deep, first thrust, the way it feels when I stretch around him... fucking magical. A tingle shoots through my body to my nipples as every cell within me activates and feels like a live wire waiting to be touched.

His forearm muscles flex on either side of my head as he grabs fistfuls of sand, slowly pulling out his cock, before pushing in again, hard and fast.

"Fuck me, Knox," I pant out. Grabbing his neck, I pull him towards me, crashing my lips to his and he kisses me back. Ravenous, full of hunger. Full of need.

He pulls away a moment later and looks at me. "Yes, coach." He winks before driving his cock into me relentlessly, sending my ass further into the sinking sand.

His forehead presses to mine, as the combination of moaning and waves crashing in the background become our soundtrack. The sun sets lower in the sky as the cool water continues to trickle up our legs, higher and higher, washing the sand away beneath us. Cradling us.

"I've always wanted to have sex on the beach," I say, catching his gaze.

"Glad I could give it to you." He smiles, his beautiful, bright, reckless smile, then bends down, pressing his lips to mine.

I tangle my hands in his hair, roaming wildly. Grabbing. Pulling. Needing to have every part of his body pressed against mine, I arch my back out of the wet, sandy puddle that has formed underneath us.

"Ev," he pants between thrusts. His lips travel down my neck before clamping on my breast, sucking and biting my nipple. I can tell he's been waiting to do that, because as soon as he sucks the first one in his mouth, he moans out in satisfaction. All of my guys like my breasts, but I'm fairly certain he likes them the most. It's why I picked out this bathing suit for our little stroll.

Goosebumps erupt across my skin as the cool water creeps higher and higher up my body. Our feet are constantly submerged while waves brush along the underside of my neck, sending shivers down my spine.

He moves his hand down my stomach towards my clit, then stops. "Shit! My hand is covered in sand. I don't want to get it on your clit and hurt you."

"She thanks you." I smile, grabbing his ass, pulling him towards me and wrapping my legs around his waist.

He jumps when the cold water from my foot drips down his ass. "Oy, that was fucking cold."

When I try to chuckle, it's cut off by my own shock. A wave just crashed right at our feet, sending water up our bodies, nearly coming to my head.

Knox hurriedly lifts my head until the water rushes away.

"I'm scared we're running out of time," I mumble, looking over his shoulder, planting a small kiss on it.

"Then I must go faster."

He lowers me back to the sand and begins to punch inside of me faster and faster, rotating his hips so he hits new spots.

"Fuck Knox."

"I've been saving this move."

I feel like I'm riding a wild bull, or rather, one is riding me. Fuck. Put a cowboy hat on him and let him grind on me.

My orgasm crashes around me just as another wave hits. Nothing like being mid-orgasm, then getting hit in the vagina with a bucket of ice water. That's what it feels like.

"Son of a bitch!" Knox shouts, before thrusting into me one more time. His groans continue, longer than I would expect to the point I think he's faking it, but then he pulls out and sits on the sand, pulling his foot up to look at it.

"What happened?"

"I think a crab or something just bit me."

"At the same time you... completed?"

"Completed?" His laughter temporarily eases his pain until another wave crashes on us.

"I think the water gods are mad we're fornicating on their beach."

"Me thinks you're right. Let's get our stuff and head back. It's probably getting close to dinner soon and I don't want the boys freaking out. Or worse, Lizzy."

Chuckling, I roll over to look up at the beach for my bottoms. Fortunately, my top is still lassoed around my neck. "Shit!" I scurry up the beach on my hands and knees and grab my bottoms, which are floating in the water, on their way back out to sea. "That was close."

I quickly stand and slip my leg through the one hole, then tie the strings on the right side, ignoring the crotch full of sand I have right now. A quick dip in the ocean should help wash away most of the sand.

Knox is standing near the water's edge looking around, still stark ass naked.

"What's wrong? Why aren't you getting dressed?"

"Ha. So... funny story."

"Knox?" I look around, but don't see his bathing suit. "Knox..."

His lips flatten into a hard line. "Yea. So me also thinks my bathing suit is gone... like Poseidon, loved it so much, he sent his little wave friends up here to snatch it back to sea."

"So you're saying he snatched it while you were getting some snatch?"

He points at me, finger bobbing up and down. "I see what you did there and usually I would high five the superb word play... but I'm standing cock out on the beach, nary a house in sight."

"Nary a house?" I look around. "Nary a bathing suit, either."

"You think this is funny?"

I shrug. "A little."

"Ev. How in the fuck am I going to get back to the house?"

"Walk?"

"With my hand cupping my cock and balls–"

I burst out laughing, "Cock 'n balls. I don't know why, but it makes me think of Christmas."

"Har, har. When you can be mature again and help me solve this problem, let me know. I'll be over here waiting."

"With nary a bathing suit, holding your cock 'n balls," I mumble out through laughter.

"I'll just take yours, since you don't seem to care." He scurries over to me.

"The fuck you will." I stop laughing long enough to stiff arm him, hand pressed flat against his chest.

"You're right, I'd never." He backs away. "But seriously, what are we going to do?"

"Can you see it out in the ocean?"

"No. I've looked. There are too many waves crashing right now, anyway."

I look off in the distance, from the way we came. "I can barely just see the house. I think."

"I'm not walking back, cock in hand. I don't need to have beach patrol cite me for public indecency.

"If they did, I'd ask for the definition of indecent, because nothing about you says indecent. In fact, I would argue that you are decent. Very decent. Well, fuck. I saw it going somewhere else in my head. Decent sounds so blah, but you are such the opposite, but like in a positive way. Like if a positive word could have a more positive opposite, that's what you would be."

"I really appreciate the pep talk, but you aren't helping," he says, looking around anxiously.

"Do you want me to run back to the house, grab a pair of shorts, and run back?"

"Very sweet, but no. It would take you too long."

"I'm going to need some more cans versus all these cants. Positivity Knoxxy baby."

"I am positive I'm fucked."

"Thank you very much," I say, blowing on my fingernails. "Or should I say fuck you very much?" He cuts his eyes at me. "Sorry. You just gave me two or three orgasms, and I use sarcasm and jokes to help me through awkward moments."

He runs his fingers through his hair, turning in a circle, letting out a sigh of frustration.

"Swim."

"What?"

"You're a SEAL. Get in the water and swim."

He looks at the water and then at the house in the distance. "That's a long way."

"Negative Nancy, let's get off the pity party bus and find a solution, because unless you want me finding a coconut laying on the ground and rigging up some sort of coconut bottom for you, then we need to get moving. We're burning daylight."

"Ok."

"Ok?" My head jerks in surprise.

"Fine. We will start walking, but as soon as I get a hint of a person getting close, I will jump into the water and swim."

"Ok. Let's go, Cab."

"Cab?"

"Cock 'n balls."

"For fuck's sake Ev."

"What?" I loop my arm in his and we start walking home. "When you get in the water, should I still pace you on the beach?"

"You could swim with me."

"Yea, fuck that. I can swim, but in the ocean. No. I'll only slow us down. Plus, I didn't lose my bathing suit."

"Keep it up, Ali. We have an entire week together."

"We always have an entire week together. We have every day together."

"Shut up." He smacks my ass, and we keep walking.

EVERLEE - CAT OR DRAGON?

ABOUT FIVE MINUTES INTO our walk, a family of four is packing up their belongings, so Knox tears off towards the ocean. He starts swimming, which, dammit if it isn't one of the sexiest things I've seen. He tries to stay on top of the water, but his ass cheeks keep poking up a little whenever the waves get low. He has a good speed at first, but fifteen minutes in and I can tell he's getting tired. Unfortunately, we're in a more populated area, so he has no other option but to stay in the water.

When we get closer to the house, I run ahead and grab a towel off the back deck, then run back to the ocean, meeting him a few houses over. He must have seen me coming because he's sitting in a shallower area, catching his breath when I get to him.

The back of my neck prickles, and I turn to find Beckett, Lizzy, and Jax on the boardwalk between the beach and the house, watching us.

"We've got lurkers," I say, handing him the towel as he steps out of the water.

"Great. Let's go get the lashings. I mean, at least the group will have something to ride me about for the rest of the week."

Flinging myself at him, I wrap my arms around his neck and give him a kiss. He kisses me back, but I know he's tired. The usual light has drained from his eyes.

When we get back to the house, only Jax is there to greet us with his arms crossed over his chest. "What happened?"

"We were playing in the ocean. A wave knocked him over and his bathing suit fell off."

His brow quirks up. "Playing in the ocean?"

I loop my arm around his and pull him into the house, with Knox following behind us. "Yes."

"And his pants fell off?"

"You act like that can't happen."

Jax looks over his shoulder playfully. "Oh, it can. But you forget I've seen that boy's ass. Ain't nothing just falling off those two Christmas hams."

"Jax McCall. Did you just make a funny?"

He shakes his head looking at me. "Why do you say a funny?"

"Because I like to. Now answer my question."

"Yes. I made a joke. Sorry, a funny. But I joke."

"Sure, at someone else's expense usually," I retort playfully, catching a side eye from Jax.

"Come on sea dog, let's get you cleaned up. Emmett will have dinner ready soon. We were organizing a little search party to come find you both when Ev snatched the towel off the deck."

"Aye, aye, captain." Knox salutes.

"I'll go with. I need to get the ocean off me."

"Doubling down? Still going with the playing in the ocean story?" Jax asks, perching his foot on the bottom stair, watching us walk up.

"There was water, fun, and sand." I toss Jax a flirtatious grin over my shoulder as I follow Knox.

He calls up the stairs, "We took the bedroom at the end of the hall. Suitcases are in the last room on the right." He pauses a beat, then continues, "Oh. Emmett said twenty minutes."

"Ok," I call back, then catch up to Knox down the hall. "Head into the shower. I'll be in there in a minute. I'm going to grab us some clothes."

He nods and walks into the last room while I dip into our luggage room. The bed frame is empty and our suitcases are lined up along the wall. After dinner tonight, I'll have to unload my clothes into drawers. I can't stay here for a week living out of a suitcase.

I find my suitcase- the hardshell case with the Eiffel tower and bright colors spread across it. Even though I've never been, it's on my bucket list of things to see and now with the hookup from Sophie... I hope it will happen sooner rather than later. Digging around in the suitcase, I pull out a pair of comfy shorts and a short-sleeve shirt that has a rainbow and a unicorn on it. First merch from Vixen that Lizzy put together.

Knox's suitcase is near the closet on the other side of the room. A dark blue hard case with the SEAL frog sticker on it. Flipping it open, I rifle through all of his clothes and find him a pair of shorts and a shirt. I don't miss the fact he doesn't have any boxers packed, or maybe I'm just missing them. But I doubt it. Boy loves to live free willy.

A couple minutes later, I'm climbing into the hot shower with Knox. Steam fills the glass trimmed walk-in shower, making the glass appear opaque. When I close the door, Knox is standing forearms against the wall with the water hitting his back.

Rubbing my hand over him, I ask, "Are you ok?"

He stands up and looks at me, smiling. "I am. Just letting the hot water soothe my tight muscles. I'm just exhausted. Did you see what the guys did?"

"With the beds?"

"Yea. They moved the other king mattress in here, so we can all sleep together."

I smile, then move over to him. "Let me wash you."

"Ev," his voice drops and his hand gently grabs my wrist.

"No funny business. I promise. Let me take care of you."

He hesitates for a second, then releases my wrist. Grabbing him by the shoulders, I direct him under the water, then pull him back out. I pump some shampoo into my hand and run it through his hair. We decided to use what they have instead of packing our own and they did not disappoint. It's some sort of bluish green coastal scent that smells like a fresh ocean breeze with hints of honey and tobacco. Once I'm done with his hair, I work the soap into a nice lather and rub the washcloth over his body.

"I love you." He's tired, and I want to just love on him and hold him. I want my funny and boisterous boy back that has Jax constantly saying, 'Shut the fuck up'.

He tilts my chin up. "I love you." He gives me a soft kiss that deepens and before I know it, the washcloth has dropped and my hands are roaming over his body.

He pulls away, chuckling.

"Sorry," I mumble, bending down to pick up the washcloth, ignoring his hard dick right there at my face. My mouth feels like it grew jets that just shot saliva in. Holy fuck.

I stand up, ignoring it. Its perfection. Until I can't. I have to clean it. It was in the ocean and sand and who knows what else. I press up against his chest, driving him back into the wall. The cold tile must sting his skin, because he lets out a hiss of a breath.

"What are you doing?" He asks through a hooded gaze.

"I'm cleaning you. All of you."

He lets out a low hum when my soapy hand wraps around his thick, hard cock.

"You were in the sand and the ocean. Who knows how dirty this is... So I want to make sure it's extra clean." My hand slowly glides from the base to his tip.

An appreciative groan escapes as his head presses back against the tile wall.

Swiping my thumb across the tip of his cock, I plant soft kisses along his neck and around his pecs. My other hand reaches down and cups his balls, massaging them, causing him to let out another moan as his hands press against the wall for support.

The wall, much like the door, is a fickle mistress.

Planting kisses down his body, I drop to my knees and look up at him, my eager mouth just an inch from his cock. His eyes are closed, but when he senses me waiting he looks down, brushing a hand through my wet locks. The water drips off his hair and runs down his face onto his body. I wish I could get a picture of him like this looking down at me. So hot.

"I want you to watch me suck you into my mouth."

His chest shudders with excitement as his cock bounces in front of me. A smile spreads across my face as my eyes lock on his, and I lean forward, sinking my hot mouth around his hard shaft. I take him deep, until he hits the back of my throat, then slowly pull him back out. His cock tastes like heaven as hints of the soap still linger. I suck him in again, faster and harder, while my hand moves to work his balls, until he's crying out.

"Goddamn Ev. I don't know what's better. The taste of your pussy or you sucking my cock."

I groan around his cock, the slight vibrations making him grab the wall again. Balls still in hand, I play with them. Tugging. Massaging.

He hisses out a string of words, but they're hard to make out and then his hands tangle in my hair, fighting to get a grip through the water, and he thrusts. Taking what he wants. I know he's close. His arousal is trickling out, coating my tongue.

As he begins to move faster, so do I.

"Shit!" His fingers latch into my hair and he gags me on his cock, hitting the back of my throat and I love every second of it. "I'm gonna-"

Before he can finish warning me, he's raising on his tiptoes and explodes down my throat, cock pressed so deep I'm fighting for air. Water from the shower hits me in the face, and my nose sucks in water, further choking me. I quickly pull off his dick and begin choking on air, causing some of his come to blow out of my nose.

"Fuck Ev!" Knox yells, pulling me up.

I'm still coughing and moaning, with tears falling down my cheeks and come dripping from my nose, sounding like some sort of strangled cat. A strangled cat who is secretly a dragon, because fucccckk it feels like I just breathed fire out of my nose.

He grabs under my chin and tilts my face to the water and begins swiping his come off while at the same time, nearly waterboarding me. "Blow," he commands.

Confused and overwhelmed, I pucker my lips and blow.

He laughs, "No, silly. Your nose. Blow out of your nose."

I'm a fucking idiot! I blow out of my nose, the burn slowly easing.

After another few minutes, the pain is gone, but the mortification remains. "Sorry. I sucked in water."

He shakes his head, laughing. "I thought I'd done something."

"No. It was me and my dumbass."

He kisses my forehead.

"Well, I think you're clean now."

"And feel like a new man." He brushes his hands over my head.

"Good. I didn't like the quiet and tired Knox. I want the one who's going to go downstairs and stir some shit up."

"He is who you shall have then, my love." His hand reaches down. "Now my turn to clean you."

"Knox, you don't have to. This wasn't a quid pro quo thing. I just wan-"

He smiles as he inserts a finger inside of me at the same time he presses his lips to my neck. "I know this was no quid pro quo... I'm just very pro pus." He nibbles on my neck. "That's Knox Latin for pro pussy. But first." He slides down my body, pausing at my chest. "I'm also pro nips."

Chuckling, I wrap my hand around the back of his head and bring him to my chest. "Suck away, my love. Suck away."

His hand slides up to cup my left breast, while his mouth circles my right, closing it around my peaked nipple. My back arches, pressing it further into his mouth, and he hums in appreciation.

"Fuck. This wasn't supposed to happen."

"What did you think was going to happen when you get in the shower with one of us?" A voice echoes near the door.

Standing there is Callum, arms crossed, ankles crossed, leaning against the door frame.

I reach my arm out to him, but he shakes his head. "Not right now. I was just sent to tell you it's dinnertime." When he sees me frown, he adds, "But don't worry. I'm very pro pus and pro nip as well." He stands upright. "Knox, hurry up, but make sure she comes."

Without waiting, Knox drops to his knees and flicks his tongue over my needy clit. My body starts moving on its own, a live wire and all it needs is a spark before I completely combust.

His mouth latches onto my pussy, his tongue sliding in as he lets out a growl. "I love this pussy so much." He fists my ass cheeks, holding me to him. Not getting the angle he wants, he grabs my leg and slips it over his shoulder, opening it up. "This is better." He dives right in and eats me like he's never had a meal before. It only takes a minute and I'm crying out his name, fingers clamped in his hair, rocking into his face. He rides out my orgasm, sucking on my clit and lapping up my release and swallowing it down.

EVERLEE - BREADED CHICKEN CUTLET

AFTER DINNER, WE DECIDE to sit on the back deck and enjoy our first night of vacation. With the constant breeze, the moonlight shining between the clouds, the sound of the waves breaking in the distance, and everyone I love in one place, it is the absolute perfect night.

To the left of the pool are large oval wicker-base couches with plush cushions that swallow you up. When Knox and I walk outside after finishing the dishes- the least we could do since we hadn't been around much in the afternoon- we find Callum, Lizzy, and Tony in the hot tub and the others sitting on the two couches. Will and Beckett are on one, and Jax and Emmett are on the other. I trod across the deck and plop down in between Jax and Emmett, while Knox climbs into the hot tub with Callum.

I plant my ass in the narrow space between my guys and throw my feet across Emmett's lap and lean against Jax. "Enjoying the night?"

"It's better now you're here," Emmett says, lifting my leg to give it a kiss on the inside of my knee.

On the couch beside us, Beckett makes a gagging sound.

"Shut up!" I glare at him.

"Oh stop! It's sweet," Will defends. "Pookie."

I make gagging sounds.

"Is that what it sounds like when you're-"

"Don't you finish that sentence," I snap at Beckett, cutting him off.

"Y'all are weird. Talking about sex so casually," Jax chimes in.

"You're in a poly pod with your brother," Beckett retorts.

"Yea, but... we're both dudes."

"And I'm gay. Ev and I both think men are super sexy," he says, patting Will's chest.

"Yes, indeed." I look up and kiss Jax's neck.

"What about me?" Emmett whines.

"And you." I sit up and give Emmett a kiss.

"Whatever. It's still weird."

"Is grump being a grump?" Lizzy chimes in.

He cocks his head to the side, staring at her, and she laughs.

"Y'all've been so good, so far."

"Y'all've? Wow! Can we contract any other words into one? You all have...Nope! Y'all've." Jax teases. "And it's because she was in her room most of the afternoon before she came down and started harassing your brother. So I had a reprieve."

"Don't you worry, boo boo grump, we have the entire week."

"Yay," he says deadpan.

Sighing, I grab Jax's hand and place it on my stomach, then grab Emmett's and place it on top of Jax's and then mine on top of both of them. Emmett looks at me, then down at our hands like he knows exactly what I'm doing. I want them together with me so badly that I can barely sit still.

Emmett promised on the plane and I do still owe them a release. Fuck, how is it possible I am this horny? I think today alone I've had... I try to count how many orgasms I've had, but lose track. That's a big fucking deal. My body shifts a little and I swear I feel Jax's body tense and Emmett looks at me.

Like they know.

Like they can sense it.

Smell it.

When I glance at Callum and Knox, they're in a deep conversation with Tony and Liz and Will and Beckett are groping each other while making out. It's so cute. I know what a big deal this is for Will. I've talked to Beckett a few times since Will has officially come out in public, and he said he's still having a hard time with public displays of affection. He's still very guarded. But hopefully this is a sign that he feels comfortable around us. I mean, how can he not?

Emmett catches my attention and nods slightly to Jax. When I tilt my head up, I see him watching Will and Beckett. I look back at Emmett and pump my eyebrows. While we've never talked about it, I think we both want the same thing, but I don't know if he'll admit he wants Jax like that. Once he says it out loud, then it's out in the world, not just in his head. And if it's out of his head and in the world, then something could happen and he doesn't want to cause problems if Jax doesn't feel the same way.

"Wait! Wait! Wait!" Lizzy shouts, and we all look at her. "You had sex on the beach?"

I blush.

"Who had that on their bingo card?" Beckett chimes.

"Do you really have bingo cards?"

"Hell yea, I do. Sexy time bingo cards are a must when we're in a sex den vacation house."

"You make us sound like sex fiends."

"How many orgasms have you had today?" Beckett retorts.

"That's unfair."

He bursts out laughing. "You don't know, do you? Because you've had so many? Unbelievable."

"Ask me how many I've had," Lizzy says, waving her hand in the air.

"No," Jax snaps.

"How many?" I glare playfully at Jax.

"Seven."

"Shit!" Beckett shouts. "Are you plus or minus that?"

I scrunch my nose.

"Jesus, fuck."

"She has four men. I have one. So unless she's had over twenty-eight, then I win!"

"Yes. That's true!" Beckett points his finger in the air.

"I'm not contesting that. It's a valid point. I'm also not the one trying to compete in orgasms."

"I gotta take my wins where I can get them," Lizzy laughs. "But seriously, who had that on their bingo card?"

Emmett pulls his phone out of his pocket and flips through some pictures. "It's on the triangle and the pentagon card."

"Pentagon and triangle?"

"Duh. There are those two and a circle. Lizzy and Tony are the circle, we're the triangle, and y'all are the pentagon."

"Wait, so she got one marked off her own card."

"I didn't know it was a thing until just now," I defend.

She puckers her lips at me. "You didn't put breaded chicken cutlet on there, did you?"

"Breaded what?" Jax asks.

"Are you serious?" She asks, looking around at the guys who are all shrugging.

I shake my head, knowing what's coming next, so I pick up Jax and Emmett's hands and clasp mine on the outside of theirs, pushing them together, so we're all holding hands.

"I'm going to be sorry I asked, aren't I?" Jax mumbles.

I tilt my head up, looking at him. "Most likely."

"Fuck."

I'm still chuckling when Lizzy pops out of the hot tub and sits on the edge and pulls in a deep breath. When we were in highschool and she learned this, I swear she talked about it all the time. "Breaded chicken cutlet. It's when you're fucking a girl on the beach, you pull your dick out, stick it in the sand, then stick it back in her."

"Fuck." Jax twists his legs and clamps my thighs together.

"We'd never do that to our pussy," Emmett says, rubbing my leg with his free hand.

"Thank you."

"Why in the fuck do you know that?" Jax asks Lizzy, taking a sip of his Old-Fashioned.

How did I miss that earlier? I hold my hand out for a sip.

"I was trying to hide it from you, you little leach."

"No wonder I missed it. Now give me." I clasp my hands together quickly like a toddler.

He sighs and hands it over.

"Thank you, love."

"Whatever," he grumbles, taking the glass back and pressing his lips to my forehead.

"Such the softy you are."

He rolls his eyes, looking at me.

EVERLEE - BAD JOO JOO

Emmett carries a pitcher of spiked lemonade with several glasses stacked in his hand, wearing a wide-brimmed beach hat with a pink flower and two sets of sunglasses.

"Love the look," Jax chimes.

"Thought you would. I wore it for you." Emmett winks.

Pushing up from the chair, I grab the glasses out of his hand and give them to Jax to pass around the group. Lizzy, Tony, Knox, and Callum run up from the beach where they've been in an intense round of bocce ball.

"Who won?" Beckett asks, pulling his glasses down on his nose.

"Still not over, but we'll win. We always do," Lizzy chimes.

"Except you haven't the last two games," Knox teases.

"Those were practice."

"In the middle of our best of seven?"

Lizzy ignores his question and reaches for a glass. "What do we have here?"

"Spiked lemonade."

"You had me at spiked."

"That's what I said when I first met her. I just walked up to her and said *spiked*! But it was in a super deep and sexy voice and she nearly melted on the spot," Tony jokes.

Lizzy laughs and punches his shoulder. "What's funny is that you are kidding, but also not."

He looks at her, confused.

"Our first conversation was legitimately you telling me the punch at Ross and Levi's party was spiked."

"No."

"Yes."

The entire group erupts in laughter.

"How could you forget that?"

"I was so lost in your beauty... I don't remember what I said most of that evening or the next day."

"Next day?" Beckett yells out. "You hussy."

"We met for coffee." Tony holds up his hand.

I clear my throat because I know the whole story.

"Ok. We walked to get coffee together."

"Z snap!" Emmett says, snapping his fingers in the shape of a Z.

"No he didn't just Z snap!" Knox says bouncing up and down. "And with all the sass of the sun hat and shades. All he's missing is a little umbrella in his drink."

Beckett chimes in, "What is that supposed to mean?"

"Now you've done it!" Callum laughs.

"I was simply saying... that Emmett likes umbrellas in his drinks. Just a fact. When did you get so sensitive, priss pot?" Knox presses.

"Priss pot? Who are you calling a priss pot?" Beckett asks standing up.

Knox lunges forward, putting Beckett in a chokehold. "You, pretty boy."

The two of them wrestle, falling to the ground rolling around. Mounting and flipping one another over.

"Boys!" I call out.

They both stop moving and look at me.

"Are you done?"

They look at each other and Beckett mumbles, "I'm not a priss pot."

"Fine, I'll leave the pot off next time," Knox says, pushing Beckett off him.

Beckett stands and reaches down to help Knox up, but when Knox reaches for him, Beckett swipes his hand through his hair. "Ooh." He laughs. "Just kidding." He reaches back down again and grabs Knox's hand, pulling him up.

"Can I have my hat and sunglasses now?" I ask Emmett, who's still standing there with the pitcher in hand.

"Yes, darling. Though I thought I looked rather fetching in it."

"So fetch."

He leans down and gives me a kiss as he plants the hat on my head.

This is how the rest of the day goes. Sitting in beach chairs under the umbrellas that Callum sat out for us, playing games, drinking drinks, and just having a general great time. Everyone is happy and smiling. Even Lizzy and Jax share a moment, teaming up for a game of bocce ball against Emmett and me.

I assumed Lizzy wanted to be on my team, but the little twat picked Jax.

God love her!

We all decide to go back to the house in the early afternoon to take showers and get ready for dinner. Beckett, Emmett and I are the first out of the shower, so Beckett and I head towards the game room to play while Emmett goes downstairs to start cooking dinner. We both offer to help, but he turns us down. He loves to be in the kitchen, with just him, his tools, and his thoughts.

"Darts?" I ask.

"Yes. If you want to get beat. I've been practicing quite a bit lately," Beckett goads.

"I'm pretty sure I can still beat you."

"We'll see."

I throw the first dart, hitting the double twenty.

"Strong start."

Beckett throws his dart and gets triple sixteen just as his phone rings. When I flip it over, I see it's mom.

"Why is she calling?"

"I don't know. I'm not a telepath."

I swipe to answer. "Hello?"

"Everlee?"

"Yea. What's up?"

"What are you doing on the phone?"

"You called me."

"No, I didn't. I called your brother."

"No. You called me. That's why I'm talking to you."

"What? No."

"Mom. Why would I be talking to you if you didn't call me?"

"Well, fiddlesticks. I was meaning to call your brother. How are you doing?"

"I'm good. You?"

"Ehh. Your dad left for his business trip just a bit ago, so I'm at the house by myself for a week."

"Oh wow. What are you going to do, you sassy little minx?"

"Everlee." The way she says my name tells me she's blushing.

"Well, let me go. I need to call your brother."

"Ok. Talk to you later. I love you."

"Love you too."

I set the phone down and Beckett is staring at me. "That was fucked up."

"Ehh. It's payback for all those times she tricked us as kids. Eat your carrots or you'll go blind. Don't swallow your gum or you'll inflate like the kid in that movie."

"Don't masturbate or your fingers will fall off."

"She never told me that one."

"Well, that explains a lot."

"What does that even mean?"

Beckett's phone rings again and before I can answer it, he snatches it and puts it on speaker.

"Hey mom," Beckett answers.

"The weirdest thing just happened. I called you. Well, I thought I did and Everlee picked up. I swear I pressed your name, though."

"You called me. Everlee was being funny."

"Hey mom," I chime in.

"Everlee!" she scolds. "Well, while I have you on the phone, Winston was asking about you."

"Mom," I groan.

"No, he was just asking how you were doing. He's with that girl he met at Easter. Tabby or something. I forget her name."

"I'm good."

"Dating anyone?"

I hesitate. "Not right now." Anyfour... different story. Semantics.

"Oh Everlee. I worry about you."

"Mom. I'm great. I have lots of friends, a great job. Life is good. I don't need to settle down and find a husband right now." Or ever. I glare at Beckett, urging him to step in.

He rolls his eyes and sighs, "What's up, mom? Do you need something?"

"Well, your dad is gone for the week and I seem to have misplaced the keys to the lawnmower."

"Mom. You don't need to cut the grass. I'm sure dad just did it a few days ago and I will do it when I'm back."

"You're at the beach, right?"

"Yea. Winslow Bay with Ev."

"So close. Do I get a visit from my daughter this week?"

Fucking Beckett.

He shrugs in defense. "Mom, it's a couple of hours away."

She sighs and I bobble my head from side to side. Part of me feels guilty she's alone, but the other part tells me she's a strong semi-independent woman who needs this time to focus on her and not Beckett or my dad.

"I suppose so. How's your place?" Her tone is soft.

"It's huge. Amazing. Right on the beach. I was getting groceries yesterday and I don't know how it came up, but the cashier and I started talking about it and she told me the locals here call this place the Sand Castle, because it's so huge."

"Wow. Sounds like y'all are going to have an amazing time."

"Yea. I'd invite you, but–"

"Oh, no. Thank you, though."

I stare at Beckett and smack his arm. Invite her? What in the fuck is he thinking?

"Listen, don't mow the grass. I'll be home Saturday and can handle it."

"Ok. Well, I won't keep you two any longer. Have fun this week."

"Bye mom."

"Bye," I chime in just before he ends the call.

He picks up a dart. "Where were we?"

"What the fuck, Beckett?" I ask, slapping his arm.

"What?"

"Inviting our mother to our sexy beach time house? What in the hell were you thinking?"

"I was just being nice. She will not come. You know she doesn't drive anywhere. Especially anywhere further than an hour away."

"Fuck!"

"I don't know why you're so worried."

"Because it would just be my luck that she shows up."

"If she shows up...then–"

"If who shows up?" Lizzy asks, walking in, putting her hair up in a bun.

"Mother."

"Your mom is coming?" She blows out a cool breath.

"No. She's not coming," Beckett asserts.

"Becks here, thought it would be a good idea to invite her."

"I love your mom to pieces, but why?"

"It wasn't even a full invite. I said I'd invite you, but..."

"But what?"

"But nothing. She cut me off and said no thanks. Because she doesn't drive anywhere!"

Lizzy laughs. "This would be the one time she does."

Beckett says sarcastically, "Ok. Everlee."

Lizzy shrugs her shoulder.

"I forgot what it's like having you both around each other for long periods of time. There's like a symbiosis that happens and you meld." He shivers his shoulders.

"I can't even play anymore." I sit the darts down.

"I feel like the real reason you're leaving is because it's been over ten minutes since you've seen your men and you're hungry for cock, but you're using this as a reason to make me feel bad." He points his finger in the air. "When you're in your sixties, I won't be inviting you to any beach parties. I'll remember this!"

"Ugh!" I stomp out of the room and down the stairs.

How does he not get that any hint of an invitation is a bad thing? Fuck. I need a drink.

Emmett is down in the kitchen, cutting up some vegetables, when he looks at me. He lays the knife down and walks over to me and cups my cheeks. "What's wrong? Who did it?"

"Beckett. He semi-invited my mother as a friendly gesture."

"Invited her... here?"

"Yes!"

He blows out a cool breath.

"He's not worried because she never drives anywhere, especially on her own, and this is more than an hour away."

"Where's your dad?"

"Some business trip for a week, so she's alone. Which is why he was trying to be nice."

"Do you want a drink?"

"Please, but first." I wrap my arms around him, pressing my cheek to his chest.

He lifts me and sits me on the counter and moves in between my legs, kissing my forehead, then my nose, then my lips. It's a soft, but passionate kiss as his hands knead my thighs.

When he pulls away, he presses his forehead to mine. "What are you doing?" he whispers.

"I was coming in here to help you."

"That's not what I mean," his voice lowers, so it's barely audible.

Oh. He means with Jax.

My pulse starts to quicken. I don't know if I want to tell him what I'm doing because I don't want him to try to talk me out of it, or say it's not a good idea, or that it won't happen. Deep down, I believe it will and want to see if it will just happen organically. Well, maybe with a small nudge to show them - him - it's ok.

"Nothing." I smile.

He pulls away, tilting his head to the side. "Ev."

All he says is my name. He doesn't push or try to stop me.

"That's weird," Lizzy announces, walking into the kitchen, pulling our attention.

"What?" I ask, hopping down from the counter.

"It's raining outside. It wasn't supposed to this week."

"We're at the beach," Emmett says.

"So? I trust my handy dandy weather guy Brad P. to never lead me astray."

"It's like a crap shoot every day for them."

"What crawled up your butt and died?" Lizzy retorts.

Emmett just looks at her from the stove, but doesn't respond.

"Well, you know what this means," Lizzy continues.

"What?" I ask, knowing good and goddamn well what she's about to say, but I'm a masochist and also need validation.

"Bad joo-joo."

"What?" Emmett barks, unable to contain himself as he dumps the vegetables into a pan.

"Bad joo-joo," Lizzy repeats, as if he didn't hear her the first time. His eyebrows perk up, waiting for more of an explanation. "Bad luck. It's a sign from Mother Nature."

"Well, my mother showing up would be bad joo-joo."

"I still can't believe my brother from another mother did that!" She shakes her head in disbelief.

"Jesus fuck. Are we still on this?" Beckett asks, walking into the room.

"Yes! It's the reason it's raining outside."

"It's raining?" Will asks, peeking around our shoulders. "It wasn't supposed to rain this week."

"Thank you!" Lizzy shouts, holding her arms out to Will. "That's why he's my beau FF."

"Wait." Beckett rubs his hands through his hair. "You're telling me you think it's raining right now, when it wasn't supposed to rain, because I quasi-invited mother dearest to our love shack?"

I look between him, Will, and Lizzy. "Yes."

"Fuck off." He flips his hands in the air. "Emmett, do you think the same?"

He looks at us, tilting his chin down with an expression that says he very much does not agree with me.

"He thinks it's because we're at the beach," I speak for him.

"A very sound and logical explanation. Much more logical than it's raining because I verbally invited our mother."

"Mother Nature works in mysterious ways. You ever drive down a road and have lots of animals darting out in front of you and then, after the sixth time, you think maybe you should slow down and then BOOM!" Lizzy claps. "A copper is sitting tucked under a bridge." She points rapidly, "Or you're driving along and you think you see a siren flashing so you slow down, for there not be one and then moments later, BOOM!" She claps again, "a copper is sitting tucked under a bridge."

"Sounds like you need to slow down or assume there's going to be a cop under every bridge you pass," Beckett chuckles.

"Not the point B. All I'm saying is that things happen."

"You're crazy." He shakes his hands in the air.

"Probably. But that one time you ignore the animals in the road or the imaginary lights, you're going to get a speeding ticket."

"Or if, you know, this is a crazy idea, went the speed limit, you wouldn't get a ticket."

"Who does that? They are mere suggestions. They should really change them from speed limits to speed ranges. Like you can drive anywhere between thirty-five and fifty miles per hour on this road."

"I'm done with this conversation."

"I'm surprised you let it go on as long as you did," Jax says, popping up from the couch.

"Have you been there the whole time?" I look from him to Emmett.

"Yep," he says, laying back down.

Well, thank fuck I didn't say anything about Jax to Emmett.

CALLUM - NEVER TELL A WOMAN TO CALM DOWN

DINNER TONIGHT WAS FANTASTIC. Everlee was quiet through most of it, with her face twisted with worry. When I asked Jax about it, he said it was something about Beckett inviting their mother to the beach house for the week... which yea, was pretty dumb, but in his defense and with everything I've heard about their mother... she doesn't leave her house. Especially without her husband. I think Beckett was just trying to be supportive and I can't blame him for that.

We spent the first fifteen minutes of dinner trying to calm her down. At one point, Beckett literally told her to calm down and I'm fairly certain that was the worst mistake he could have ever made. Had Knox not grabbed the bowl of fruit from in front of her, I'm pretty sure it would have been emptied on his lap.

After dinner, it was still raining, much to everyone's dismay, so that put a damper on outdoor activities.

Beckett and Will still got in the hot tub and Lizzy and Tony played a game or three of shuffleboard in the game room.

When Everlee first mentioned this trip to us, I was concerned because I didn't want it to be the kind where we all have to agree on something and then do it together. This was nice, though. We all sort of do our own thing and we can invite others along if they want to. I do enjoy the group dinners though. It was nice to hear about everyone's day.

Most of it was spent together, but Will and Beckett took a walk in the afternoon during low tide and walked to the end of the island, where it meets up with another across a small inlet and saw dolphins feeding on the beaches. They said the dolphins were circling fish, then would push them up on the strand and leap out of the water to eat. We looked it up, and it's called strand feeding. Everlee's eyes lit up like a Christmas tree, so we're all going to head that way tomorrow afternoon to see the dolphins.

With everyone doing their own thing tonight, the guys and I decide to head back to the room to rearrange it a little more. We had taken the second king mattress out of the other room and brought it in here, but it's really cramped with the dresser. Since we have the other room designated as our closet, we decided this morning to shift the dresser and corner chairs into our room's walk-in closet. Emmett had the brilliant idea of taking a picture of the room beforehand so we can put everything back where it belongs. I'd hate to get a fine for moving furniture around.

Thirty minutes later, Everlee is walking into our room just as we're putting the final touches on it. Well, final as it can be. We have two large-ass mattresses taking up a majority of the floor space, but moving the dresser allowed us to run the mattresses down the left side of the room in front of the closet and window, allowing a small walkway to the bathroom on the right. We put all the pillows from both rooms along the wall to make a row of pillows. It's not the circle bed that we usually sleep on, but there isn't enough space for all of that.

"Lookin' good guys," she says, pouncing onto the bed.

"I hope you're talking about us and not the bed," Jax says.

She puckers her lips and taps her chin.

"You seem to be in a better mood." Jax slips his shirt off and tosses it to the corner of the room behind the door.

"I am. Well, kind of. I'm trying not to freak out. It's been several hours since he talked to her, so tomorrow will be the tell-tell day."

"So we better make the most of our time then, is what you're saying?" Knox hums, walking over to her on his tippy toes, looking like a sprite little fairy.

A smile spreads across her face. "That sounds exciting, but I'm a little tired. It's been a long day."

She flops onto the bed and we all look at each other. Her words are not matching her actions, because she's rubbing her legs up and down, looking at us with those pouty lips.

"Ev?" I growl softly, with my cock twitching in my pants.

"Hmm?" She's biting on her bottom lip and I can feel the energy in the room shifting.

"I need to get my pajamas out of my suitcase," she yawns.

"Let me, darling. You just get all the rest you can right now," Knox cheers, flying out of the room. His unspoken words were *because we're about to fuck you into the night.* If by some chance the heavens spite us and her mom shows up tomorrow, then we need to get our sexual fill now.

"They're red."

"Red?" Knox asks, poking his head back into the room with a low gravel in his voice.

"Red?" I ask, completely confused.

"Ev." Jax is nearly humming right now with restrained excitement, and it's making my cock twitch as well.

"Red," Emmett says matter-of-factly. "Sorry. Everyone else was saying it, so I felt left out."

Everlee laughs, rolling onto her stomach, kicking her feet into the air. Her already short shorts ride up her ass more and I start salivating. Without thinking, my hand is gliding up her leg, inching ever closer to the curve of her ass. Just as I'm about to touch it, Knox bursts into the room.

"Everlee McKinley!" His face is red. From blushing?

"Knox Fisher," she calls back defiantly, with a hint of con-fusion.

He's holding something behind his back and under his shirt, but I can't quite make it out. "Is there something you need to tell us?" he asks in an accusatory tone.

"I didn't think there was, however, by the way you're acting, I feel like I should say yes."

His lips pinch into a flat line and his head tilts down. "Are we not satisfying you? Giving you what you want? What you need? When you need it?"

Her brow furrows, and the hint of a smile curls on her lips. "What are you talking about? Of course you do."

"Then why do," he pauses, looking behind him down the hall, then steps forward and shuts the door, "then why do you have this?" He yells pulling his hand around in front of him.

Her large green monster cock.

She gasps, then growls. "Lizzy. I swear to God! I left my luggage open on the bed when I was getting ready for the Stars and Stripes party."

She stands from the bed and saunters over to him slowly. He's fucked.

She stands on her toes and wraps her arms around his neck, kissing just under his ear. "Do you want to use that on me?"

He licks his lips, nodding.

"Did she at least pack any lube?" Everlee asks, already for-giving Lizzy for sneaking it in.

He stutters out a no as her hands gently glide under his shirt and up his chest, pulling it over his head.

"Shame on her," Everlee teases.

"I got you, boo," Emmett says, walking into the bathroom.

She turns to Emmett and laughs. She's like a drug.

I walk over to her from the bed and wrap my hands around her waist, turning her towards me, so her back is against Knox's chest.

"Oh no," he feigns. "Not her backside." He laughs a deep, playful laugh. "Psych! Back side, best side!"

"Here, here." Emmett walks back into the room, waving the bottle of lube in the air.

"Here, here," she mumbles, fisting my shirt and lifting it over my head. Her hands and her gaze travel down my body, feeling like silk on my skin. Her hands rest on the band of my shorts and with her chin tilted down, she nibbles her bottom lip, while her dark, sensual gaze settles on my face.

"I'm going to suck that lip out of your mouth. You drive me crazy when you do that," I pant out.

She doesn't stop, and continues to watch me.

Defiant.

Daring.

When I move to kiss her, the smell of sun and coconut swirl around me, causing my head to swim. God, she's intoxicating. A drug created especially for me, to torment me and drive me wild. My love for her will be the death of me, but my God, it will be glorious.

Knox, being the ass he is, ruins the moment by taking the massive green dildo and inches it over her shoulder and pokes me in the neck with it, like he's playing a game of pool. Asshole.

"We're going to have fun with you," I say, running my hands up her stomach and slipping her shirt over her head. Her breasts bounce, dropping with their natural weight, as she stands there before us.

"I love your fucking breasts," I mumble out, grabbing them in my hands.

"I love fucking your breasts," Knox says behind her, making her giggle.

"Shut the fuck up," Jax says. It's been almost an hour since he's said it, so it felt about time.

"What? I do." He presses up behind her and loops his hands around her stomach and down her shorts.

"I love watching you come undone," I moan, heat boiling inside of me.

"Do you want to watch her now, Callum? Do you want to watch me finger fuck our girl until she comes all over them?"

No more playful Knox. There's a fire in his eyes.

She lets out a gasp and arches her back, pressing her breasts into my hands while her head falls back against his chest. Her hand snakes up Knox's body and wraps around his neck for support, and she lets out another moan. "Take me."

"We will love, but not yet. We're going to make you come so much tonight it will take the rest of the week for your body to recover."

She whimpers out, her knees buckling as she clamps down on her bottom lip.

"We can't see what he's doing to you love to make you moan so much." I drop down and slowly grab the top of her shorts and glide them down and over Knox's hand. He's buried two fingers deep while his thumb rubs on her clit. "Such a beautiful pussy."

"If I was an artist, I'd paint it and hang it in our house," Emmett says, slipping out of his clothes and climbing onto the bed beside Jax.

She looks over at him and her eyes... they flash for a minute, but then it's gone.

I drop to my knees and rub my hands up the back of her legs softly and slowly, then grab an ass cheek with each hand and breathe onto her clit.

"Oh damn numanum," she moans, legs getting weak again.

My cock is so ready. Ready to escape the confines of these pants. Ready to feel her hand, her mouth, her deliciously tight pussy around it. Choking it. Sliding into her slick arousal.

"Lizzy got seven orgasms in one day. I want to give you eight in one hour. Starting now."

EVERLEE – IT TAKES TWO

HIS WORDS NEARLY MAKE me come. The power this man. Hell. These men have over me is... unhealthy, but at the same time, so fucking healthy. Callum pulls Knox's thumb away, while he moves in slowly, so fucking slowly, and runs his tongue over my clit.

"Talk to her, Jax. I think she wants to hear what we're going to do to her," Callum commands, before passing his tongue by again.

A moan escapes before I can catch myself.

"Do you want me to talk to you, love? Tell you we're going to fill every hole on your body with our come?"

A whimper. I need a cock inside of me now.

Stretching me.

Fucking me.

"She likes that," Knox says bending his fingers and hitting that glorious spot.

My knees buckle, but Callum's hands latch on, holding me up.

"There's one," Knox whispers, placing his lips on my neck.

Jax commands, "Knox, suck her off your fingers while Callum fucks her pussy with his tongue, drinking up her arousal."

Without words or hesitation, he removes his fingers from my needy little cunt and glides them up my body right in front of my lips, then sucks them off right in my ear. His groans cause a wave of pleasure to float through my body, and then another hits me as Callum eats me like the goddamn pro he is.

Another wave is building. It's too soon. Too fast.

"I want to take this pretty little ass of yours," he says, brushing the hair off my shoulder. "Can I take her ass, Jax?"

He looks at Emmett and they pass a silent exchange through their gaze and my stomach tightens and I nearly come. Emmett's waiting for Jax. So they can take me together. Hell yes!

"Yes. Take her ass, while Callum takes her pussy."

Emmett tosses the lube over to Knox, who catches it with one hand, while his other fondles my breast, rubbing my nipple through his fingers, applying just enough pressure for me to feel it in my pussy.

When I close my eyes for a second, Jax barks at me. "Eyes open, love. I didn't say you could close them."

His commands light my skin on fire with the control he has over me. Desire pools within making me want to obey him so I open my eyes slowly and stare at him. The exhibitionist in me wants to watch him while he watches me being fucked by these men, but the voyeur inside of me wants to watch Emmett and Jax fist their cocks.

The click of the cap echoes behind me and a moment later, Knox's hand is gliding down my ass, and then between my cheeks.

"Come for daddy," Knox commands, pressing a lubed finger at my forbidden entrance.

Callum slips two fingers in as he continues to suck on my clit, driving me completely crazy. When I glance over at Emmett, my heart stops beating for a second. Jax is leaning over, his cock on Emmett's leg as he's whispering something.

Fuck me. I thought they were kissing.

Fuck!

I whimper out and Knox twists my neck, taking my lips in his as he swallows my moans down. "We can't have you letting the entire house know what we're doing in here."

"I'm pretty sure they already know," Jax says, sitting up.

I want to know what he was saying. I want to know what Emmett was thinking with Jax's cock so close. The idea of them fucking and me watching... my stomach tightens at the thought. To watch Jax's face while Emmett sucks him off. Visions of it play in my head and I nearly come.

"I need... to lie down. Legs..."

"You're going to ride their cocks while they stand," Jax commands.

Knox presses a finger in and I buck slightly in my stance. He gently and slowly pushes me over so I'm bending at my hips while Callum tosses his shorts across the room.

"So tight. This ass is so perfect, like it was made for my cock."

He works my ass, rubbing and stretching. He applies more lube to his fingers and inserts a second and continues. After a few more minutes, I hear the familiar click of the cap and then feel his cock at my entrance, like a shuttle waiting for its launch sequence. In my head, I count down. Five... four... three... His stance widens... two... he places a hand on the center of my back... one... his other hand grabs my hip... blast off.

He pushes in slowly.

Images of a shuttle slowly lifting from its base, shoots through my mind.

He pauses at the tight ring of muscle, letting me adjust to his size, before he pushes all the way in to the hilt. His hands glide up my back, pressing firmly like he's fighting for control within his own body. He pulls his cock out, except for the tip, reapplies more lube and then presses in again, this time a little faster.

"Your ass feels so good." His hands grip around my hips as he presses in again, each time getting faster and faster until need consumes us both and I'm pressing back into him.

"Oh Knox. Yes. Give me more."

"Stop," Jax commands, but we don't listen. "Stop," he repeats, his voice more stern.

We both look up, slowing to a stop.

A smile spreads across his face.

"Callum, lift our girl and hold her in your arms while you both fuck her."

Callum walks over and Knox helps lift me into Callum's arm, his cock still pressed inside of me. When I move to wrap my legs around Callum, Knox lets out a whimper. "You can't do that, babe." His hand brushes across my breasts. "Your ass clamped down like a vise."

"Sorry... not sorry?"

He pinches my nipple playfully and I buck, his cock hitting my tail bone.

"Ouch!" He barks.

"That was your fault."

"Please don't break my cock."

"That could also ruin the vacation," I say, going back to our conversation from yesterday. I lean my head back on his shoulder, while Callum notches himself at my entrance.

"Yes. Most definitely."

Callum presses in slowly. "You're so tight."

Once I'm fully seated on both of their cocks, they adjust their arms around me, keeping me at a good height sandwiched between them.

"Goddamn. It's the perfect Everlee sandwich," Jax moans.

"After they load me full of their come, I want you both in my pussy." My gaze flickers from Jax to Emmett, back to Jax. He looks at Emmett, then nods without saying anything. Even though I'm fairly certain that's what he's waiting for, I still wanted to offer it up so he could think it was my idea, if he wasn't ok admitting out loud that's what he wanted, yet.

Callum and Knox move in unison, thrusting me up and down on their cocks. The pressure, the fullness almost too much to take.

"Do you like that?" Callum grunts out.

"Yes!" I fucking love it. I lean forward and wrap my arms around Callum's neck, pressing my chest against his. "Fuck me harder," I plead.

"Hold her for a second, Knox."

They pause as Callum loops his arm under my leg and grabs my ass. "Much better."

I smile, because this gives me more control as well.

"Ok, Knox. Let's give our girl what she wants and fuck her so hard she won't be able to walk tomorrow."

"Yes, sir," Knox says, and I quiver with lust.

Taking Callum's lips, I press my tongue into his mouth and wrap my hands around the back of his head. His free hand glides up my back and grabs my hair, pulling me backwards. "Don't forget about Knox."

I turn my head to the side, the only direction it can go with the hold Callum has on me, and find Knox there waiting for. His hand grips around my neck, with his thumb notched under my chin, holding it in place, bending me backwards a little more.

His kiss is wild, reckless. Hungry.

It takes my breath away as they continue to fuck up into me, causing my entire body to spool like a rubber band ready to explode.

Callum latches around my breast.

"She likes it rough, Cal, suck her hard," Jax commands.

He hesitates for a second and then his teeth clamp down as he sucks harder. A pain travels down through my stomach to my clit, as I moan out into Knox's mouth.

"I think I'm about to fucking blow my load watching you," Emmett cries.

When I glance at him, his hands are pressed into the bed and he's gripping the sheets, like they're his life raft.

"Fuck," he groans out again, his hips thrusting in the air.

God, what I wouldn't give right now to see Jax suck him off.

The image flashes in my head and that's all I need. I fucking explode, screaming out.

"Goddamn," Callum says, pulling his cock out. "She's squirting."

I moan out, arching my back at the same time Callum drops my legs, which is the wrong fucking time because I'm like a newborn giraffe. My legs buckle, but Knox's cock inside of my ass prevents me from falling to the ground, although it getting shoved further in my ass only amplifies the orgasm.

"Holy shit," Knox says, looking over my shoulder. "Get down there Callum!"

"No. I need you in my mouth," I whine.

"Eiffel tower?" Knox asks.

"Yes," I pant out. "Just hold me up."

"I would never let you fall, babe." Knox presses his hand to my back and bends me over. I would have happily bent over on my own, but the fact Knox is controlling me sends shivers through my body and makes me hot as fuck.

"Suck my cock," Callum commands, placing his hands on my head and guiding me down. "Do you want your face fucked, love?"

"Goddamn right."

"I love you," Knox whines, thrusting his cock into my ass, sending my mouth around Callum.

Callum sucks in a breath as he hits the back of my throat and I clench around him. His hands twist tightly in my hair as he takes control and presses in again before pausing. He's savoring it. The power.

Clamping my fingers around Callum's waist, I steady myself. "That's a good girl," Callum says, his free hand rubbing under my chin. "Look at our good girl, boys. Taking our cocks like the queen she is. So eager for them."

I moan out my appreciation around his cock and suck him in.

His back arches and he loses the battle of control for a moment. "Such a good fucking girl."

His praises are about to make me come again.

I don't see or hear anyone move, but a second later, I hear a vibration.

Dead.

Knox presses the green monster inside of my cunt and I fucking lose it. It's moving in circles deep inside of me as the vibration causes my entire body to tingle in delight.

"Holy fucking shit. Oh my God! Oh my God!" Knox yells out.

"Keep it together, Knox," Jax warns.

"I... oh... fuck. It... shit... touching. Damn it." His need unleashes, and he's fucking me hard and fast, his hands clamping onto the side of my hips. Using my right hand, I grab the green machine as gravity pulls it out of my pussy and press it back in, praying Callum won't let me fall.

Knox presses in and my leg muscles start to shake and then he's cussing out a string of words as he slams into me one last time, filling me with his warm release. My... shit... I don't know what orgasm it is, but it hits me hard and fast.

"Hold her, Knox."

My eyes literally roll into the back of my head, and I'm pretty sure I just passed out for a minute. But like a kid on a sugar rush, I pop back up and suck Callum's cock into my mouth, abandoning the monster to fall onto the floor.

"Everlee," Callum sighs.

With Knox's hands around my waist, holding me up, Callum locks his fingers in my hair and thrusts fast. I reach up and grab his balls and he lets loose, shooting down my throat.

"Oh," he cries out, his body still rocking back and forth like it doesn't know his cock has stopped moving.

We all collapse to the mattress, breathing heavily.

Giving us a minute, Jax walks over. "You aren't done yet."

I smile. "Yes. Operation Awakening, commences."

"She's like the energizer bunny. She keeps going and going and going."

"If only you were too," Jax snaps. "Then you could go, go, go get the fuck out of here."

"I'm rubber, you're glue, whatever you say."

"Seriously, shut up."

"I'm going to go to the bathroom and wash up, not because you asked me to, but because I'm making the choice."

"No. Don't leave," Jax fiends.

"I'm going to clean up quickly, then grab us all a pitcher of water. I feel like we're going to need it," Callum says.

I lay on the bed for another moment, trying to regrow bones in my body, waiting for Callum to leave. I'm trying to keep the moans to when the door is closed, although it wouldn't surprise me if the rest of the house heard us after my little squirting incident.

Callum walks through wearing a pair of light gray joggers low on his hips. Oh, mama Mia. The thin fabric does little to hide his large swinging cock within, coupled with his whole display of tattoos.

"You're moaning," Jax says.

Callum looks over his shoulder when he gets to the door and winks at me. "You three have fun."

Knox slips out right after him, with a hand towel wrapped around his cock. He mumbles something about using the other shower and grabbing clothes.

It's just the three of us.

My stomach is twisting into a bundle of excited knots. That or Callum's come is growing wings and flying around in my stomach.

I don't want to push too fast, but I've been thinking about this for a while. There are so many things I want to do, but I have to take it slow.

"I can't wait to take both of you."

"Me too," Jax and Emmett say in near unison.

I close my eyes, savoring this moment for a minute. "What do you want, Ev?" Jax asks.

My gaze shifts to Emmett, whose chest puffs up, but he doesn't speak.

"First. I want you both in my hands, then in my mouth, then in my pussy. I want you both everywhere, together."

Emmett looks at Jax, waiting for him to shoot it down, but he doesn't. He simply says, "Ok."

Fucking right, doggy!

Control yourself Ev.

"Lube," I staccato out, like a doctor asking for a scalpel.

Emmett hands it to me, still not speaking.

Flipping the cap open, I squeeze some lube onto the palm of my hand, lay the tube down, then rub my hands together, coating them. "I need you closer, so I can get your cocks in my hand."

"Here," Emmett suggests, moving to the opposite side of Jax, so they are sitting in front of one another.

"Yes. Now lay back." They were still too far away. "Scoot closer, so your asses are touching."

Jax looks at me without speaking, then scoots. I glance at Emmett and watch his eyes roll into the back of his head, but Jax can't see. When he opens his eyes, he looks at me and smiles, so I toss a wink back.

"Very nice," I hum out, sitting beside them with both of their cocks in front of me, hard and ready for attention.

"You two were such good boys watching me get fucked earlier, and now it's your turn."

Jax interlaces his fingers behind his head and looks up at me with his stomach muscles clenching, hardening the lines of his six-pack. He swipes his tongue over his lips and I just want to kiss them!

In time.

The mattress presses down when I shift onto my knees and grab their cocks in my hand, stroking them from base to tip.

EMMETT - WHEN HANDS ROAM

OH MY GOD. SHE'S stroking our cocks so painfully slow and his balls. His balls are touching my balls. If one of us farted, it would likely pass into the other's ass. Like the school grade card game suck and blow. Only this would be the opposite. I shouldn't be thinking about this right now.What is wrong with me?

No. I should be focused on Everlee, rubbing our two cocks together. She's hot for our cocks and not in the singular, but literally the plural. I saw her watching us earlier. The hope, the longing in her eyes.

Damn. I wanted it too. I'd give my left ball if Jax reached over and grabbed my cock. I was so close to exploding and he knew it, too. Fuck, he could have probably just started reaching for it and I would have blown my load.

I shouldn't be thinking about him like that. We're family. We don't fuck, well, like that, anyway. Sure, he's taken me from behind, which he hasn't done recently, and I don't know why. Does he not like it, because I was pretty sure he did. Not enough to want to do it on our own, but it was always nice when we could line up and fuck Everlee together. I'd almost wish for that tonight, but I desperately want to feel his cock in her pussy with me. Maybe that's why he stopped, because he likes the way my cock feels against his?

I love her with everything inside of me. I want to fucking load her with my come, with our come and make pretty, pretty babies with her. We can't. I get that, but shit. The idea of shooting my come inside of her makes me so damn hard, it hurts. The longer I'm with her, the more I'm beginning to think I have a breeding kink. A shiver runs down my spine and my balls start to tighten. No, Emmett. Pace yourself.

"You like this?" she asks.

She's not looking at me and my breath stops. I don't hear a response, but she smiles with a light giggle. She turns to me, "Do you?"

I tilt my chin down. Such a stupid question. She knows I love it. That I want more. I want everything.

"I love both of your cocks together. It makes me so," she raises on her knees, as she nibbles on her bottom lip.

She is so goddamn sexy.

"Fucking horny."

She looks around and her eyes land on something. Following her gaze, I see her green machine.

"Yes, baby," I moan, reaching my arm out for it. My leg shifts and swipes across Jax's and I feel his ass cheek brush against mine and I almost explode.

The sensations. They're too much.

She smiles at me when I hand her the dildo, and flips it over, removing one hand from our cocks as she focuses and turns it back on. She lowers herself on it and her back arches and her perfect tits reach out towards the sky.

"I want your breast in my mouth," I moan out, watching her.

"So take it." She's slowly bouncing up and down on her toy as her hands slide up and down us, slick with our arousal and lube.

"Gladly." I shift to sitting up and gently grind my balls into Jax's. Not on purpose.

Well, maybe just a little.

But fuck. I can be a selfish bastard, too.

My left hand presses into the mattress behind me, offering me support, while my right wraps around her waist as I take her breast in my mouth.

"Yes, daddy."

My eyes cut to hers and she just chuckles and shrugs. "It just felt right."

A moment later, Jax is sitting up and when he grinds his ass back into me, I jerk. The feeling. I about pulled a DMX and lost my mind.

My eyes catch his and he's watching me, like he's trying to dissect what I'm thinking. What I'm feeling. Pretty sure it's all over my face, but for good measure, I rock my hips forward, thrusting my cock up in Ev's hand and watch him.

I'm not that big of a badass. I shifted under the guise of needing to get closer to Ev, so yes. I'm a scared little bitch.

Everlee presses her tit into my mouth further and Jax joins, sucking her other one.

"I can't wait until you're both in my pussy, fucking me. I want you to fill me with your cocks and then your come." She lets out a moan as she stops bouncing, and just grinds on her dildo.

Judging by the slight wobble in her sitting, I can tell it's waving and licking her cervix because it's so deep inside of her and I'm jealous. I want it to be me.

Her moan lowers, and her hands pump faster. She's close. I drop her breast from my mouth and grab it with my hand as I suck her neck. My legs curl around Jax, my heel pressing into his ass for balance. He mimics me, scooting closer, and I bite. I bite into Everlee and she cries out.

Of course she would like it.

Jax does the same, wrapping his legs around me, pressing his heel to my ass as he reaches around her back, his arm latching onto mine as he sucks her neck.

Fuck it.

I grind.

I move my cock in her hand and my balls against his.

He's been matching me, move for move so far. How far will he go?

"Jax, Emmett. Yes." Her head falls back and I pinch her nipple hard as she screams out as her orgasm rips through her.

She clamps down on our cocks and we're both fucking her hand grinding against one another.

Pinch me.

I'm dead.

Jax is grinding against my cock. His hand is latched onto mine. His balls. His glorious fucking balls.

I explode, thrusting my cock into her hand. She comes back down from her orgasm and uses my release to coat our cocks and she continues to pump. "Come on, Jax. Be a good boy and come all over his cock."

"Fuck me," he cries.

"I am," I say.

He looks at me and Everlee wraps her arms around our necks, abandoning our cocks as she presses her lips to Jax. Without thinking, I grab them and continue where she left off.

I'm touching Jax's cock.

And he's not stopping me.

Everlee moves from Jax to me. Her lips are still wet with Jax's kiss. She pulls us in closer, her hips grinding down, as her breasts brush against us.

A second later, Jax's hand grips around mine and our cocks.

Without pulling away from Everlee or making it a big deal, I kiss Everlee harder. All of my passion, all of my excitement, all of my everything flows into her. I love her so much.

Jax jerks under our grip and as his warm come shoots out, some of it lands on my chest, but most on Everlee's.

"Now it's your turn again," Jax says, dropping our cocks and pushing her back. He pulls the green machine out of her and tosses it across the room.

"Emmett," he pauses, staring at me for a minute. "Lick my come off her chest."

She sucks in a breath and pauses, looking between us.

My eyes narrow at him. Is he trying to dom me? Do I hate it? Do I love it? Am I trying to stop myself from over analyzing what this all means?

"Yes, sir," I say, bending over her and slowly running my tongue along her stomach and up to her breast. I let out a moan for good measure.

"What about the come on your chest, Emmett?"

Rocking back on my hind legs, I look down at the two small lines on my chest.

"I should get it," she says, moving to sit up, but Jax presses his hand to her shoulder.

She freezes, and I forget how to breathe.

Everyone is quiet. I think my heart has forgotten how to beat.

"I'll do it," Jax says after a long pause. My head tingles like it's being squeezed into a vise.

Did he?

I lean back a little further, inviting him in. He crawls over the top of my legs, his cock gliding along the inside of my thigh. His face is inches from my chest. It's not the first time his cock has touched my leg or that he's been this close to my chest, but this feels... different.

Intimate.

He hesitates a second and I can almost feel his heart pounding out of his chest as he leans in agonizingly slow, his eyes locked on mine. His warm breath dances across my skin like silk, wrapping me in its softness.

His warm, wet tongue presses against my chest as he slowly swipes up, his tongue flicking into the air at the end. He moves to the other small streak closer to my nipple and does the same, but this time flicks my nipple ring with his tongue when he's done.

And I'm hard again.

"I think I just came," Everlee says, panting, eyes glassy.

Jax sits back, holds my gaze for a moment, then turns to Everlee. He pushes her back and climbs on top of her, his now hard cock passing by her wet pussy. "Did you enjoy watching me lick my come off E's chest?" His voice is low and gravelly.

"Yes."

"Does it make you wet?" He inches closer to her neck as the tips of her nipples graze over his chest.

He's magnetic to watch.

"Does it make you horny?"

"So horny."

"Do you want to be a good girl now and ride both of our cocks?"

She pants out a breath as her breasts press into his chest and her heels dig into the bed. His lips clamp around her neck and he's sucking so hard, I can see her skin tenting under his lips.

Her fingers latch onto his back as she thrusts her hips into him.

She likes him rough. I'd seen the aftermath of their times together, but never in person. Her nails dig in, leaving indentations in his skin causing him to release her neck and buck up.

"Ev," he warns, and she smiles playfully.

"I want your cocks in me now."

He looks over his shoulder at me and I'm so turned on my dick feels like it's going to fall off. "You ready E?"

The words 'Yes, daddy' want to tumble out of my mouth and now I understand why Ev said it earlier. It just feels right. "Yes." Daddy. That will be my little secret right now.

"Do you want top or bottom?"

He's giving me a choice? The little devil in me wants to ask him what he wants because I know and Everlee knows. I'm just not sure he knows, or if he does, is willing to admit it yet. But the angel in me wins out this time like it always does.

"You know I'm a bottom guy." So many meanings to unpack with that one.

Jax climbs off Ev and when she sits up, she grabs him under the chin and gives him a quick kiss, before she crawls over to me and pushes me backwards on the bed. She pumps her eyebrows a few times before taking my cock in her hand and guiding it under her pussy.

"Can you feel how wet I am for you? Can you feel their come leaking out of me?"

With my cock notched at her entrance, I buck my hips and slam into her, catching her off guard. "Can you feel my cock buried deep in your tight little pussy?"

"Damn E," she pants, relaxing her legs and following my hips down to the bed. "Your cock feels so good."

"Show me how good."

She tilts her head to the side, presses her hands on my chest and raises off me, before sinking back down.

"Your piercings... have I told you I loved them?"

"Not today."

"I love them and I love you." She falls forward on my chest as my hands dig into her waist. I thrust my hips hard and fast into her delicious, hot, wet pussy. I have to stop before I lose control. I want to see where this goes tonight.

"Jax?" I ask.

He nods, and crawls over on his knees, and plants himself between our legs, the outside of his knee brushing against my thigh.

She presses up slightly. The little voyeur in her loves to watch me when Jax presses in the first time. I think it gets her off almost as much as it gets me off.

I feel his knuckles brush across my skin as he lines up his cock at her entrance. Her eyes catch mine as we both wait with eager anticipation. His cock presses in slowly, rubbing tightly against my dick, and my eyes roll back in my head.

My head is spinning.

I'm dying.

This is heaven.

Every time it feels like this, but this time it's... different. More intentional, more feeling.

When he pulls out, I moan out, clamping my hands around Everlee's ass, bringing her as far on my dick as she can go.

I love her so fucking much I want to scream it from the rooftops.

He pushes in again.

JAX - JUST A LITTLE LOWER

GODDAMN IT. I'M GOING to fucking blow my load and we just started. His ribbed cock is like... fucking amazing. I was going to be more eloquent with my words, but there's no need. Straight to the point. His cock is brilliant!

I shouldn't be thinking about these things.

Pressing in again, I have to bite my bottom lip to stop from moaning. I know he loves it, and her. I catch the way they look at each other, like they're keeping a secret, only I know what it fucking is. Big whoop.

And last night. In the kitchen. I was lying on the couch and I heard her come downstairs and make a beeline for him. They share this connection, that has been getting stronger with every passing day. I'm not jealous.

Well, not a lot.

Her and I have our connection. I mean, I guess she has it with each of us, all different in our own ways, but I don't know. Something about their glances, speaking without talking... ugh!

I love the feel of his cock.

I push in again. Her pussy is tight around us, hugging them, but she's more relaxed now.

"Such a good girl taking our cocks, aren't you?"

She presses back on us and I can't help but smile.

"I'm going to fuck you both now."

She gasps and E's eyes fall on me. Curious.

I know I'm playing with fire, but right now I don't care. I'm buried in her pussy with his cock and nothing else matters. I can let down my guard with her, with them, if only for a minute.

"You want to fuck us too, E?"

He smiles.

He thrusts his hips up and my breath catches. I'm not going to last long, but I should. I was holding back from my orgasm earlier because I wanted to be hard enough to fuck her. I didn't know watching E lick my come off her chest was going to make me harder than a brick in two seconds flat.

And then me.

What the fuck was that? Licking my come off *his* chest?

AND THEN THE NIPPLE RING!

Why is it that when you yell at yourself in your head, it's still just as loud as when you're not yelling?

His fucking nipple ring. It's laying there, staring at me, waiting to be flicked again. I'd heard that the sensations when someone plays with it are amazing. Was it amazing for him?

Everlee's hands slide up his arms and she interlaces her fingers in his and stretches them above their head, elongating her body, giving herself, her control, over to me. It's a rare gift, and one that I'll gladly take.

I grind into her, burying myself to the hilt, and my eyes roll into the back of my head. E is grinding his cock, slowly, savoring the feel, the moment.

Wanting to bask in it as well, I lean over and run my hands up Everlee's arms and interlock my fingers with Emmett's, enclosing her hand.

In this new position, Emmett and I grind together in perfect unison. Pressing in, pulling out.

Her knees dig into the bed as she helps ride our cocks. She gets faster and faster, and I know she's getting close.

Releasing my right hand, I loop it around her waist and rub circles around her clit. When she bucks, my hand slips and brushes against the base of Emmett's cock.

Fuck. Shit. Damn.

Nope. That was a mistake. An accident.

My hand retreats to her clit as I continue to rub, pushing her closer to her orgasm. Her pussy is quivering, eager for its next release, and I know when she comes it's going to be her biggest yet. They always are when E and I fuck her.

Our bodies press together as one, and there... just... not even an inch away is...

Clearing my head, I slam into her harder and she yelps, shifting again. And again, my hand slips.

That was not on purpose. That was out of frustration.

But...

What would it feel like... to feel us moving inside of her?

My stomach clenches into knots. Just do it. It's not like you haven't touched his cock before. But this just feels different.

Before I can stop myself, I add a second finger and rub on her clit. She's grinding down on them, her body sandwiched between E and me as her moans get louder and louder.

"Yes, baby. Come for us," I urge.

My hand drifts down just a little further, and I can feel his cock enter her and then pull out, sliding along the tips of my fingers. I release my other hand from E's grip and move her hair out of the way and start planting kisses on her back. Nibbling on her skin, trying to ignore the fact that I'm letting my fingers graze his cock.

She likes that.

E catches my eye, and he's staring at me.

I close my eyes, savoring the feel of my cock inside of her and my fingers brushing the top of his cock. So hard.

My two fingers inch down a little further so they form a v around his cock. He's brushing past my fingers as he enters her over and over again. My cock is aching, it's so hard.

"So close."

Fuck.

I've been so focused on him and his cock that I forgot about her. I pull up my hand and find her clit and circle a few times and a high-pitched moan tears through her. Her back straightens, her pussy strangles our cocks and I explode at the same time as E. All three of us are moaning as our orgasms rip through us.

"E. Shut her up. The next county over is going to hear her."

He shifts to sit up and his cock twitches inside of her against me and I let out a growl.

She's still moaning, her body is ridged and her pussy still has a chokehold on our cocks.

E wraps his hand around the back of her neck, looks at me, and takes her lips in a hungry kiss. Passionate. Angry.

She fights him at first and then melts into his kiss. She always does and a second later, her moans stop, her body goes limp, and she crashes onto E. We all fall to the bed, panting like we just ran a marathon. Her cheek is laying on his chest as his hand rubs her back and she rubs circles around his nipple ring.

I wait until my heartbeat slows and pull out of her and flop on the bed beside them, staring at the ceiling.

What the fuck was that? What was I thinking? I'm going to fuck everything up.

Goddammit!

I roll off the bed and head into the bathroom.

That can't fucking happen ever again.

Take all these thoughts. All these feelings and blow them up with a big fucking missile.

Closing the door, I lean against it and look at the ceiling, and then my hands. Specifically, the two fingers that were fucking both Everlee and E.

Fuck!

EVERLEE – MORNING AFTER

LAST NIGHT WAS... WOW. I don't think I've ever had as many orgasms as I did last night and that last one.

Holy forking shirtballs! I thought my body was going to be frozen. Literally every muscle in my body seized and a moan coming from somewhere inside of me just kept coming out. Like I don't understand how because it wasn't coming from me. It was like I'd been possessed by something and it was moaning for me.

Shit!

Was it my soul? Was my soul moaning? Did it have an orgasm? A soulgasm?

Had my orgasm been so powerful it transcended the plane of... what? Life? Reality? The living and the... not death, but like that place where souls are just hanging out. Was she moaning? I assume she's a she, because I'm a she. Does a soul have a sex?

Why in the fuck am I thinking about the gender of my soul?

"Here," Lizzy says, handing me an ice pack.

"What's this for?"

She looks at me, face full of sass, with a hand on her hip. "I figured our pussy needed it."

"You know, it's really weird that you claim my pussy as yours."

"How in the fuck can't I after last night? You were moaning so loud, I felt it in my bones. I thought I was having an orgasm, but no. I was sleeping. Do you know how it makes me feel to wake up with tears in my eyes from a glorious orgasm only to realize that I wasn't, in fact, having one? That I could feel no tingling twat, no pulsing pussy, no nothing. So is it weird?" She shrugs, "But after last night, I'm pretty sure the whole damn house felt like they were in that room with you. Shit!" She claps her hands. "Imagine how Beckett and Will feel. They are gay dudes and had to experience your orgasm. A female orgasm." She grabs a bowl for cereal down. "Have you no shame?"

"Are you done?"

"Not quite. I'm like your orgasm. I'm going to keep going and going and going until you begin to question yourself."

"I'm sorry."

"Don't be sorry. I mean maybe a little, but you do you. Bring your whole orgasm to the house, to the beach. Pretty sure some sea animals were getting laid last night because of you. It was like a boinking beacon."

"You need to stop." I laugh, scooping another spoonful of Honey Nut Cheerios into my mouth.

"Buttttt I wooooonn'ttt."

"I get it. I won't orgasm anymore for the rest of the trip."

"Oh, damn." Her spoon falls, clanging onto the counter.

"What?" I ask with a modicum of concern.

"You just put that out into the universe."

"I was joking."

Her eyebrows lift. "You don't joke about that. It's Monday. Tomorrow is the fourth. There will be fireworks tomorrow and now you won't have your own."

"I'm pretty sure I will orgasm again before the end of the week."

She shakes her head, face taut with concern. "I don't know."

Setting my spoon down, I grab her wrist. "You're serious, aren't you?"

"Ev. Look outside. It's still raining."

"It's more like a fine mist."

"It wasn't supposed to rain at all. Even the weather app shows it's sunny."

"So you think there is just a small pocket of rain above our house because of my mother? You sound coo-coo-ca-choo."

"And you don't?"

"I know you're not being serious."

"I mostly am."

"What can I do to retract the whole no orgasm for the rest of the week comment?"

"Well, you can stop saying it. That's for damn skippy. I don't want that bad joo joo rubbing off on me."

A sigh escapes as I pick up my spoon again. "Well, hopefully the rain will stop and my mom doesn't show up."

"Hello love!" Knox calls across the room, walking in from outside. "Man, it feels great outside. There's just this little patch of rain here, but once you get down the beach like half a mile, it clears up. Weirdest thing."

"Don't you fucking say a word." I point at Lizzy.

There's no way.

Jax walks in a moment later, wiping his face. He's been quiet since last night. After we finished, he stayed in the bathroom for quite a while. Emmett was confused and didn't really say much.

Figuring we needed to give Jax space, Emmett and I went into the other bathroom, where we took a shower and he cleaned me. He's always so gentle and so loving with me. By the time we got back to the bedroom, Jax was asleep on the mattress.

Knox and Callum were still downstairs talking to Beckett or Will, not sure if it was just one of them or both. I think they'd forgotten about the jug of water they were supposed to bring up, which was ok. I would have appreciated it, but at the same time I felt... last night felt... different. Jax felt more...

explorative. I felt his fingers near the end. It was like they were searching out Emmett's cock, but he was still scared.

Was he mad at himself for giving into temptation? Is he still mad?

When I woke up this morning, he was already out of bed and gone.

"Did you boys have a pleasant run?" I try to keep my voice as light and airy as possible.

"Yea," Jax mumbles, walking over to the counter to grab his extra-large water bottle.

His shirt is off and there's sweat dripping down his body, disappearing into his dark elastic waistband. His leg muscles are tight and bulging, and there's a small amount of sand still left on the top of his feet.

"I'm going to go upstairs and take a shower." He sets the empty water bottle back on the counter and walks upstairs.

"What's wrong with him?" Lizzy asks. Even she knew enough not to crack any jokes right now.

"Nothing," Knox defends. "He's always like this after long runs."

"How long is long?"

"This morning we ran for fifteen miles."

"Fif- what?" Lizzy stutters. "On the sand?"

"It was hard and wet."

"Like your-"

"Lizzy!"

She rolls her eyes playfully. "I was just teasing. Obviously."

"Obviously."

Knox walks over and gives me a loving kiss on the head. "You look beautiful today."

"I just rolled out of bed a few minutes ago."

"You wake up beautiful."

"Gag me with this spoon," Lizzy teases, pressing her spoon into her mouth.

"Give it to me," I say, holding out my hand.

"Don't threaten me with a good time."

"You would like it, wouldn't you?" Knox laughs.

"I'm going to take a shower as well. Get all this sand and sweat off me."

"Or don't. I think it's kind of sexy."

Lizzy makes another gagging noise, and I cut my eyes at her.

"What? Y'all are so cute it's sickening."

"Why did I invite you?"

"Beach please. We wouldn't be here if it wasn't for me."

"You're right. What was I thinking?"

"Obviously you weren't."

EVERLEE - STRAND FEEDING

AFTER THE BOYS GET showered, we meet back downstairs and decide to take a walk to the end of the island to see if we can find the dolphins strand feeding. It takes us close to forty-five minutes to get there, and we wait about twenty minutes before we decide they aren't coming. We get three steps towards the house and several people start excitedly whispering, so we turn back around and see several dorsal fins peeking up through the water.

I don't think I've ever been so excited. The little girl in me is screaming and jumping for joy. Dolphins! It isn't the first time I've seen a dolphin, but that doesn't matter. Every time feels like the first time. They are so magical. The way they dip under the water, gliding along effortlessly.

There's at least five and a baby! I about scream and melt into the sand when I see its little fin pacing its mother. Following the lead of others, I sit down on the beach and just watch the dolphins come into the little inlet and swim around for a bit. I've never seen a strand feeding before, so I don't know what to expect, but fortunately I sit near an older woman who must live on the island or has been out here many times. She's whispering to a little girl about what the dolphins are doing.

She's telling us, well her, the complete process from start to finish and says we're sitting in the best place. I'm shocked to find the boys are also sitting on the beach, knees brought up to their chest, arms wrapped around them. They look like my bodyguards, close enough to know me, but not close enough to be intimate. Lizzy, Tony, Beckett and Will walk further into the inlet and watch the dolphins swimming at the other end.

"Here they come," the lady whispers excitedly, pointing. She stands up and takes a few steps back, so I follow. "We don't want to move around a lot or speak."

We're standing about twenty feet back from the strand and the guys quietly walk over to stand beside me. I reach out and grab a hand and realize it's Jax's. He looks at me and gives my hand a little squeeze, almost like it's an apology for being so quiet last night and this morning. I pull his arm, and wrap it around me and wrap mine around him, resting my head on his shoulder. He plants a soft kiss on top and we just watch and wait.

"They're getting ready," the woman whispers. A small crowd has gathered around her, and Lizzy and Tony walk back over and stand behind us.

The dolphins are circling, getting more aggressive, swimming faster and faster.

"They're lining up," she says.

And then whoosh! They press forward, all in unison, and push an enormous wave of water and fish onto the strand. Their bodies lay on their side as they eat the fish, then wiggle back into the water.

"Holy sh-irtballs," I correct and whisper, seeing the little girl in front of me. "That was amazing."

The dolphins circle again, rounding up the fish and a few minutes later, press them onto the beach again. They do it one more time, then swim further into the inlet.

The older woman tells the little girl they are done for now. They're going to swim around for a bit, then head back out to the ocean.

I look at the guys, then grab Jax's hand, interlacing my fingers in his. For some reason I feel like he needs more. More attention. More love. Just more.

"That was pretty freaking cool," Knox says bouncing up and down as we start to walk back.

Jax just looks at him but doesn't speak while Emmett and Callum walk up ahead. Tony and Lizzy are behind us waiting for Beckett and Will to catch up with them.

My stomach growls and Knox gives it a little rub. "Do we need to get her fed?"

"Yes. She's starving."

Knox walks with us for a few minutes, then bounces backwards to talk with Beckett and Will about something. Still uncertain about Jax, I look up at him and he looks back. "You good?"

"Yea, I'm good." He smiles.

I nod, wanting to ask more. Wanting to press. But I know that's not Jax's style. If and when he wants to talk about it, he will. Last night felt... different, and maybe we pushed him a little too far. Although to be fair, we didn't ask anything of him, but perhaps the energy... he felt that and was responding to it. Who knows?

"Hey!" Knox announces, running back up to us a few minutes later.

"What?" Jax chomps back.

"Will and Beckett think they can beat us," he thumbs over his shoulder and we all look at Beckett, laughing.

"Unlikely. Doing what?"

"A race back to the house. They think they are in better shape than us."

Jax looks at them, then at me. I can't help but smile, because I know how competitive he is and, selfishly, I just want to see him take his shirt off and be all hot and sweaty.

"You got this, babe." I pat his butt.

"You won't be mad at me when I beat your brother?"

"Not at all. It will be good for him."

He throws his head back, laughing. And my God, is he beautiful? "Fine."

Knox jumps up and down and we stop, letting Tony, Lizzy, Beckett and Will catch up to us. Callum and Emmett must have heard the commotion, so they walk back towards us with a silent, but quizzical brow.

"What's going on?" Emmett asks, watching Knox and Jax take their shirts off.

I reach out to grab them. "Beckett and Will want to race Knox and Jax back to the house. SEALs versus firefighters."

"Good luck to them."

"That's what I said!" Knox chimes, more excited than a kid in a candy store.

Jax leans over and touches his toes and, of course, several beach goers have stopped to watch what's going on. When four insanely attractive guys have their shirts off and start stretching, you know something is about to go down.

"We seem to be drawing a crowd," Callum says, looking around.

"All the more people to see Becks get his ass spanked." Knox stretches his arms across his chest.

"Did Will tell you I liked that?" Beckett says, cutting his eyes at Will, who shakes his head.

"Ew," I cringe.

"Kinky," Knox laughs, patting him on the shoulder.

"Don't you dare ew me after what I had to listen to last night. I legitimately thought you were dying at one point. I have never heard something so... so... loud, deep, and squeally all at the same time."

"Is squeally a word?"

"Fuck. After last night, it one hundred percent is. Like those noises didn't even sound human. I literally was tearing out of my room thinking some sort of animal had gotten into the house when Callum and Knox stopped me."

"Are we going to race or talk about orgasms?" Jax interrupts.

"Are you really asking my opinion or just pretending?" Knox asks, then quickly backs away from Jax's hand. "What? I thought it was a valid question."

"Shut–"

"Yea, yea. I get it. Not a real question."

"So first to our house's boardwalk or first team to the boardwalk?"

"I think, team," I chime in.

Everyone shrugs in agreement.

"What do the winners get?" Beckett asks.

"I don't know. What do you want to give up when you lose?" Knox chides.

Beckett tosses his head back in laughter. "Good point. What do you want, Will? I want it to be something good when we win." Will shrugs, then Beckett thinks about it some more, then holds his finger up in the air. "For the rest of today and tomorrow, losers have to play servers to the winners. Basically be their little bitch boys."

"Oh, you just guaranteed our win. Jax won't play servant to anyone." He looks at me, "Well, outside of Ev, of course."

"No cheating or holding anyone back. Just a clean race," Will says, looking at Beckett.

"Why in the hell are you looking at me?" Beckett puts Will in a chokehold, rubbing his knuckles on his head.

Will grabs Beckett by the legs, taking him down, before popping back up.

"Oh. We're totally going to win." Knox is running around in large circles, thrusting his arms into the air.

"Is it too late to change partners?" Jax asks.

"Man." Knox swipes the air, then draws a line in the sand with this foot. "Let's go, bro!"

"Coming darling," Beckett sweeps across the beach in a fantastically dramatic fashion.

Watching my guys with Beckett makes my heart swell. The way that everyone is here and melding so well together. It's like these guys- my guys- are long time best friends of Beckett's. I don't know how I got this lucky, but man, am I thankful. Rich was never like this with Beckett. In the time we were together, we may have hung out with Beckett three times, and two of those times were the holidays. I knew Beckett wasn't a huge fan of Rich while we were dating, but it wasn't until we broke up that he unloaded all of his thoughts and feelings on me.

Beckett hated him, and that was before he found out he was cheating on me.

They were like oil and water.

Rich always had his nose in his phone and was always working, or so he said. But these guys... they're like brothers from another mother. I would have never dreamed of going on a couple's vacation with Rich and Beckett and Lizzy. This just proves that things happen for a reason. You may not know what that reason is when you're going through it, but there's always a reason. The storm before the rainbow.

Jax and Knox are lined up on the left, and Beckett and Will are lined up on the right. Callum, Emmett, Tony, and Lizzy are standing behind them, while I'm in front of them in the center. Being very car racer girl like, I hold up a shirt in the air, letting it dangle towards the ground with my fingers.

"When this touches the ground, you can go."

"Let's go, Becks!" Lizzy shouts from behind.

"What the heck, Liz?" Knox asks, throwing his arms in the air, flabbergasted.

"I love you too, but Becks is my boo boo brother and Will is my beau FF."

"We'll talk about this later!"

"Fine! Let's go Knoxxy baby!" She looks at me and winks and again, my heart is nearly exploding with love.

A group of about fifteen people are now standing on the edge watching, mostly groups of females. Possessiveness creeps in, but then I relax. These are my guys and they only have eyes for me. Look on women... get your fill!

"On your marks, get set..." I drop the shirt and they're off.

I turn around as they breeze past me, sand flying in the air as their feet dig in.

"Oh, this is going to be close," Callum says, walking up to me.

"It will be on Knox to win or lose it. Jax won't let himself be beat," Emmett says, walking up.

"He went for a long run this morning though," Tony says, joining the group with Lizzy holding his hand.

I glance at Emmett and he looks at me, then Callum.

"Shall we head back to see who the victor will be? I need to know which team I need to bribe to let me partake in the benefits of the win."

Placing my hand on my brow to block out the sun, I squint into the distance to see if I can tell who's ahead, but they're too far for me to tell and getting smaller by the second.

"We still have like a thirty-minute walk back," Lizzy moans. "Damn it!"

"What?"

"We should have made them race, but carrying us on their backs!"

"So you wouldn't have to walk back?"

"Yes."

"There's always tomorrow."

Tony gets down on one knee in front of her.

"I'm already marrying you."

"Yes. Please don't have a second wedding. I don't know if I can survive the first." Emmett laughs.

"You tease!" Lizzy bats the air and Emmett just pumps his eyebrows.

"No. I was getting down so you can climb on."

"My hero." She climbs on and Tony stands up, shifting her weight to better position her. "My sexy man!"

Emmett lowers down on one knee.

"Oh my God! Are you proposing?" Lizzy squeaks.

"Fuck, Lizzy!"

Emmett cuts his eyes from me to her.

"Right. Sorry. I forgot. I just got excited."

"We know," Callum deadpans.

"I was going to let you climb on. I can't let Tony show me up."

"He could never," I whisper in his ear, before climbing on.

Emmett stands with ease and shifts me in his arms.

"Well, this is awkward," Lizzy says, looking at Callum.

"All good here."

"Of course it is. You like to watch," Lizzy teases.

"Lizzy. Will you shut your mouth?"

She laughs, then smacks Tony in the ass. "Yee-haw! Let's get 'ta movin' cowboy!"

"Ooh baby!" Tony skips down the sand with a cackling Lizzy on his back.

I smack Emmett's ass.

"You want me to run after them?"

"No. I just wanted to touch your ass."

"Touch it anytime you want, love."

EVERLEE - CHICKEN

- -

JAX AND KNOX WON, but according to Beckett, it was very close. If you ask Will, it wasn't that close, and Beckett gave up near the end.

We decide to spend the rest of the afternoon at the house, relaxing on the deck and playing in the pool. Beckett has been alternating between the hot tub and the pool when he isn't fetching snacks and drinks for Knox. Jax hasn't really asked for anything, and likely won't. He just didn't want to lose.

"Becks darling. Could you please get me a refill on my sparkling water? This time I'd like three pieces of pineapple in it."

"You love you some pineapple. No wonder Ev-" Lizzy starts, but I cut her off.

"For the love of God, Liz, don't finish that sentence."

"What? I was going to say, no wonder Ev loves you so much since you like pineapple too!"

I narrow my eyes at her and she cackles.

"Oooh. I say we have a chicken fight. It's been such a long time since we've had one," Lizzy says, floating on her back around the pool.

"I always beat you."

"Like once."

"Are you talking about the number of times you won?"

"Har har. I mean, if you're scared, just say you are."

"I'm not scared."

"Who do you want to be your bottom?"

I chuckle, shaking my head from side to side. "E?"

"Yes, love?"

"You want to be my bottom?"

"Is today Monday?"

"Yes?"

He winks at me.

"Oh. I get it. Yes, it's Monday, and yes, you'll be my bottom."

He hops into the pool and dives under the water between my legs. His beard brushes along the inside near my pussy as he grabs me and pulls me under the water. His hair is floating up and his arms are waving back and forth to keep him under water. He winks at me, then swims up to get some air.

"So, are we ready?" He asks, flipping his hair out of his face.

"Oh yeah, baby!" Lizzy shouts, clapping her hands.

Emmett dips under the water again and swims between my legs, hooking my legs around his shoulders before he stands up. I let out a small scream as I bolt out of the water, my hands clamping onto his hair and my feet tucking around to his back, locking me in place. Tony lifts Lizzy into the air, but she's more prepared, so she ascends his shoulders in a more graceful manner.

Lizzy grabs onto Tony's hair and starts riding his neck, "Yee-haw pony."

"Is this a new fetish of yours?" I mumble and her eyes grow wide like maybe I've said something I shouldn't have, but fuck if I know. Plus, if I did, it would serve her right. She says something she shouldn't say at least once every thirty minutes. And the difference is she knows she shouldn't say it and still does. Mine was an accidental slip, however, now I'm curious.

"Shake hands," Callum directs.

"Yes, daddy," Lizzy says and Callum tilts his head down at her. She doubles down and blows him a kiss.

Thank God everyone is so confident in their relationships. Trust is so important.

"Let's go, babe!" Emmett says, squeezing my legs.

"You got it Ev. Let's go!" Callum encourages.

"I didn't realize how much this sucks until right now."

"What sucks?"

"You have an entire team cheering you on."

"So do you babe!" Tony says, squeezing her legs. "See?"

"What?"

"Go babe!" Tony says. "You got this hot stuff," he continues in a deeper voice. "Oh my God girl, you look so hot and are totally going to crush this," he says in a higher voice.

"Aww babe. You're so sweet." She leans over to give him a kiss but topples off of him, knocking them into the water. She pops up, gasping for air. "That didn't count!" She points her finger in the air.

She climbs back on his shoulders, and the game begins. During the middle of it, we decide to do best out of five rounds. The first three happen pretty quickly. I knock her off, then she knocks me off two times in a row. The fourth time we struggle for quite a bit and she accidentally knocks my bathing suit top off my right breast, which is embarrassing, but I don't give up.

Never give up! Never surrender!

I quickly fix it, then we lock arms again, pushing and shoving. I do a whole matrix move, then pop back up, knocking her off.

We're tied two to two.

"Next one wins," Callum announces.

All the guys are back and sitting around the edge of the pool. Knox tries to get a round of betting going, but it doesn't go anywhere, so he has Beckett and Will make him and Jax a cheese tray with three pieces of cheese, four grapes, and two crackers. He's just fucking with them, but they don't complain.

When they walk inside, I nod to get Knox's attention. "You have to cut back. It's only been a couple of hours since you won."

"I will. I was just trying to get him to complain at first, but they're so agreeable. He knows how to lose a bet, and I can respect that."

Jax shoves his arm, and he falls over into the chair.

"Last round. Here we go!" Callum says, clapping his hands to start the round.

We go back and forth for several minutes. Lizzy wants this. I can see it in her eyes.

"Get his nipple, babe!" She shouts.

"Dirty."

"You didn't say they can't touch. It's a strategy."

"She's right," Callum calls.

"Whose side are you on?"

"I'm on the side of the game."

"Traitor," Emmett mumbles, before he screams. "Didn't know I was getting a purple nurple. Geez!"

"Go again!" Lizzy shouts, riding his neck.

"Next time he lets go of her leg to twist my nipple, push them hard. We're going to attack."

"Strong side. Weak side," Lizzy grunts.

We push and shove a few more times, arms locked, each of us leaning back into the water or pulling forward.

"Attack!" Lizzy commands.

"Shit!" Emmett shouts, running backwards into the water, but he can't move fast enough. Tony clamps on, causing Emmett to yelp!

"Don't get a hard on E." Jax enters the roasting and Emmett just glares at him. Jax tosses his head back, laughing, and I let out a sigh of relief.

He's going to be ok.

We're going to be ok.

Damn it!

I'm not paying attention and Lizzy catches me off guard. Emmett and I fall back into the water and when I pop back up, Lizzy is cheering around the pool while Tony carries her around on his shoulders like a trophy.

"Good job, Liz."

"What happened? You seemed distracted."

"Nope, all good. I was expecting you to do something else, and I was wrong." I didn't want to admit what I was actually thinking about. I feel like we're on shaky ground as it is, and I want Jax to get solid ground beneath him.

She cheers some more.

Dinner comes and goes and we all hang out in the hot tub for a little or cuddle on the huge chairs. After a while, Jax stands up and asks me to go on a walk with him, so I do. It's dark except for the moonlight, which is fairly bright and almost a full moon. We can't have flashlights on the beach after nine because turtles are still coming up to nest on the beach, and if there are bright lights, it may confuse them.

He's silent for a while.

I don't know why he invited me on the walk or what he wants to talk about, so I wait for him. With him, you don't push. When he's ready, he will speak.

We continue walking for several more minutes, then he reaches out and grabs my hand and interlaces his fingers in between mine. Still no words.

I'm dying to ask what's going on, what's been on his mind all day. Last night. Does he regret last night? Does he not? I want to tell him he shouldn't, but I also don't want to pretend like I know what happened. Something did, but I'm not sure. The only thing I know is that I can't push.

"I love you," he says, so quiet that it almost sounds like the waves washing back out.

"I love you, too."

He stops walking and pulls me into him, dropping my hand and cupping my cheeks. "I love you so much, Everlee. I hope you know that."

"I do, babe. What's-" going on? What's wrong? What happen last night? These are all the questions I want to ask, but can't. So I just kiss him. I wrap my arms around his neck and he lifts me into his arms. My ankles lock around his back as my heels dig into his ass. The kiss is deep. Intense. Passionate. Full of emotion.

He pulls out of the kiss and presses his forehead to mine. "I…" He hesitates, then stares at something in the distance.

"What?" I whisper, feeling the hairs on the back of my neck start to rise.

He slowly sets me back on the sand and grabs my hand, strolling up the beach.

"What?" I whisper, looking off in the distance. There's something large moving, and my heart starts to race.

He pulls me in front of him and wraps his arms around my waist and holds me there.

About fifteen feet in front of us is a sea turtle. She's huge. At least three or four hundred pounds, and she's digging a hole in the sand to lay her eggs.

I'm in complete awe because I've never seen it happened before. We stand there for a while, watching her, then slowly slink to a sitting position. Jax positions me between his legs and continues to hold me, never breaking his grip on me.

The turtle continues to work the sand forever, digging down deeper and deeper. She hovers for a moment, then paddles the sand back into the hole.

She laid her eggs.

I turn to look up at Jax, the moonlight causing his eyes to sparkle as he looks down at me and smiles. He kisses the tip of my nose and we turn back and watch her slowly make her way back to the ocean. It takes forever, and she pauses several times to catch her breath or regain her strength. As she gets closer to the water's edge, we stand and follow her, still keeping our distance, and then watch her hit the water, then swim off.

"Holy… wow. That was amazing," I say breathlessly.

"Yea. That was pretty amazing." He looks up at the moon, then says, "We should probably get back. It's late."

"Yea." I don't know why he wanted to go on the walk or what he wanted to say, if he wanted to say anything at all. Perhaps he will tell me whatever is weighing on him when he's ready. All I can do right now is to be a rock for him. Support him and love him through whatever it is.

BECKETT - SURPRISE

THIRTEEN.

That is the number of hours I, we, have left of being Knox's little bitch boy. Even though Jax also won, he's not taking advantage of the situation as much as Knox is, or at all, really. And to be fair, Knox has cut back quite a bit. I think Everlee said something to him, because he went from asking me every five minutes to get him something to every couple of hours.

Everlee has calmed down with the whole *the world is ending and mom is showing up*. She was pretty antsy most of the day yesterday, but finally started calming down near the end.

Today's the fourth and we're going to have fun!

Lizzy, being Lizzy, has gone all out and has an entire basket full of goodies. Light up necklaces, headbands, glasses and more. Pretty sure she raided the entire party section of the store and bought anything that had red, white, and blue on it, or looked like it belonged to the holiday. She's been on us all day to stay decked out.

One thing I've learned about Ev's guys is that they love her big. Like super big. Anyone who would willingly be trapped in a house for an entire week with Lizzy must really love her.

I've seen snippets of her relationship with the guys when I've visited, but nothing like spending nearly every waking hour with them.

I really like them. They are all so different, but God. They rotate around Ev. They are the planets to her sun. I love that for her so much. I hated dickface and when she told me they broke up, I was equal parts sad and happy for her. Sad because she was going through all that hurt and pain, but so happy for her because she was finally done with him. The thought of her marrying him terrified me. She was convincing herself she was happy with him and they would have likely gotten married, had two point five kids, bought a house and lived for several years in a blissful-like state, but it would have ended. He was always a dick, in more ways than one. I'm just glad he showed his true colors to her before it was too late.

Then when she told me about the guys, well, let's be honest, she never really had to tell me, because the chemistry between the five of them is electric. Anyway, when I found out about her little polypod at Easter, I was nervous. It's a lot, but they seem to have most things figured out. They are still relatively young in the relationship, but from what I can tell, they are stronger than some couples who have been together for years.

"What do you think they're talking about?" Will asks me, nodding at Lizzy and Everlee bobbing in the ocean.

"I have no idea, but with those two in can't be good."

Will lets out a throaty laugh. Damn, he's a handsome man, and he's all mine. The last couple of months have been a complete whirlwind as I've helped him through the whole coming out in public. He told the firehouse first, and they were super accepting. I'd like to think I helped pave the way for future firefighters who wanted to come out, but that's also the selfish prick in me wanting to take credit for someone else's accomplishments and successes and really any general positive thing.

"You want to toss the ball around?" He nods to the football perched on the top of Ev's Rainbow colored Bogg bag.

"Sure!"

We've been on the beach most of the morning playing bocce ball and throwing the football around. At one point, all the guys were tossing the football, talking about the most random shit. It was a great bonding moment, then Knox had to ruin it with a request of pineapple water from the house.

I've noticed he hasn't asked for an alcoholic drink. Without asking him, or really anyone, I'm trying to figure out why. They've talked about him drinking and I've seen him take a sip here or there of Ev's drinks, but he never has one of his own. I can't help but wonder if he's a recovering alcoholic, which I don't think so based on everything else I've seen, although I'm sure everyone goes through it differently. But there's something there, but again it's none of my business unless it effects Ev and from everything I can see he's head over heels in love with her. Emmett would be tied or a very close second. Callum and Jax seem to show their love in a different way, which is fine. Because again, everyone is different.

Will and I throw the football back and forth for a little before our group grows when Tony joins. A few minutes later, Ev and Lizzy are walking back up with smiles on their faces.

"Knoxxy baby," Ev says, perching herself on his lap, crossing her legs.

He's been basking under an umbrella reading a book for the last hour, not making a peep. Emmett and Callum have been talking about their businesses and Jax has been playing some logic puzzle books. Seems like it's something he recently picked up from Ev.

"What do you need, my love?"

"We're hungry."

Shit.

"I see. Would you like some turkey and ham rolls with some freshly cut fruit?"

"Sounds delightful."

"Do you want it brought out here?"

Her finger makes circles on his chest. "You know me so well."

"Yes, I do." He wiggles his fingers in the air. "Ding, ding, ding."

Twelve hours.

"Yes, my darling Knox," I say with a British accent. It was his request.

He rubs his hand on his stomach. "I'm starving."

"I'm sure *you* are," I snipe back quietly.

He chuckles. "Would you be a dear and get me some turkey and ham rolls-"

"With cheese," Lizzy whispers.

"With cheese and bring them out here?"

"Anything else?" He's forgetting the fruit and I don't want his stupid ass to remember too late and make me go in again to get it. It isn't that far of a walk, but it's far enough when you don't want to do anything but sit and do nothing.

"Ah yes. Fruit, cut up."

"How many rolls would you want?"

He puckers out his bottom lip, rubbing his chin. "I'm thinking ten of each."

"Wow, you really must be hungry."

"Famished."

I close my eyes and take a deep breath and start to walk towards the house.

Knox calls after me, "Darling."

I think these are becoming our pet names for one another. "Yes, Pookie."

He tilts his head to the side and whispers, "So sweet." He huffs a moment, "After this, you will be released of your duty to me."

"Really?"

"Yea. Ev may have had a better offer."

"I can only imagine." I toss a quick glance at Ev and she's pumping her eyebrows. Aside from being a pain in the ass most of the time, she's a great sister, though I'd never say it out loud!

"Does anyone else want anything while I'm going in? Will and I can get an assortment of goodies and we can have a little picnic."

"Yay Fourth of July picnic!" Lizzy shouts.

"I wasn't finished. For everyone but Lizzy."

She hisses at me and throws her fingers up like snake fangs.

We make the three-minute walk up the beach and across the private boardwalk to our house. It really is a great freaking house.

We walk in and the house is deathly quiet, as echoes of seagulls and the chatter from our friends fade away.

Will walks over to the fridge to pull out all the meat and condiments and I can't control myself.

"Hey," I say in a low voice.

He stands up slowly, like an animal in the wild who knows they're being watched, but he doesn't turn around. "Beck, what are you doing?"

"Nothing."

He looks over his shoulder and flashes his brilliant white smile. "It doesn't seem like nothing. You have the dropped shoulder swagger with your sexy time voice."

"Ooh, my sexy time voice?" I repeat, lowering my voice.

He sets the armful of items on the counter.

"We have the house to ourselves," I say, taking a step closer to him, then pause.

"We do." He smiles. I find it so cute how slightly uncomfortable he is right now.

Closing the distance, I pull him into my arms and press my hardening cock against his and I smile. "You seem happy to see me."

"I'm always happy to see you."

"Are you?"

He leans in and kisses me, taking control of the situation. "Do you want to go to the bedroom?"

"No."

"You want to do it out here?" There's a slight note of panic in his voice.

"Is that a problem?"

"What if someone comes home?"

"No one's going to come home and if they do, let them watch. I'd say they could learn a thing or two, but they all seem to be a bunch of kinky fuckers."

"Beck."

I kiss his neck, sucking his fevered skin into my mouth.

"Beck."

I moan out as I swipe my tongue across his neck, then reach my hands down the front of his bathing suit and latch onto his hard cock.

"Beck."

"I know that's my name." I plant kisses down his chest, looping my fingers in the top of his pants.

He presses his hands on the counter with eager anticipation. I love this man's cock. It's so perfect.

As I drop to my knees, I pull his pants down. "Oh, hello there, friend." I blow a warm breath around his length, being sure not to touch it.

He growls out.

"Now who's eager mceagerville?"

"Shut the fuck up and suck my cock like a good boy."

"There he is!" I smile and wrap my hand around his hard shaft, sucking him into my mouth. A bead of his arousal swipes against my tongue.

His knuckles are clenched around the edge of the counter.

I slide off his cock and look up at him. "Are you ok?"

"I just really don't want anyone to come home and see us."

"Babe. This is payback for Easter. Do you remember when we were at my parent's house in their kitchen? They could have come home any minute, but you didn't stop."

"I can now see what a mistake that was."

"You haven't yet, but you will." I suck him back into my mouth again until he taps the back of my throat.

"Damn Beck." His hands fall from the counter and latch into my hair.

Fuck, yes! I love when he takes control. I look up at him through my lashes and he looks down all sexy like and growls at me. I think I just came in my pants some.

My hand works the base of his cock, while I continue to suck him in.

"Yes, baby," he moans out, urging me on.

DING DONG.

"Babe. Someone's at the door."

"Wrong number."

"It's not a phone."

I continue to suck, harder and faster.

DING DONG.

"I think we should answer that."

I growl to a firm no.

DING DONG.

"Hello? Is anyone inside?"

I stop sucking, and my balls shrivel up immediately. "Oh, fuck!"

"What?"

"Fuck, fuck, fuck, fuck, fuck!"

"What?"

I stand up and adjust my pants around my now limp-ish dick. "Pull up your pants. Fuck!" I yell out, walking over to the door.

I take three deep breaths, hand on the handle, then twist.

Standing before me, weekend bag on her shoulder, wearing an enormous hat flapping in the breeze with a nervous smile on her face, is trouble.

"Hello mother."

EVERLEE - MOTHERASS

Knox's fingers run up and down my spine, sending shivers through my body, while Emmett has perched himself at my feet under the shade of the umbrella.

"This is great," Knox says, pressing his lips to my shoulder.

"It is. It really can't get more perfect than this."

"We have taco Tuesday tonight and I'm super excited to help! It's going to be totes faboosh!" Lizzy chimes.

"Help? Your ass better be in there cooking with me."

"I had Beckett buy bagged shredded lettuce so your wee little fingers wouldn't have to chop lettuce, and he also bought diced tomatoes, sliced peppers, and shredded cheese," Emmett adds.

"O-M-G. Y'all are so cute! He didn't want you cutting and dicing, so he bought it all prepared for you."

"I wasn't trying to have anyone cut themselves this week."

Lizzy tosses her head back, laughing.

"I was talking about you," Emmett laughs.

"Emmy baby!" Lizzy shouts, swatting at him.

He rolls to the side, dodging her hand and chuckling.

"Where are the boys?" Knox looks over my shoulder. "Beckett will not get a tip."

"I'm sure they'll be out in a minute." I look towards the house, but don't see anything. It has been a while. A prickly feeling tingles on the back of my neck, but I ignore it. I was worried all day yesterday for no reason. We're going to have a great day and the rest of the week.

Relax Ev!

"It's my fault," Knox says, throwing his hands in the air.

"Likely," Jax chides, walking over to us. "But what specifically are you talking about?" He tosses me a wink, and it warms my insides.

He's been doing better today, less...stressed? Worried? I don't really know what the right word is, but he just looks better overall.

"Beckett. I forgave his debt for the rest of the day and then he goes and takes advantage of me."

"Did he know he was supposed to come back out?"

"Yea, we were going to have a picnic. It was his idea," I say, shifting a little on Knox's lap.

"Maybe he's still getting it ready?"

"It's been over thirty minutes," Lizzy chimes in.

"We could go help him?"

"Who wants to do that?" Knox says with a grimace.

I turn around to face him, running my hands up his chest. "I would be forever grateful if you helped." My stomach gurgles, so I stand up in front of him.

"How grateful?" He leans in towards my stomach and plants kisses on it.

"Fucking horn dogs! The whole lot of you!" Lizzy shouts, grabbing Tony's hand to walk back towards the house.

"You didn't answer my question," Knox whispers against my skin, his lips barely brushing it.

I look down at him, as he's staring at me between his lashes, looking like every bit of the badass surfer boy.

He pumps his eyebrows a little, then drags the front of my bathing suit down.

"Knox! We're in public."

He smiles and slides his other hand up my thigh and dips his finger into my bathing suit, brushing it across my pussy. "Is that why you're so wet?"

"Fuck you," I pant, voice shaky.

"Yes, please." He slides his finger out and wraps both hands around my ass, bringing my hips closer to his face. He takes in a deep breath and I cringe.

"I just got out of the ocean. There is going to be sand and salt all up in my lady bits and who knows what else."

"Ceviche."

"Shut the fuck up. Gross." Jax wraps his arms around my waist and pulls me from Knox's grasp. "That was Lizzy level of stupid shit to say!" He swings me around and I can't help but laugh.

Knox leaps from his chair and runs after us while I'm still strapped to Jax's chest like a tandem skydiver. After a few circles, Knox stops and Jax sets me down.

"So I'm really starving and now really horny. Thanks to Knox."

"At your service," he says, bowing and tipping his invisible hat.

"How about this? First one back to the house gets to shower with me!" I take off running towards the house.

"Dibs!" Knox yells, running.

"Shit!" Jax mumbles, running after him.

I'm slow on the sand. It feels like lead weights have been strapped to my ankles, but I push through, because food and orgasms wait for me! Lizzy must hear what's going on because she pauses on the deck and looks at me running like a loon across the small boardwalk.

"What's going on?" she yells.

"First one back gets–"

"Oh!" she shouts as realization hits her after she sees the guys running towards the house. "Count me in!" She grabs Tony's hand and starts running.

I'm a few paces behind her and see her fling open the back door, then freeze. We all nearly run into one another like they do on those cartoons when fast moving objects meet a wall. That wall right now being Lizzy.

She turns and looks at me, her face drained of all its color, like someone died.

"What?" I ask in a panic. Did something happen to Beckett? Is that why they never came back out?

I step forward and walk into the house and see what she saw.

Fuck.

Something did die. My pussy. My orgasms.

My heart leaps into my throat and I can't breathe for a moment. My jaw clenches, my skin is clammy, and I think I'm going to puke.

Knox, unaware of what's going on, pushes through and yells, "I'm first! I- shit!" He shakes his head quickly. "Obviously, I didn't shit. Sorry ma'am."

Ma'am.

Mother.

My mother.

Standing in the middle of our luxury sex shack on motherfucking Fourth of July.

Fucking Beckett.

My eyes dart from my mother to Beckett, who is standing just behind her, holding her suitcase in hand with her hat tucked under his arm. His eyes are wide with panic and apology and nearly every other emotion the human can experience.

"Mom," I say slowly, realizing I haven't greeted her at all yet.

"Everlee," she drawls.

"Mama McKinley!" Lizzy says, swooping into the room, arms spread wide, with a huge grin on her face.

"Lizzy." My mother smiles as she gives her a warm and welcoming hug.

"I didn't realize you had... so many people here." She looks between Beckett and me nervously, then points her finger to her chin. "Wait a minute." She points it rapidly in the air.

Fuck.

"You're the boys from Easter. I thought I recognized you. Took a minute with all the," she waves her hands over her chest, then puffs out a breath. "Woo. Yep. Definitely didn't recognize you at first. So many tattoos," she points to Callum, then looks at Emmett. "And... a..." she points at her breast and her brows rise on her face. "Looks like it hurts."

Emmett shakes his head awkwardly and just mumbles something incoherently. What does he say? Yes, it hurts, or no, it doesn't and it turns me on. He's screwed either way.

Knox steps forward, holding out his hand. "Nice to see you again, Mrs. McKinley," he smiles.

I can't help but watch him take her hand in his and then I freak out. Those fingers were just brushing along my pussy not five minutes ago. Jesus fuck, I'm going to hell. If I wasn't before, I'm sure as shit going now. Hello back door to hell, party for one.

"So funny story... turns out that they actually live down the road from Lizzy."

"Small world," Beckett chirps awkwardly.

"Well, how about that! You boys just keep showing up."

Dear God, Hi it's me Everlee. I know I only reach out to you when I need something or if I'm having an org... fuck, get it together, Everlee! You can't pray to God asking for help and talk or even think about the word orgasm! Having an org... anization problem. Those darn lids. You can never find the one you need. It's always lost. And then you try labeling the containers with the lids, but then somehow that doesn't even work. I mean, really, why is it so hard? Everlee!

How am I yelling at myself in my head? I'm seriously like a squirrel in a nut shop.

Focus.

Focus on the prayer to get you out of this god awful situation.

Shit! Is he still listening to me? I started praying, but never ended it with an Amen, so does that leave everything open in between? Like if I need a pause, should I say Amen, to cut the feed off.

The feed?

What in the fuck is wrong with me?

I'm spiraling.

My whole body feels like a piece of ice that's been dropped into a volcano.

Hey G buddy.

Fucking help me.

Shit.

Amen.

No. Too late.

Amen should have been said before the shit, not after.

"Everlee?" Jax asks, moving to put his hand on my back, but pulls away.

Soul crushing ache.

I want to reach out and touch him. Them.

AMEN!

GODDAMMIT!

"Beckett," I grit through clenched teeth, trying to maintain any level of calm and cool. "Can you please help me with something outside?"

He tilts his head to the side. "Can one of them help?" he says, pointing to my guys.

My lips flatten into a hard line. "No. They can't."

Will nods and pushes him along. "Go outside and help your sister."

"But I don't wanna," he whines.

I have half a mind to snatch him by his ear and drag him outside.

"Beckett. Go help your sister," our mother urges.

He sighs and starts walking towards me, but I point to the front of the house. I don't need her to see me yelling at him through the glass on the back wall.

"Lizzy."

She perks right up, with a combination of pity and fear in her eyes.

"Please introduce my mother to... our friends."

Friends.

I'm going to fucking murder my brother.

Just as the front door closes, he holds his hands up. "Ev."

"Don't you fucking say one word to me!"

His lips pinch together.

"What in the fuck were you thinking?"

He stares at me, lips still pinched.

"Fucking talk!"

His eyes pulse for a second. "I didn't know. You said not to, then you're asking me questions. You're scaring me right now."

"Good!"

"I'm sorry Ev. I had no idea she was going to show up. Obviously."

"Obviously," I snipe back.

"I was just as shocked as you were when she showed up knocking on the door."

"Were you shocked?" I push against his chest and he lets me push him backwards. "Shit Beckett!"

"I know. I know."

"Why is she here? What happened? How did she find this place?"

"We were talking about all of that when you all got home. She said she was lonely and realized how she never does anything without dad and she wanted to be more independent. Something about it being Independence Day and hers... Anyway... she got to the area, and asked them where this house was and since everyone knows about it... it wasn't hard to find."

"Of course."

"How can I fix this? If you want me to ask her to leave, I will. I'll be the dick kid."

My growl of frustration makes the birds nesting nearby flutter away. "Fuuuck. No. I'm not going to ask her to leave."

"I really didn't think she was going to show up. I swear. She literally never goes anywhere."

"Yea, I know," I say, my tone softening. Even though I was nervous, I never thought in one million gazillion years she would have showed up. "Fuck. Shit. Motherass. Cunt bag. Titty tangler. Schlong a dong, fuck!" I yell out, kicking the pebbles on the ground as I stomp back into the house.

When I push the door open, mother is standing there with her bag in hand and Lizzy and the guys behind her.

"What's going on?" I ask.

"I can leave. I shouldn't have just showed up. That wasn't right of me. Y'all are having a good time here with your friends. You don't need me here messing it up."

"No," I say, cringing with myself for trying to talk her into staying.

A loud crack of lightning echoes behind me, followed by a rumble of thunder. I try not to laugh, watching Beckett high step it into the house, trying not to piss himself, screaming like a two-year-old.

"What the fu-dge was that? Where did it come from?" He peeks his head back out of the door, looking at the sky, then shuts the door.

"Weather is a fickle friend," Knox says ominously from the kitchen.

"You're not going anywhere. At least right now. It's raining or lightning apparently, and you just got here. You've been driving all morning. Stay. Have some lunch and we can re-assess."

"Are you sure?"

No. "Of course. Beckett and Will were preparing us some food for a picnic, but judging by the weather, it's probably a good idea we weren't outside."

"Small miracles," Beckett mumbles.

"I'm going to go upstairs and take a quick shower while Beckett finishes getting everything ready."

"Do you need any help?" Mother offers, following him into the kitchen.

Lizzy catches my eyes and her lips twist and she mouths, 'Sorry'.

Trying to keep it together, I wink at her, then look at my guys. They have a mixture of looks on their faces and parts of me are breaking inside.

JAX - FIXING IT BACK

THE ROOM IS SILENT as we all watch Everlee walk upstairs. Her face. It's breaking my heart and makes me want to punch a hole through a wall. I need to go outside for a minute to calm down. Losing my shit in front of her mother wouldn't be the best thing to do, especially since she already looks at us the way she does. It's not fear, or disgust... but it's something.

"I'm going to get our stuff from the beach, since I don't think we'll be going out there anymore."

"Let me help," Emmett offers, hesitating and waiting for my approval.

After a second, I nod. I don't know why I waited. I wasn't trying to be a dick or make it awkward, but that's the way things have been lately. Awkward. And it's probably my fault. Actually, I know it's me, but I don't know how to change it or fix it.

The rain is pouring down, but the lightning and thunder seem to have stopped, which is a good thing. Fairly certain Everlee would kill me if I got hit by lightning. She would bring me back to life, just to kill me again. Darling, fiery angel that she is.

"So that sucks," Emmett says, walking a pace behind me.

We haven't talked much, which sucks because I miss talking to him. He's the only one who just lets me be me. Callum tries to fix whatever he perceives is broken, Knox, in general, is a little shit, though he can be a strong rock when I need him to be. And I try to never need him because... well, that would mean I'm having a moment and I don't like having moments. Moments are for the weak. Not Jax fucking McCall.

Emmett just gets me like no one else does. He presses when he needs to, calls me on my shit when I need it, and is just fucking there.

I shouldn't have done what I did. It was the wrong fucking thing to do, and it can't happen again, but I'm scared to tell him that because I don't want him to think what happened was wrong, because it wasn't.

"Yea."

"Poor Ev. She's probably losing her damn mind right now."

"Yea." I realize I'm being short, but I'm not trying to be. I just don't know what to say. Having her mom here fucking sucks. Ev is going to retreat inside of her shell and again our happy little butterfly is going to disappear. Although if she were a butterfly, she'd be a black butterfly with a skull on its back because she is a kinky little fucker now and I love it.

"Load me up."

"What?" I look over at him and he's standing in a starfish pose, with his arms open wide.

"There's a lot of stuff. Slide the bags on my arms, throw the towels on me. Load me up. I am but a mere vessel for your future work of art."

I can't help but laugh. "You're a dumbass. You're close to Knox level craziness."

"Jax," he says sternly. "That's a low blow."

"Shut up and get over here."

He steps the three paces and his hand grabs my wrist. "Are we good?" His voice lowers with a look of concern on his face.

I smile and pull my wrist from his grip and shove his shoulder. "Yea. We're good."

He nods, then resumes his starfish pose. The rain starts pouring, and it takes us about five minutes to get all the bags and towels hung and draped around him. The rumbling in the distance lights a fire under our ass. He walks back to the house with the waddle of a penguin, looking like some sort of swamp monster. I'm left with the random things, like the bocce ball set, football and a few starfish Everlee and Lizzy found this morning.

When we get back to the house, Beckett, Will, and Knox are putting together a large platter of fruits, cheeses, crackers, and sandwich meats for a buffet style lunch. Lizzy and Tony are talking about wedding plans with Mrs. McKinley in the living room while Callum walks around the area, tidying things up and setting the table for lunch.

I'm soaking wet and need to change. Emmett must have taken the bags and towels into the laundry room to dry because I don't see him, only wet footprints on the floor leading down the hall.

"Mrs. McKinley, I'm heading upstairs. Would you like for me to take your things up and place them in a room?"

Lizzy stops talking and looks at me and her face falls.

"You can call me Donna, and that would be lovely. Thank you..." her words fall off as she tries to remember my name.

"Jax."

"Jax. That's right," she smiles, but doesn't say anything else.

Her bag feels like a lead weight in my hand as I walk with it up the stairs. It's a representation of the constraints that are now placed on the rest of the week. No more smiles from Ev, no more flirty touches, or inappropriate jokes. No more holding her, cuddling with her, or sleeping with her.

Turning into the first room, I move to set her bag on the bed.

Emmett pokes his head in. "The one across the hall is better. It has a Jack and Jill bathroom with the bedroom closest to the main bedroom."

"Shit."

"What?"

"The bedroom with no mattress because of our little love nest? Thank God she didn't walk up here on her own." We walk across the hall and place her things on the bed. "Do you want to help me set the rooms up?"

"No," he pouts. "But I will."

We move to our bedroom and lift the mattress off the floor and put it back on the bed frame in the room which adjoins to Donna's. Quickly, but quietly, we deconstruct our room, moving the bed back into place, along with any furniture we may have moved. The room looks simple now.

Plain.

Uninviting.

Emmett heads back downstairs to check on lunch while I sit on the bed, trying to get out of this funk. Trying to find the positive in this screwed up situation.

It's stupid to be this upset about something.

Right?

I love sleeping with Ev, but I also really love sleeping without the guys. I don't mind the group sleeps, but it's what we do almost every night. Who knows... this could be good for us. Although, doing the math, that means two of us have to share a bed.

A quick flash of Emmett passes through my head, but I quickly dismiss it, pushing it away. Knox and Emmett will take the other two bedrooms up here and share a bathroom, while Callum and I bunk up in here together. Not ideal, but makes the most sense.

But none of us will be with Ev and the thought alone reignites a fire inside of me. Why am I having such a hard time with this?

Because you're scared, my subconscious unwelcomingly chimes in.

I'm not scared.

Scared that with her mother here, she will see why this is a bad idea. Why you all can't be together? Scared she will want safe. Normal. Not this, not you all. Which is reckless and taboo.

As if hearing my thoughts, Ev slides open the pocket door of the bathroom and is standing there, wet, head to toe, with a towel casually wrapped around her. The steam is billowing out of the bathroom while the water head in the shower still presses water out.

"What are you doing?" Her eyes grow wide as sadness sweeps across her face. She takes in the room and it hits her.

"Jax." She reaches her hand out to me, but I just stare at her.

She looks so sad and broken... and red. Her eyes are red. She's been crying.

She lightly stomps her foot on the ground, shaking her hand like a child would do when they aren't getting their way and words are just too hard to use.

Her towel drops to the floor and I freeze, mesmerized by her beauty.

This is such a bad fucking idea.

But I don't care.

My feet carry me across the room as I reach out for her hand.

EVERLEE – FIDDLESTICKS AND BISCUITS

WHY IS IT THAT hot showers make you cry when you're feeling emotional? It's like the best cries always happen in the shower. Is it because of the noise? It helps drown out the sorrows? Is it because you can just let the tears stream down your face without having to feel guilty for wiping them away?

The hot water pelts on my face while I stand there, letting it wash away all of my emotions. We were having such a good day. A wonderful week. And it's all gone.

Part of me hates I feel like this. Hates that I'm so upset my mother is here. I should be happy, welcoming. This shouldn't be filling me with rage and sadness. Beckett's not. He's bummed, but I think it's more guilt. Guilt for me because of my situation. Because I'm too much of a coward to tell my parents the truth about my relationship. Part of me is scared I will lose them, but the other part of me fears I won't but that things won't ever be the same. And of course that's silly to say, because things will definitely not be the same either way, but it took a lot for them to... accept is the wrong word, but understand maybe? Beckett's situation. I don't know if they would try as hard for me.

Maybe that's what I'm scared of. Fear of rejection from my parents. Fear that I will have the definitive proof Beckett is their favorite. When my parents found out they were pregnant with me, they were surprised. They were, of course, married, because having sex before marriage was a big no-no for them, *and could you imagine with four guys at the same time? My subconscious chimes in.*

Anyway, they've always loved me, but it just felt different. With me, I was an oopsie. With Beckett, he was planned. For some reason, after me they had a hard time conceiving, so it took them three extra years after they were ready to get pregnant with him and they were so excited. Over the moon. I wonder sometimes if that's how they were with me?

I pound my fist against the shower wall and resume my crying. Why am I so emotional right now?

A large thump from outside the room catches my attention. Sticking my head under the water, I let it rinse the tears away. Why? I have no fucking clue. Obviously, I'm not thinking clearly.

I grab the towel hanging beside the shower and wrap it around me. When I get to the door, I'm taken aback and another wave of emotion hits.

Shit!

The room is put back together the way it was, and Jax is sitting on the edge of the bed with his head in his hands. He must have heard the pocket door slide because he turns to look at me, eyes hollow shells of what they used to be.

"What are you doing?" he asks, staring at me, his eyes searching my face.

"Jax." I reach my hand out to him, eager to touch him, to feel him. He looks so sad and confused and I know we're feeling the same pain even if he won't admit it. He continues staring at me without moving, so I stomp my foot and shake my hand. I know it's childish, but I'm scared if I open my mouth again, I will cry. And I don't want to cry anymore. I mean, it's just my mother at a beach house. Ugh!

The need to have him touching me, inside of me, consumes every inch of me so I let my towel fall to the ground.

A small bit of joy dances through my body when his eyes pulse wide for a second and his jaw slacks open.

A moment later, he's walking across the room, eyes on fire.

His hand circles the back of my head as his lips crash to mine, pushing me back into the room. He kicks the door closed, only hard enough for the latch to click, as his hands rove my body and his tongue gently assaults my mouth. His kiss is deep. Fast. Passionate.

His hands quickly work his bathing suit down as he continues to move us into the shower. The hot water hits our head and runs down the small gap between our bodies, our lips never separating. When he pushes me against the tile, it feels like ice against my skin, taking my breath away.

"I need to have my cock inside of you."

"Samesies."

He lets out a low throaty chuckle and leans down, placing kisses on my neck, working his way down to my breasts.

A moan escapes and my back arches.

"You have to be quiet. We're right over the living room," he whispers, switching breasts.

Right above my mother.

Needing him inside of me, I lift my leg and hook it around his waist. His hard cock presses at my entrance.

"Jax, fuck me." I reach my hand down and run it over his length before lining it up at my entrance.

He latches onto my neck, sucking on my skin. I love when he does this. It shoots a tingly feeling down through my nipples. "With pleasure." His hand clamps firmly to my waist and he slams into me and holds. A wave of euphoria passes through me. He feels so good. "You're so fucking tight wrapped around my cock," he whispers on my skin.

His words do things to me. Good things. Great things.

My hands clamp onto his back, my body eager for more of him while the shower continues to rain on us.

He pulls out and slams in again, pausing before he repeats, getting faster and faster each time. Consumed with passion and the need to go even faster, he presses into me then lifts me onto his cock and presses my back against the wall. "I want to bury myself so deep in your pussy that you feel me for days."

"Do it," I moan out against his neck. "Impale me with your cock. I need you so fucking bad. Make me drip with your come so that I feel it all night."

His breath stutters. "You're so fucking perfect."

With my legs thrown over his arms and his arms wrapped around my back, he has full control over the speed that he slams into me. He moves faster, sending his cock into me so deep it feels like he's bruising my lungs.

I'm trying not to moan, but it's nearly fucking impossible.

"Kiss me," he commands.

Without hesitation, my lips latch onto his and he swallows every delicious moan. My orgasm is building faster and faster as the pressure from inside couples with the friction of my clit rubbing on him. We're both close, need tipping the scales into this wild frenzy.

"I fucking love you so goddamn much."

His cock and his words send me over the edge. My orgasm slams into me, and I come undone in his arms, riding every delicious wave around his enormous cock. Removing my lips from his, I bite into his neck and suck his skin.

"Can't... do... that," he puffs out between thrusts.

"Why?"

"You'll leave a mark."

I growl out in frustration, but I'm interrupted by his orgasm exploding inside of me. His cock pulses as he slows to a stop, keeping me perched on his cock.

"I love you too."

He looks at me and smiles.

"This week may have changed, but my love for you and the guys hasn't changed a single bit. I'm not going anywhere. We will get through the rest of this week, plus it may be kind of fun to sneak around. Stolen glances and kisses here and there."

"There's nothing fun about stolen glances. They'll only make my cock ache that much more to be inside of you."

I wrap my arms around his neck and squeeze tightly, pressing my breasts against his chest.

He pats my butt as he unhooks my legs from around his arms and stands me back up.

"You probably need to finish washing quickly. You've been up here quite a while."

I snarl at him and he laughs.

"Here. Let me." He grabs me by the shoulders and guides me under the showerhead and runs his fingers through my hair. He grabs the shampoo and squirts some into his palm, rubbing them together, before rubbing them in my hair while massaging my scalp.

"Your fingers are heaven."

"You have no idea."

"But I do," I say, turning around to face him.

He looks at me, both of us just staring at one another for a moment before he tilts my chin up and steps against my body, pushing me back into the water so he can rinse my hair.

Ten minutes later, I'm walking downstairs wearing my fun and flirty Fourth of July dress with my wet hair pulled into a bun on my head.

"Everything ok? You were up there for a while," my mother asks, standing from the couch. Lizzy is behind her humping the air and I ignore her.

"Yea. I had to use the bathroom beforehand and you know how I get with those logic puzzles. Can't get off the toilet before I finish it."

She laughs. "It's not good to do puzzles on the toilet. Or read. It compresses things down there that shouldn't be compressed and could give you..." she stops talking and looks around, remembering she's not at home. "Things." She raises her brows and tilts her head down knowingly.

Hemorrhoids. That's what we were talking about.

"You're right," I say simply, praying to God we get off this topic.

"Lunch is ready!" Beckett calls from the kitchen.

"Thank God!"

"I was waiting on your diva ass to get out of the shower."

"Bec–" Mother starts, then stops, holding up her hands in apology. "I'm sorry. You're on vacation. Cuss away." She pauses, then says, "Damn it! Ass!"

Lizzy and I look at one another, then burst out in giggles.

Mother does not cuss. Like hardly ever.

We were at the store once and she was leaning over to get something and smacked the back of her head good on the shelf above. It damn near knocked her out and all she said was fiddlesticks and biscuits. If it was me, the store would have thought they were under attack by pirates. I would have likely made up a new cuss word and said it so loud and so many times that people around me would have thought they missed out on some new word.

No. Mother does not cuss.

Well, apparently until now.

EVERLEE - 4
LETTER WORD

THE HEAT OF THE sun pulls me from my sleep as my hand roams the bed looking for warmth, but realization hits.

I'm alone.

Callum's scent dances around me like a cruel joke. A wish, a memory of what once was.

Rolling onto my back, I open my eyes and stare at the ceiling fan, unmoving. Is it stupid to miss the spin of the blades? It's the first time I've slept without a fan on in months and I miss the low hum.

My legs carry me toward the bathroom, because I'm still too mopey to walk with purpose.

And tired.

I feel like I tossed and turned all night. After dinner last night, we all sat in the living room and talked about random things. Beckett and Will talked a little about the firehouse, while the boys talked about their businesses, except for Allure. Probably not the best topic of conversation. Of course, mother latched onto Bo's because she loves to cook. She even volunteered to come up and visit, saying she's been meaning to, so we could go to Bo's. At times the conversation was great, felt normal and natural, but then I'd remember there was a veil over the entire thing. A truth that could never come to light.

Just before ten, we walked onto the beach and found a spot to watch the fireworks. It was dark outside because even though it was nearly a full moon, it was deep red and low on the horizon. I had envisioned the night a lot different- me cuddled in the middle of all my guys, nestled between someone's legs, watching the fireworks. Instead, it was me on a towel with Lizzy and Tony nestled, and the guys scattered around. Mother was with Beckett and Will, and would occasionally pick up a conversation with Emmett.

Jax and Knox were near the water's edge with their heads together and I was dying to know what they were talking about. And then Callum. He sat closest to me and occasionally in between the fireworks lighting up the sky, his hand would reach over and rub against mine. Just the light brush of his pinky. A gentle reminder he was there.

My rock.

When I get downstairs this morning, Teddy Swims is playing on the Bluetooth speaker in the kitchen and mother and Emmett are moving around the kitchen like a pair of synchronized cooks talking about something, while Callum sits at the table working on a crossword looking hot as fuck. He's wearing a pair of dark blue bathing suit shorts with a white t-shirt v-neck that only mutes the tattoos under his shirt and does nothing for the two full sleeves of tattoos he has on his arms.

Tony, Lizzy, Beckett and Will are spread out between the two couches watching the end of an episode of Schitt's Creek where David and Patrick are trying to find their wedding location.

Beckett glances at me and gives me a quick nod before looking back at the screen, and I can't help but wonder what his thoughts are on marriage. Not the act of marriage, but marrying Will. Will is the only guy he's had a steady relationship with and they are so great together. Callum watches me from the table, so I walk over to talk to him. When I get near him, my body buzzes, eager to touch him, to feel him touch me.

But we don't.

"Where's Jax and Knox?"

He looks in the kitchen and my eyes follow to see mother mixing something on the stove, talking up a storm to Emmett. Callum's hand drops from the table and rubs up the back of my knee, causing goosebumps to erupt across my skin. My body hums with excitement at his touch and my eyes snap shut to relish this feeling. He keeps his eyes focused on the crossword, pen tapping on the table like he's deep in thought. "They went for a run this morning. They should be back soon." His words and his tone are casual, but the energy radiating off of him is delicious and... dangerous.

His hand snakes further up and my legs buckle as I lean onto the table for support. I look under my arm to see my mom still at the stove stirring away, still talking Emmett's ear off. He catches me looking, and a sly grin spreads across his face before he tosses me a quick wink.

Callum's hand continues to travel up until his index finger slips just under my shorts and brushes over my pussy. He looks at me knowingly, as I try to hide the shock on my face.

What in the actual fuck is he trying to do?

"No panties," he whispers, running his finger up to my clit.

"You ass," I grind back.

He sits back in the chair, his right arm still casually resting on the table with his eyes focused on the kitchen. On my mother. "You haven't seen me be an ass yet," he winks, and my skin erupts with fire.

We are playing a dangerous game, but I can't walk away. I can't move. I'm frozen in place by a combination of fear and lust. Fear that my mother will catch us and fear that he will stop. My lungs forget how to work and my chest burns, reminding me to breathe.

"You're so wet," he whispers, scraping his teeth over his bottom lip.

He is the fucking epitome of a sex king right now. Leaned back in the chair, arm propped on the table, hand up my fucking pants playing with my pussy with my mother feet away.

My eyes roll into the back of my head. This man. He will be the death of me. Right here in this dining room.

He twists his arm so he can insert his finger inside of me.

Holy fuck.

Holy fuck.

He's fingering me in the middle of the dining room with everyone around. Unless the group on the couch leans up and looks over the back of the seat, they won't see anything but Emmett and my mother. MY MOTHER! They can just glance over. There's a small island between us, but I don't know if it would do much to hide anything.

My pulse is racing.

And I'm so turned on right now.

So fucking horny.

He tries to reposition his hand, but can't quite get the configuration. This would be a brilliant time for me to walk away, but do I?

No.

My greedy little cunt turns to give him better access, and he fucking eats it up. He knows he has me right where he wants me. In the palm of his hand.

Literally!

"Ooh," he hums, looking up at me in approval. "Who's being a good girl?"

Before I can answer, he pushes another finger into me.

"You know the rules."

My heart flutters. No sounds, or he stops.

Are we really doing this here?

"Yes sir," I whisper.

"Good girl," he mouths.

My stomach clenches and my breasts swell as my orgasm quickly builds inside of me. Something about the way his fingers pulse in while his thumb works my clit, and the fact we are in the middle of so many people...

"I can hear how wet you are and I just want to drink you up," he whispers and I clench, strangling his fingers with my pussy.

He chuckles softly.

"Is Everlee making fun of me?" My mother asks and we freeze.

Emmett jumps in immediately. "Mrs. McKinley, you didn't finish telling me about your soufflé."

Chancing a glance, I look over my shoulder and see he has her turned away from us.

He sees me looking but doesn't acknowledge it.

Callum pumps his eyebrows at me when I look back at him. He's so fucking hot right now with the muscles in his arm flexing as he fucks me.

My orgasm is close because my body starts to grind on his fingers. I glance at his shorts and see his hard cock eager to get out and join the party. The image of me pulling out his cock and falling to my knees to suck it in my mouth sends me over the edge. My legs shake and a wave of euphoria sweeps through my whole body as my pussy pulses around his fingers.

"Did you say something?" My mother calls.

Callum's hand drops from my shorts as he readjusts himself.

"Everlee?"

When I turn to look at her, she's staring at me and my heart drops. Fuck me.

"Yea?"

"What is it?"

"What?" I asked, confused.

"I thought you said something to me."

"Oh. No."

"Emmett," Callum calls.

"Yes?"

"Ev was trying to help me out, but we're stuck. What's a four letter word for each of a number of strips forming a framework for enclosing a pane of glass?"

"Came," mother bellows out, proud of herself.

Some god awful sound leaves my body as I almost crash to the ground.

"Are you ok Everlee? You look a little flush. Sit down."

A chair pushes out from the table right in front of me as Callum nods.

"Thank you, Callum. Such the gentleman."

Yea, the gentleman who just made your daughter come not even fifteen feet from you.

"Came. That's it. Perfect."

The back of my neck prickles and when I follow the direction, I see Lizzy perched with her chin between two cushions, staring at me like a baby peacock trying to play hide and seek.

Shit. Mother ass. Did she watch us? That fucking little dirty freak.

My eyes narrow to thin slits at her and she smiles, then rolls back onto the couch and into, presumably, Tony's arm.

EVERLEE - GIRL TALK

<hr>

AN HOUR AND A half later, we're walking onto the beach. The sun feels warm and welcoming on the skin, and the skies are bright blue without a cloud in the sky. There's a slight breeze coming off the ocean that feels nice against my skin. The dangerous breeze that doesn't let the sun heat your skin so you forget you're getting sun.

Knox is bouncing down the boardwalk in front of us with a smile spread across his face. The sun has to be jealous of his radiance and bountiful energy. Being around him makes you feel... happy and at peace. Aside from Jax, everyone around him smiles in his presence. It's a rare gift.

"Right this way, Mrs.-"

She holds her hand up, stopping him. "Knox," she scolds.

He laughs, "Sincerest apologies. Right this way, Donna." He sweeps his arm wide. "I've set up a chair for you under this umbrella so that you may partake in all the beach sights away from the sun."

"Oh Knox. You didn't have to do this. Ev, your friends are so kind."

"They are."

"I set you one up too Evy-" He stops mid-sentence, realizing he was about to call me our special name.

"Evy? Such a unique nickname."

"Yea." I don't know what else to say. I'm really trying not to be rude or short with her, and I know it keeps coming out that way, but I just don't know what to say. I feel so guarded. Like every word, every sentence can be used against me, or reveal my secret. Part of me just wants to say fuck it and spill the tea because it's only been one night, but I miss my guys. I miss the connection, the closeness. I just miss them.

She takes a deep breath and sits in the chair and I take the one beside her.

"Where's mine, Knoxxy?" Lizzy coos.

He pulls his lips. "Beside Evy, of course."

"Evy and Knoxxy. So cute," Mother says, setting her bag down and digging out a puzzle book.

"Logic puzzles?" I ask.

"Yes. I saw you playing them at Easter and I thought they looked interesting."

I dig in my bag and pull out my book and show it to her.

"The same one." She smiles, tilting her head to the side. "I'm stuck on puzzle sixty-nine."

"Being stuck in sixty-nine is the worst," Lizzy chimes in and I cut my eyes at her.

I didn't miss the *in* versus *on* in her sentence. She's trying to be clever and make a joke about the one time I told her about doing sixty-nine in the bedroom with Knox and we tried to use rope and somehow got tangled up and stuck. It was super fun when Jax found us and teased us verbally, then teased me sexually before he undid the ropes. He, of course, made sure I was ok first, but damn.

"You play these too?" Mother asks cheerfully.

"God no. I don't have the patience. I just remember the one-time Ev was stuck."

"In this book? Can you help me?"

"Lizzy is being Lizzy." I snarl at Lizzy before I turn towards my mother.

Mother's brow furrows, and she tilts her head to the side like a dog does when you ask it a question.

"She's confusing the situation."

"I'm not. I remember it like it was just last week." I see the smirk dancing across her lips as she digs a book out of her bag.

"Jax could probably help," Knox offers with a light gleam in his eyes. I want to run over and put him in a chokehold, but before I can, he's throwing his shirt on the ground and flittering off to join Jax near the ocean.

"He seems fun and so full of energy."

"He does have a lot of energy."

"So you can't help me?"

"No, Lizzy was talking about volume two."

"Volume two?"

"Yes. You have the third volume."

"Third?" She flips the book closed and sees volume three right under the title.

"Well, I'll be."

"Yea, these are a little harder."

"Do you ladies need anything to drink? I'm going to run back inside and make a few pitchers of drinks."

"That delightful concoction you made last week would be wonderful. The one with the pineapple," Lizzy chirps.

If I leapt out of my seat and tackled her to the ground right now, I feel like that would be super obvious that something else is going on and all of her comments have another meaning. This one being that the night he made those delicious drinks, the guys and I ended up having sex in the kitchen because they were eating and licking fruit off my body.

I should just stop telling her about my sexy times with the guys and then she can't do stupid shit like she's doing now.

"Ok. I will make that one and bring a pitcher of water out as well."

"These men are so thoughtful. Even the tall, dark, and handsome one over there." She nods towards Jax. "What's your thoughts on him? Or any of these guys?"

"What?"

"Well, you seemed to be drawn to them at Easter and then you're here together. Seems like you hit it off at Easter."

"They live just down the way from Lizzy and own a bar on the same street as her."

"I hear you, but I don't know. Seems like you have a chemistry of varying levels with these men. They are all very handsome and in fantastic shape. Do you find any of these men suitable?"

"Are you trying to set her up, Mama McKinley?"

"Well, she doesn't seem to like the men I find for her." She huffs, "Granted, none of them are this good looking."

"You think they're good looking?" Lizzy presses. She's nearly leaning across my lap to talk to my mother.

"Well, I'd have to be blind not to think that and then honestly, I'd have to feel them with my hands and..." she starts fanning herself and Lizzy laughs.

"We should have a contest. We have to be blindfolded and you have to feel the men to determine which one is the hottest."

"No," I say sternly, looking at Lizzy, wondering what in the fuck she's doing, then turn towards my mother with shock, realizing she was thinking about it.

"No, no, I couldn't." Mother blushes.

"But you wanted to, though."

"I didn't *not* want to." She giggles.

I'm in shock. I've never seen this side of my mother. The relaxed, dare I say, carefree version of her. She's always in a tussy, going here or there, always 'on'.

"Didn't *not* want to do what?" Emmett asks, walking back out with two pitchers and plastic cups.

"Nothing," I snap, the tone betraying my irritation with Lizzy. I feel like she's purposefully trying to spill the beans on this little love nest situation.

Knox is running back up to us, his golden locks bouncing in the air.

"What's up, buttercup?" Lizzy asks.

"We're going to go on a run. Anyone care to go with?"

I thought about it. Perhaps we could find a quiet spot on the beach and I could let them have their way with me, but the chances of that happening again, this late in the morning, would be slim to nil chance. Plus, having an orgy on the beach is a lot harder to hide than just one on one. Plus, the boys looked like they wanted to actually run, and I can't keep pace with them.

"No thanks," I say.

"Yea. I'll join," Emmett says, sitting the tray down.

"Tony will be down in a little and we're going to head to the dolphins."

"Dolphins?" my mother inquires.

Lizzy, in typical Lizzy fashion, falls to the ground and re-enacts the dolphin strand feeding we saw, then goes on about how amazing it was and regurgitates all the facts the older woman told us. She ends it with an invitation to join them.

"I don't want to barge in on your time with Tony. I feel like I've already barged in enough."

"Not at all."

"Oh, hey!" Knox yells and then runs onto the boardwalk to meet Will and Beckett. He throws his arm around Beckett's shoulders and starts moving his other hand rapidly as he's talking. Likely trying to convince him to go on a run, or more likely trying to start some sort of bet or contest.

Moments later, Beckett is nodding and laughing while Knox is jumping up and down.

"Beckett seems to get along with the guys really well. Did they just meet?"

"What?"

"Beckett seems pretty comfortable with the guys, your friends. It's not weird for him being here with them?"

"Because he's gay?"

"Goodness no. Give me a little more credit. I just mean you have your friends here and then Beckett. I didn't know if he felt like the odd man out."

"Beckett and Lizzy are practically siblings, and no… I don't think it's weird for him and no, he met them when he came up to visit."

"Oh. That makes sense."

Knox, Beckett, and Will are walking by a minute later, laughing. "Last chance, ladies, if you want to join us."

"I'm afraid I wouldn't be able to keep up with all you beef-cakes, plus I'm fairly certain that if it hasn't already, it will turn into another race and I don't want to get left behind."

"We'd never leave you behind, love!" He claps, then darts off across the beach towards Jax and Emmett. "Let's go bro!" He shouts to Will and Beckett behind him, then does a cartwheel into a back handspring.

"Wow."

"Have you talked to dad?" I ask, watching the guys stretching on the beach.

"Yes. I spoke with him last night and texted him this morning. He was very surprised I showed up."

Weren't we all?

"He said he's been having long days and nights. Meetings all day, then dinners and networking into the late hours."

"Busy, busy."

"Thank you for letting me stay," she says, grabbing my arm. "I know you probably weren't expecting it. Heck, neither was I. But I was sitting at home and I kept thinking about you and Becks and going to the beach when you two were so small and all the fun we had and I just… I just missed that. Before I knew what was happening, my feet were carrying me to the bedroom to pack a suitcase and then to the car to drive here. On the way here, I just kept thinking… what am I doing?" She laughs at herself. "But then I said, what would Everlee do? She would just go. She wouldn't be afraid to take a leap and just go." Her face falls and her demeanor changes. "You've always been my free spirit, my wild child. Sure, Beckett has his moments, but you. You've never let fear of the unknown hold you back. You see an opportunity and you just go for it all in. It makes you more likely to get hurt, but you don't let that stop you. I have no idea where you get it from, but I admire you. I look up to you."

"Mom," I chirp out. My throat is tight, holding back the tears, and I can feel Lizzy crying. She's trying to read her book, but I hear it in her breathing.

"I know I give you a lot of shit about finding a husband, but it's just because you're so amazing. I don't want the world to miss out on you. I want you to find a man who can give you everything you deserve, and it's a lot. Honestly, I don't know how one man can do it, but I know you'll find him."

I don't look at Lizzy, but hear her rotate her entire body away from us so all we can see is her back.

"Thanks mom. I want you to know, though, I may never get married and you have to be ok with that. That doesn't mean that I won't be in a relationship that fulfills every need and desire. It just means we won't be married."

"So no grandchildren?"

"Mother." I grab her arm. "This may come as a shock to you, but I'm not a virgin."

I ignore Lizzy's restrained snicker.

"Well, I know that." She closes the puzzle book on her lap, her hands fidgeting.

"And I may or may not have a child in the future. I'm not going to let my marital status dictate that. There are plenty of single women out there who are raising families on their own."

"I know... I just... You're amazing and I want to have little you's that you bring around so I can spoil and love."

"Don't discount Will and Beckett. They can find a surrogate."

"I volunteer as tribute." Lizzy says, turning around. "Shit. Not in a weird way. That sounded weird. I was just trying to say that it would be pretty cool to be part of your family because y'all are so great."

I'm speechless, still getting over the fact she wants to be their surrogate. Not even knowing if that's what they want or if they are even in that place in their lives. I really feel like this train derailed a while ago.

"Lizzy, you are part of our family. Blood or not. You can be born into a family, but you can also choose one. And I believe God chose you to be in our lives. I know you have your mother and father, and they are wonderful people, but you have always felt like part of this family from the very first time you stepped foot in the door."

"Mama McKinley, you're going to make me cry... again."

"I don't want to do that, sweetie."

"What did I miss?" Tony asks, walking up to us.

"Just... girl talk," mother says.

"If you aren't ready for the walk, we can wait," Tony offers.

"No. I'm ready." Lizzy stands and wipes her face and tosses her cover-up on the chair.

She's wearing one of my favorite bathing suits on her. Red and white striped bottoms with a halter top with cherries on it that ties in the middle. I have one similar, but opted for the bright pink string bikini today. My skin has gotten some sun on it the last couple of days, so the pink really pops.

"Are you sure you don't want to come, Mama McKinley? It's so cool to watch."

"Well, actually. If you're really ok with it, it sounds pretty cool."

"Absolutely!" Tony leans down and offers his arm to help her up.

"Do you want to come, Everlee? You'll be here by yourself."

"No, you go. I'm going to stay up here and work on my tan."

"Watch the tan lines, girl. You've worn a different type of bathing suit every day. You're starting to look like someone wrapped you up in rope, then left you hanging around."

The quiver in her bottom lips tells me she's proud of herself. How many more little inside jokes or jabs is she going to say for the rest of this week?

"Thanks."

"You know I got you, boo."

They walk away, getting further and further down the beach and I feel this weight leave my chest. My mother has never been an openly affectionate woman. She wasn't closed off, but she also was never the friend mom that other girls have. I guess you could call it a tough love, which was so hard for me to understand when I saw her with Beckett. She was always so gentle with him, and I never felt that. She would probably say that she was trying to toughen me up for the real world, and it worked, I guess. I had no qualms about leaving and starting my own life somewhere else. It could be the same reason that Beckett can't or won't leave.

After our talk about weddings and babies, I feel like we're in a better place. I got what I needed to say, well, at least some of what I needed to say, off my chest. Hopefully, this will mean she doesn't try to set me up on anymore dates.

A hand slides down my cheek to my neck and I nearly jump out of my seat, ready to attack whoever thought they could touch me.

CALLUM - UNDER THE SEA

THE HOUSE IS EERILY quiet. Just before I went up to take a shower, Emmett was fixing some pitchers of drinks to take out for the ladies, and Will and Beckett were... sharing a moment in their room. I guess their moans and grunts make up for the ones we were causing a few nights ago with Everlee.

The summer breeze filters through the back door, fluttering the curtains. When I walk over to look outside at the beach, I notice Everlee sitting by herself. I quickly grab a piece of pineapple out of the fridge and pop it into my mouth while I walk out to meet her.

She's quiet, lost in her own world, and doesn't hear me walking up. Needing to feel her skin under my touch, I run my finger down her neck.

She jumps and I can't help but laugh.

"Callum?" she asks, turning around.

"Were you expecting someone else?"

"No. Not really, I guess. I just assumed..." she shakes her head. "You didn't go out with the guys?"

"Well, I guess not."

"Yea. That was a stupid question," she says, standing up.

"What are you doing?"

"I'm going back to the house. Lizzy said I need to work on my tan and called me out about all the weird tan lines. So I'm going to do it in the privacy of our house."

"Hmm. Do you want some company?"

"Do you want to watch me tan?"

"I can watch you sit and read a book and be happy."

She rolls her eyes at me, and I admit, what I said was probably a little corny, but I don't care.

She grabs her bag and tosses it over her shoulder. "You want to watch me walk away?"

"You know I hate to see you go, but I always love to watch you walk away."

She throws her head back, laughing, before she tosses a flirtatious glance over her shoulder. My cock twitches as I watch her ass sway from side to side in that cheeky, bright pink, string bikini. Desire ripples under my skin as I fight the urge to rip it off her body and press my cock inside of her, claiming her. But I don't know where her mother is and I don't want to come across as an uncontrollable sex feign, although that's what I feel like around her.

Fuck!

I stay five paces behind her the entire way back to the house and I swear she has an extra sway to her hips to fuck with me. And it's working. She gets under my skin in the best and worst way possible. It's like she's my obsession.

Last night was hard. Not only because I had to share a bed with Jax, but because I could hear her tossing and turning all night. I could almost feel her searching out for us, needing us. Unable to take it anymore, I rolled out of bed and padded across the floor to her room, where I snuck into her bed and cradled her. She immediately rolled into me, tossing her leg over mine, and found her favorite little spot in the crook of my neck.

I sat an alarm for my phone in case I fell asleep. I didn't want to deal with the explanation or blowback of her mother walking in and finding me in her room in the early morning.

Although, I guess it's better than her finding all five of us in bed.

She finds a lounger and sits her bag down, then spreads her towel on it. She looks over her shoulder, making eye contact with me, as she unties the back of her bathing suit top. My stomach tightens and my cock stirs, growing eager to be closer to her.

She smiles as she lets the top fall to the deck.

I casually sit down, trying to hide my erection from her. I don't want her to know the control she has over me. Hell, fingering her this morning before breakfast took everything I had not to snatch her wrist and drag her upstairs.

She looks behind me at the beach and then undoes the string of her bottoms and lets those fall. What is she doing? My hands clamp onto the chair beside me to hold me in place.

Satisfied with my reaction, she lies on the chair, chest up and closes her eyes.

That's it.

No words. Nothing.

She shifts, arching her back in the chair to get more comfortable at the same time a gust of wind blows off the ocean. Her nipples harden and I feel like they are seeking me out like the periscope of a submarine. Obviously, I know they're not, but that doesn't mean they don't make my mouth salivate.

"Where's everyone at?"

Her eyes open and she tilts her head up ever so slightly to look at me. "Lizzy, Tony and my mom went to look at the dolphins and the others went for a run. Why didn't you go?"

"Didn't want to run, and I had to call Sammie. She left me a voicemail this morning about some of the talent she'd found for Eden's soirée we're planning for next month. And then after that, I took a shower."

"I had some ideas about the little soirée," she says, lifting herself up on her elbows.

"I'd love to hear them." Over the last couple of weeks, she's taken to her role of part owner. She's finding her place and shedding all the doubts that held her back. I love to watch her grow in all aspects of her life. She's almost unrecognizable from the girl that walked into Vixen months ago. No. That girl was reserved, shy, broken. She had some fight in her, but it was all directed at external forces. That jackass who laid hands on her still causes my skin to simmer. I hadn't seen him at the club again, and it's for the best. If he tried to come back, I'd shove him up against a wall and beat him until he was unconscious. My hands clamp tighter on the chair rails as I focus on Everlee, letting the anger seep out of me.

For her.

For her, I'd do anything. Give anything. She's wound herself around my heart and has a vise grip on it. The broken girl before has turned into someone who is bold, confident, and not scared of taking risks. She has her moments still when self-doubt creeps in, but that's why we're here. We push it out, allowing the hole it left inside of her to fill in and harden.

She continues our conversation, pulling me back from my thoughts. "We can talk when we get back home. I'm in vacation mode right now."

"Trust me. I can tell." My eyes rake across her naked body and my cock twitches.

She smiles then lays back down and I watch her. I fucking watch her like the love sick creeper I am. Only I'm not a creeper. I'm hers and I'm giving her exactly what she wants.

Her calves rub back and forth as her thighs clench.

A stuttered breath slowly blows out of my chest as my cock hardens and throbs, pushing to get out of my pants, but I don't move. Her left eye twitches a little and I can tell she opened it to look at me. To see if I'm watching her.

Her hand drags up her body as the tips of her fingers circle around her breast.

"Everlee," I growl out a warning.

"What?" She doesn't open her eyes, but the smirk on her face gives away her intentions.

"What are you doing?"

"I'm tanning."

"Are you?"

"Yes." Her hand travels down her stomach as her legs open wider, exposing her glistening pussy. She's so wet I can see it from here.

Fuck.

My pulse is thumping hard in my chest, and my cock is screaming out, needing release.

Desire cuts through me like a knife, but I restrain myself from tearing across the deck and shoving my cock in her needy little cunt. No. She wants me to watch, and that's what I'll do. But as soon as she even hints at wanting my cock to ravage her, it's gloves off. I slide my pants off and resume my place back in the seat, fisting my throbbing cock in my hand and swiping the bead of arousal down my shaft. Slow and steady.

Her finger dips inside of her, causing her head to press into the chair and her peaked nipples to jut into the sky. My mouth salivates at the thought of wrapping around her, my tongue flicking her nipples, before my teeth clamp down and suck her in.

Slow and steady.

Her fingers move with precision, as she drags them out, coated in her wetness as she rubs them over her clit.

She moans out and I wait for my name to dance on her lips, but they don't. Not yet, anyway. She's teasing me and I love it.

Her wanting gaze locks on me as she continues to rub her clit, her teeth biting into her bottom lip. She is all kinds of sex wrapped up in a fucking bow for me. I want to feel her tight pussy wrapped around my cock. I want to feel her pulsing around it as she comes. I want to feel her breasts rubbing along my chest as she moans in my ear.

Fuck.

I want it all.

My hand is flying over my cock as I lose control. Shit! I need to stop before I come.

One more pump, then I release and grab the fucking arms on the chair like they are my lifeline. Like I'm on a roller-coaster and hanging on for dear life. My ass is still pulsing, thrusting my cock into the air like a male dog who's been fixed, humping the air, searching for a place to put his cock.

She watches me, her fingers stilling. The air between us changing. She stands up and walks over to me, her breast eager for my lips.

"Why did you stop?" she asks, standing in front of me.

I lean forward in the seat, my mouth inches from her delicious pussy. Her breath catches as she watches me, eager to feel my tongue licking up her arousal. But I don't.

She steps a half step closer, her leg rubbing along the inside of mine.

"Can I help you with something?" I try to sound as apathetic as possible, knowing that we're in an intense game of sexual tango. Who can make the other break first?

"No." Her eyes glance at the beach.

She's looking for her mom. I know she wants to sit down on my cock and have me claim her, but I won't. Not until she's asking. Begging for it.

Her hands glide through my hair before she latches in and jerks my neck back, so I'm looking up at her. She watches me, her eyes twinkling with mischief as a smile spreads across her face.

"Do you want to taste my pussy?"

"Do you want me to?"

Her eyes thin to narrow slits. She steps closer and climbs into the chair, placing her knees on either side of my thighs and slowly starts to lower herself so that her needy little cunt is right above my cock. I can feel whispers of her arousal touching the head, but she doesn't sink down and it would be so easy to push up inside of her right now and claim her.

"Do you want to fuck me, Callum?"

I smile at her. "Do you want me to fuck you, Everlee?" My hands glide up and down her spine, causing goosebumps to spread and her nipples to grow even harder if that were possible. My will is beginning to wane.

She thrusts her hips forward and lowers, so my cock slides along her backside and my pulse stutters. She's good, so fucking good.

Her forearms drape on my shoulders as she leans in, pressing her breasts against my chest. Her cheek brushes along mine. "This puts us in a very odd predicament. What will happen if everyone comes home right now?"

"Well, I guess you would have some explaining to do with your mom."

She lets out a low hum, the words breezing by her like the warm wind blows across the deck. Her lips kiss along my neck for a brief moment before she sits up and looks at my cock, rubbing between her ass cheeks, yearning for friction.

Hell, I'm fairly certain I could explode up her back if she does that just a few more times.

"You are so beautiful," she says, running her hands over my tattoos. There's a lot of them, each of them with their own story. Like the one she's rubbing her fingers over now. "What's this one mean?" She cocks her head to the side. "If you want to share... I know they can be personal."

I brush her hair behind her ears and cup her cheeks. "Everlee. All I have is yours. My heart, my home, my body. I will share any and everything with you." I kiss her collarbone and she arches, so eager to feel my mouth on her breast and I'm reminded of this little game we have going on. She does this and I pick up on them every single time. Usually it's the breaking eye contact first. She did it the first night I saw her at Vixen.

Intoxicating.

"That's a shield. It was one of my first tattoos. I got it to symbolize protection. Protection for my brother and I."

"Why is it over your heart? I am sure there's a meaning to that."

I smile. "Yes. It was to protect our hearts from ever loving anyone again, so we didn't get hurt. But I guess I should get another layer on top of it with a crack in the shield because you've torn down all our walls. All of our protection. We are bare to you. Exposed."

She leans over and kisses my tattoo and again her ass rubs along my cock and a puff of air escapes and with it, all that was left of my willpower.

I grab her cheeks and lift her head, crashing my lips to hers. The kiss is strong. Powerful. Like two waves crashing into one another, each trying to consume the other. Our hands wildly rove over one another, searching. Feeling. Needing.

She pushes up on her knees and my cock swings back towards my chest and she lines herself over it, but pauses. A low chuckle reverberates in my chest.

"Do you want me to fuck you?" I ask.

She looks at me, that devilish grin on her face. "Do you want to fuck me?"

My, how the tides have turned.

"Very fucking much." I grip her hips and slam her onto my cock, and nearly explode inside of her after one thrust. "Oh my God Everlee. You feel so fucking good." Her pussy is already quivering. She presses up and I slam back into her again. "I can't wait to feel you come around my cock."

"You won't have to wait long." She grinds her hips down, rubbing her clit against my body, and she shatters a second later, throwing her head back as pleasure rips through her. My mouth latches around her breast and I bite on her nipple, sucking her orgasm back through her body.

"Oh God, Callum," she moans out. "Harder." Her hand holds my head to her breast while she grinds on me. "More." She continues to bounce, but her growls are frustrated. Wanting.

Pushing off her chest, I pat her butt. "Come here."

"Where are we going?" She quickly glances back out at the beach. Another quick glance to make sure there isn't a sighting of her mother. She doesn't stop me, so we must be in the clear.

"Get in," I command, pointing at the pool.

"In there?"

I use my dom voice. "Get in."

Her eyes grow wide and she smiles. "Yes, sir."

She hops in and I fall right after her. She leans against the edge of the pool, but I grab her hair and redirect her to the middle. "Can you hold your breath?"

She looks at me excitedly and nods.

"Everlee," I scold, then pinch her nipple.

"Yes, sir," she breathes out.

"Good. Hold it until I come." I bend her over and push her head under water and punch my hard cock into her tight, wet pussy. I grab her hips, digging in and pound into her as fast and as hard as I can with my hand wrapped around the back of her neck.

A few bubbles float to the surface of the pool, but she stays down, like my good fucking girl. My skin prickles as a tingle shoots down my spine, causing my balls to tighten. "Oh, goddamn." Her pussy quivers around my cock as she unleashes another orgasm, causing mine to rip through me, feeling like the most explosive thing I've ever experienced. Tangling my hands in her hair, I yank her out of the water and she looks like a mermaid, breaching the surface, gulping in a lung full of air. With my cock still spearing her, I pull her back, wrapping my arms around her chest as our mouths find one another.

"I love you so much." She breathes, twisting her body and tucking her leg between our bodies so she could turn around and face me.

"My little gymnast." She's still sitting on my cock as it continues to pulse inside of her.

"I want your come in me, Callum. I want it all. I want everything."

She pauses, looking at me like she didn't mean to say those words. Like it's a truth she didn't know herself until this moment. I know what it means, what she wants, and it may be the only thing I can't give her. We can't give her. A pain lances inside of me.

Her face contorts. "Not now, or soon. But fuck. I love you with everything inside of me. It hurts."

I kiss her hard and fast, needing to shut her up. I will give her anything and right now, if she keeps talking, I will give her this, but I can't.

A human bird call echoes from a distance away.

"Fuck!" Everlee stammers, climbing off of me.

"What was that?" The hairs on the back of my neck are standing on end, because I know what that was. Rather, who that was.

Everlee leaps out of the water, ass up and tits on the floor, stretching over to grab her bathing suit as she slithers back into the pool. I do the same, quickly beaching myself to grab my shorts as I pull them back into the pool and slip them on.

"Fucking strings!" She has her top around her neck, but her back is still untied.

"Here, let me help." My fingers work swiftly to tie her bathing suit on the back, while she simultaneously works on the one by her hip.

Another bird call, this one much louder. They're on the boardwalk and I can hear her mother talking about the dolphins.

"There."

"Shit. I can't get this fucking tied."

"Enjoying a pleasant swim?" Lizzy asks, stepping on the deck just in front of Tony and Donna.

No words form on my tongue, causing Lizzy to smell the air, then pump her eyebrows.

Fucking sixth sense.

EVERLEE-MERMAID POWER

MY FINGERS ARE NERVOUSLY fumbling with the strings on my bathing suit and I can't for the life of me get the fucking knot to stay. What am I? A fucking three-year-old? "Shit. I can't get this fucking tied."

"Enjoying a pleasant swim?" Lizzy asks, stepping on the deck just in front of Tony and mother.

Callum and I just look at her and she smells the air, then pumps her eyebrows.

Great. Add this to the list of things she can give me shit about.

I move to the side of the pool and stand there casually while Callum swims to the other end.

"Nice swim darling?" Mother says, walking across the deck to stand on the same side of the pool as me.

"Yea. I was getting hot on the beach, so I thought I'd get some laps in." As I'm saying the words, the waves caused by Callum's little swim to the other end of the pool shifts the strings on my bottoms and I feel them slowly start to slide down my leg. Trying to stop the inevitable pussy moon - I don't know what you would call it- I press my hip to the side of the pool, hoping to pin my bathing suit against it to prevent it from falling.

But it doesn't work.

It continues to slide down and land by my ankles.

My gaze shoots to Lizzy, who sees the bright pink bottoms down around my ankles and then to Callum, who is at the other end of the pool licking his lips like the feral beast he is and I swear his gaze alone makes me hot.

Mother, fortunately, being on the same side of the pool as me near the door, can't see anything below my breasts, which fortunately are covered by my top.

"Maybe I'll join you for a swim," Mother says, walking towards me.

"Dude! I totally beat you," Knox yells over his shoulder, running up the boardwalk before stopping to look at everyone. His eyes go from me, to my mother, back to me, then down to my bottoms lying on the pool floor. "Well, hello." He pumps his eyebrows.

My face flushes red and my tongue presses into the side of my cheek as I shake my head. "Delightful walk?" I ask, trying to sound as casual as possible.

Callum makes laps in the pool, swimming from side to side and I can't understand why he's doing it, but he should stop. My bathing suit swishes back and forth at my feet and I'm scared it will just swish right into the middle of the pool.

"You boys should jump into the pool and cool off!" Mother chimes.

"I would love to get in there," Knox says, stepping forward.

"What's going on people?" Beckett asks as his eyes move down my body to the floor of the pool. He screams out in a high-pitched squeal, clasping his hand to his mouth, then tries to regain his composure. "Sorry. I thought I saw a bee."

"Becks. They are more scared of you. You are huge," Mother scolds.

"You're right, mom. I just forget sometimes." His cool gaze settles on my face. "Whatcha doing, sis?"

My tongue runs across my teeth. "Just going for a swim. I got hot on the beach."

"I bet you did."

"Come on and join us Becks," Mother says, walking towards the ladder.

"Wait!" Beckett yells as Knox jumps in, splashing everyone.

"What Becks?"

"I think I got a scrape on my foot. Can you look at it?"

"You are a grown man."

"I know, but... please."

Jax mumbles something in his ear as he brushes past him and if I had to guess, Jax called him a pussy, then his eyes settle on me and a smirk crosses his lips.

"Beckett's a big boy. Let me help you in the pool, Donna," he offers, lending out a hand.

"Thank you." She takes his hand after she squeezes his biceps. "So strong. What does this tattoo mean?" She points to the frog on his chest. "It looks familiar."

He glances at me, then turns to my mother and explains how it's a tattoo he got while he was in the SEALs. Distracted by his story, I jump when I feel a hand brush up my leg.

Knox.

He pulls my bathing suit up and ties both strings around my hips in a matter of seconds, then gives my ass a pinch before kicking into the middle of the pool, breaching the surface.

He's so beautiful. Radiant. I want to swim over to him and climb on him and press my lips against his until we're falling under the water. Speaking of. Holy shit. Orgasm under water. I was nervous at first and then so fucking turned on I had an orgasm hit me out of nowhere.

"Knox was in there with me." Jax points.

"Really?" She pumps her eyebrows. "I've always found military men so... sexy."

"Mom!" Beckett and I both say at the same time.

"What? I can look, but not touch. I mean, I guess I'm touching you, but technically, you offered your hand."

Jax chuckles, helping her into the water.

"Want to play Crossnet?" Knox asks.

"I'm getting out," Callum says, climbing to the edge.

Mother smiles. "I'll play. I used to love playing volleyball when I was younger."

"Excellent!" Knox thrusts his fist in the air. "Ev?"

"Sure."

"We got three, we need a fourth."

Beckett snickers and I cut my eyes at him.

"Jax?" Knox asks.

"Hard pass."

"Emmett?"

"I'm going to go inside and fix lunch for all of us."

"Fine. If you're going to beg me. I'll play," Lizzy chimes, plopping into the pool.

"Ooh Knoxxy is outnumbered," my mother says.

We all look at each other, surprised. This is not the same woman I'm used to seeing. This one is so much more relaxed and easygoing.

"It's ok. Surround me with beautiful women and I'll be a fortunate man." He looks at Jax. "A little help, brother?" He points at the Crossnet in the deck's corner.

Jax's eyes squint at Knox and had my mother not been here, Jax would have likely told him to fuck off, and Knox knew that. "Sure thing, brother." His words are thick and laced with a hint that payback will come back to bite Knox in the ass.

He slides the net into the pool and then drills the ball at Knox's head.

"How is your mother doing?" Mother asks and all the guys look at her. "Ms. Mary Mae. I saw her at church last week and she had a wrap around her wrist."

Jax back straightens. "What?"

"Oh. I'm sorry. I thought you knew." When no one speaks, she continues. "Yea. She was cooking a casserole for the church and apparently burned her arm pretty badly. She, of course, didn't get it looked at and had to end up going to the doctor for some antibiotics because it got infected."

"No. We didn't know."

"Oh. Well, it's not too serious. She probably didn't want to bother you all."

"I'll go call her now," Jax says, walking inside.

"J. Let me know," Knox says, all humor dropped from their banter.

Jax nods and dips inside the house.

"I'm sorry. I'm sure she's fine. I was just trying to make small talk. I find it so interesting how small the world is. Of all the people that could have opened a club down the road from Lizzy. You all grew up just a town over. How serendipitous."

"It is kind of crazy to think that," Lizzy agrees.

"Yes, it is." I say, jumping up and down. "Now, who's ready to play?"

Knox's eyes grow wide as he gets distracted by my bouncing bosom.

"Careful," Lizzy warns. "I'd hate for your bathing suit to fall off."

There it is. Her little jab.

Cutting my eyes at her, I splash her with water.

"I don't see how you aren't always worried about that. I'd be terrified that something could accidentally snag it and then boom!" Mother says, laughing.

"Boom!" Lizzy repeats, clearly having fun with this. "Has that ever happened to you, Ev?"

"Something accidentally snagging my bathing suit and it falling off? No." Because it wasn't an accident. It was very much on purpose and some of the best sex I've had, which is saying a lot.

She scrunches her nose at me, dropping her tease for now. "Let's go, bro! How do we play?"

JAX - BOY TALK

THE LARGE CREAM-COLORED ORB in the sky dances on top of the waves as they crash onto the sand, and the constant whoosh whish soothes my restless soul. When I left the house after dinner, the group was starting a game of poker. Lizzy had found a large case of chips and a few decks of cards. Then the ladies started throwing out games like baseball, follow the queen, high Chicago and seven card no peek. I was almost in when I thought it was going to be Texas Hold'em, but after all those other games and it being dealers' choice... I don't think I could sit there and listen to Lizzy explain the rules to me and honestly, I didn't want to have to learn those games to play. It put me at a disadvantage, which I don't like.

I've worked hard in my life to master everything I choose to do or be part of and having Lizzy teach me... No.

Just no.

"You didn't want to play the games?" The voice is familiar. Hesitant.

Emmett.

He pauses behind me, waiting for the invite to sit down. Things have been a little off between us since our night with Ev. Not in a bad way, just... different.

"Come on," I say, patting the sand beside me.

He sits down, bending his knees and wrapping his arms around his legs. "It's beautiful out here." He stares at the moon, the light making the few gray strands in his beard sparkle like diamonds.

"Yes, it is."

He slowly turns his head to look at me, but doesn't speak. After a few pushes and pulls of the moon on the ocean, he asks, "How was mother?"

I let out a puff of air. I'd been holding it, as cliche as that sounds, because I didn't know what he was going to say or ask or think. I was literally holding my breath, as if that would stop time. It doesn't. It just makes it awkward as fuck when I breathe again. Which is not what I like to be. Awkward AF, as Lizzy would say.

Christ. Why am I thinking about Lizzy?

Because I've been around her too goddamn much in this house.

"She's good. Taking her meds. She goes tomorrow for a follow up with her doctor to make sure everything's ok."

"Wonder why she didn't tell us?"

"She's not going to call all of her children and tell them she burned herself. Do you call her every time you burn yourself?"

"I'm a professional. I don't burn myself," he says, straightening his back and sticking his nose in the air.

"Fuck off." I shove him hard, and he rolls to his side on the sand.

"What the hell?" He lunges at me, knocking me down, as he falls on top of me.

We freeze and stare at each other for a second before he pushes off. "Sorry."

We both sit back up. "For what? Getting sand on me?" I brush off my arms and resume my spot in the sand I had prior to him walking out here.

He hesitates a moment. "Yea."

A silence fills the air again, so much so that I have to look to see if he's still sitting beside me.

"I miss her," Emmett says, staring out at the water.

"Ms. Mary?" I always had a problem calling her mom. She was our mom for all intents and purposes, but she wasn't at the same time. I don't know if I ever allowed myself to truly let her in because I was scared she'd leave.

Emmett did. He let her in. He's obviously not as afraid as I am. I could feel myself starting to creep down that dark rabbit hole of emotions and feelings and thoughts that I've pushed away and hidden for years. But I have to continue to push them down. Live in the present.

"No," he moans. "Everlee."

"You miss her?"

"Yes. Unlike some of us on this beach, we have not had sex with her in a long time."

"A few days."

"Which is a long time. Hell, even when she's on her period, we still have fun."

"Did you hear about her and Callum?"

"Bits and pieces." He starts chuckling. "Lizzy has been singing some song about under the water most of the afternoon, so I assume she's teasing Ev. I've noticed she's been doing that quite a bit and I find it very amusing. But don't tell Ev that."

"That you like seeing her in a constant panicked state? Scared to say or do anything that may reveal something to her mom. I mean, her mom has to know something's up. Right? She probably doesn't assume that she's with all of us, but something. Right?"

"Do you want her to know *something*?"

"Fuck yea I do. I love Everlee and I want her to have it all. Everything she wants. I want to give that to her. I want us to give that to her. If that means her mom," I shrug, "and her dad have to know, then so be it."

"Wow. I've never heard you... just say you love her like that."

"Fuck off." I shove him again, but not as hard. "I do."

"I know you do. I've seen it for a while, even if you haven't."

"Are we really that pussy whipped?"

"Yes," he says without hesitation.

"True."

He's hesitant, before he speaks. I know there's something on his mind he wants to say, but he's scared to. My pulse thumps heavy in my chest with anticipation. When he starts talking, I suck in another breath and hold it.

"I think I am going to want more with her."

I look at him and exhale. That's not what I expected, but I'm neither relieved nor disappointed. "More?"

"More. I'm not saying anything soon. But she's it for me. For us. She completes us. Makes us whole. We are a family because of her." He holds up his hands. "Don't get me wrong. I'm not saying we weren't before because you three guys are my family. I love you all so much, but her. She's like a beacon of light shooting straight down in the middle of us from the sky. She completes us in such a way that I didn't even know existed. It's like pieces of me were broken and she fits perfectly in those cracks." He sighs and stops.

"Wow." I hesitate before I speak again. "Don't quit cooking to be a poet."

"Shut the fuck up, asshole." He shoves me hard and I topple over into the sand, but this time he doesn't apologize, nor should he.

He's my friend. My best friend. Callum is my brother. Knox is like an annoying fucking brother and Emmett. He's my best friend. I love him with a different kind of love than the others. He gets me in ways the others don't. Hell, that I don't, sometimes. He knows me and I know him. "I love you. You know that?"

He looks at me, eyes focused, and his lips quiver. "I know, and I love you too."

We both look back out at the ocean and just sit in silence for who knows how long.

EMMETT - ALL IN

WHEN JAX AND I get back to the house, it's just after one in the morning and most of the house is still up and playing cards. Beckett and Will seem to be the only two missing, and Everlee nods to their room.

I pull up a seat between Donna and Lizzy while Jax pulls up a stool just behind Everlee. He sits perched, thighs spread wide with his palms pressed into the seat between his legs. A goddamn dreamsicle I want to suck in my mouth.

Nope.

Should not be thinking that.

Pretty sure bi-awakening is not on the BINGO cards, which I noticed are no longer tacked to the front of the fridge. It took me a day to realize they were missing, even though I noticed something was different in the kitchen. Just couldn't put my finger on it until this afternoon.

He catches my glance and stares at me a moment, then looks over Everlee's shoulder and whispers something to her. She giggles, then nods at Callum, who has a stack of chips in front of him looking like a mafia king in front of his spoils. I learned a long time ago not to bet against Callum in cards. He has a wicked mind and is a lucky son of a bitch. Although, looking at Everlee's pile, I'd say she could be the only one to give him a run for his money. Knox and Lizzy are almost out of chips, and Donna isn't far behind.

"Let me see what you got?" Knox jeers, trying to look at Everlee's cards.

She laughs and pulls them closer to her chest and Knox's eyes pump before he can catch himself.

"Cheater, cheater."

"We have to beat Callum."

"I know. That's my plan."

"Good luck, love." Callum chuckles.

Her eyes widen as she glances between Callum and her mom, but Callum doesn't react. He just tosses in his chips.

"Aww boo boo," Knox says, batting his eyelashes. "Are you trying to distract me with your little pet names?"

"Whatever it takes.... Love."

Everlee's lips twist into a smile. She's radiant. Glowing.

"You know," Everlee starts, then pauses. "If you wanted to beat Callum, you could just give me your chips."

"Or you could give them to me, if we're giving away chips," Lizzy chimes in.

"I'm not giving my chips to anyone. If you want them, come and get them."

"Then watch out, because here I come," Everlee teases, rubbing her hands together.

"You shouldn't announce when you're coming. Let it be a surprise," Lizzy smirks.

"Drinks, anyone?" I ask, pushing away from the table.

"I'll take one of your fruity concoctions," Lizzy says.

"Make that two!" Everlee chimes.

I look at the group, but no one else speaks up.

The roars and laughter of the crowd echo behind me while I make our cocktails. I was going to make an Old Fashioned for myself, but decided it would just be easier to make the same drink for all three of us.

Knox starts yelling about something and Everlee is taunting him playfully and laughing along with the rest of the table. Even Callum. If I had my phone, I would take a picture of this moment and save it forever. Everyone is so happy and carefree. Donna is a lot more chill than I expected and even though we're having to hide who we are, I'm thankful we can still be around Everlee and have this moment.

When I get back to the table, I set Everlee's drink down, press my hand to the back of her chair and lean down. "You need to kick all their asses."

She smiles, turning to me, our face inches apart. "I plan to."

"That's my girl," I whisper, then pull up and accidentally brush along Jax's leg.

When I sit back in my seat, Lizzy leans over and whispers, "I'm pretty sure she's wet and if she were wearing panties, they would have incinerated her." She pats me on the arm. "Good boy."

My skin prickles and I find Jax watching Lizzy and I, with a look on his face, I can't place.

Everlee wins the next three hands in a row, knocking Lizzy out and Knox has a few chips left, while Donna has improved her chip stack a little.

"What did he give you? Some kind of unicorn magic?" Knox takes Everlee's drink and tips it back. "Peach and orange. Sex on the beach." A smile plays on his lips.

"Isn't that your fave Everlee?" Lizzy chirps. Knox and Lizzy are like two peas in a pod. Each serving up the spike for the other.

"I do like sex on the beach, but Emmett's Old Fashioned's are my new fave."

"Your dad loves sex on the beach," Donna chirps. "The drink. Although..." her voice quivers playfully. "I imagine he'd like the other, too."

"Mom!" Everlee shouts, blushing ten shades of red.

"Mama McKinley, you rascally rabbit," Lizzy cheers.

"Oh my God. Whose deal is it?" Everlee asks, trying to get the conversation back under control.

"What?" Donna asks innocently.

"Mom," Everlee sighs into a whisper.

"My deal!" Knox stands and swipes the table, bringing all the cards to him. "That is a good drink." He takes another sip of Everlee's drink. "They may be my new favorite. Less sand between my butt cheeks."

The table erupts in laughter again as everyone seems to have a case of the late-night giggles. Even Jax and Callum are chuckling. I wouldn't call it a full-on laugh, but their lips are parted into what some would describe as a smile with a soft shake to their shoulders.

"Fucking hell." Everlee throws her hands up. She's the only one not laughing, although she should be the one laughing the hardest, since they are talking about her and Knox. We had to listen to Knox complain the rest of that entire night about finding sand in his ass.

The table eventually settles. Lizzy and Tony turn in and it's just the five of us and Donna. Everlee passes glances at me throughout the night and I know she wishes her mother would lose so it would just be the five of us, but her mother went on a hot streak and won six times in a row, depleting a bulk of Everlee's chips, and wiping out Knox.

"I'm so tired," Everlee whines, looking at her watch. "It's after two in the morning."

"We can call the game if you want. I'm tired too. The walk to the dolphins today wore me out."

"Yes, please," Everlee moans, pushing back from the table.

"I'll take the win," Callum says, his eyes flaring.

Everlee pauses, her eyes locked on Callum, her ass pressed against Jax. "No. You do not get to win by forfeit. Let's go. One last round. All in. Winner takes all." She looks at her mother who nods, then to Callum.

By this point, they all had roughly the same number of chips. He may have a touch more if they were to count them, but it's close.

"Unless you're scared."

Callum pushes away from the table, palms pressed in as he stares at her. The chemistry is floating back and forth between them like a hot wire. "Love, I'm not scared. I will play. But just so you know. I play to win."

"So do I. Love." Her words are very punctuated.

"Well, well, well. Somebody get me some water, it's getting hot in here," Donna says.

And like being snapped back to reality, Everlee shakes her head and stands up, pushing all her chips into the middle of the table. The neck of her shirt gapes open just a little and her breasts are so fucking close. My cock twitches, but I'm sitting right next to her mom, so it would be awkward as fuck to get a boner. Shifting my cock back into submission, I stand up and take a step back, and Jax nods his head at me with a knowing look.

I flip him off and he chuckles, licking his lips.

Fuck me.

My cock twitches again, but for a different reason.

I need to get this shit under control.

Everyone is standing, for different reasons obviously, as Everlee deals the last hand. Her aim for leaning over the table is to distract Callum and I think it's working because he has to keep shifting where he stands. Knox and Jax head to his side, eager to support him and see his cards.

Or so they say.

They, too, want to torture themselves with the little display Ev is putting on right in front of her mom. It's the exhibitionist in her. Pulling at her. Making her walk that dangerous line between truth and secret.

She flips the last card and an evil fucking smirk twists her lips.

She has him, and she knows it.

"One card away from a pair," Donna says, flipping over her cards.

"You show me yours and I'll show you mine," Everlee taunts, waving her cards in the air.

Donna's gaze narrows on her daughter and flickers to Callum. There's no way she isn't picking up on the flirting and subtle, rather, not so subtle, sexual innuendos that have been flying around the house all afternoon.

"One at a time, highest card you have," Callum says.

"Fine." She holds a card up in the air. "One, two, three."

They both flip an ace and the dining room is filled with oohs and ahhs. Knox being Knox is so pumped he's jumping up and down on Callum's arm.

"You both have a pair," Jax calls. "It will come down to kicker."

Callum flips his card. "King."

Everlee bites her lips.

Callum taunts, without thinking, "Next time, babe." But I don't know if anyone heard it except for me, because Everlee slaps down her card.

"Ace!"

"Trips. Everlee wins," Jax cheers.

Everlee jumps up and down, her breasts lifting her shirt, revealing hints of her stomach.

I'm going to have to rub one out tonight. Too much stimulation.

"Good night all," Donna smiles, grabbing her glass.

"I'll clean up, mom," Everlee says, reaching over and taking the glass.

"Oh, thank you, darling. See you all tomorrow morning. Good game all." She waves her hand, then walks up the stairs while Everlee grabs the glasses. She glances over at her mom and then looks back at Callum and crosses her arms and slaps them on her legs. "Suck it!" She mouths, picks up the glasses and walks into the kitchen.

She doesn't see or hear Callum coming, but the rest of us do.

CALLUM - CIRCLE JERK?

SHE'S AT THE SINK in those short shorts and that top that hugs her like a fucking dream, taunting mc. And then at the end, bending over so her breasts were on full fucking display.

Dirty.

And then she tells me to suck it with that flirtatious fucking grin. My cock is hard in an instant. I give Donna the courtesy of waiting until her door clicks shut before I move over to claim what's mine.

Everlee may have won the cards, but she's my fucking prize.

The glasses clink in the sink, but before she can turn around, I'm there pressing up against her, pinning her to the sink. Leaning forward, my cheek against hers, I whisper, "Suck it?" My voice is low, with a restrained urge to fuck her where she stands.

I'm feral for her, unable to control myself right now.

She sucks in a breath, no doubt feeling my hard cock pressed into her back, then turns to look at me, her lips brushing against my cheek. "Yes."

A low growl reverberates in my chest, and she eats it up. Her head presses back into my shoulder as she grinds her body against my cock.

Fucking hell.

My hands snake around her hips and slip under her shirt and grab her breasts hard.

She lets out a moan, but I use my other hand to clamp it over her mouth. "You know the rules, baby girl. You make a noise, I stop."

"Yes sir." She presses her head back and turns it, her lips searching for mine.

"That's my good girl." I remove my hand from her mouth and slip it into her shorts. "Fuck me, you're soaking wet." I pull my fingers and shove them in her mouth. "Suck." She grabs my hand and wraps her tongue around my fingers, and sucks her arousal off.

"Do you want the others to watch me finger fuck you?" I ask her, feeling the guys at my back.

She nods and I smile.

"Of course you do." I shove my hand back into her pants and press my finger inside of her, then turn us as one. "Jax. Come, lift her shirt so you all can look at the wonderful tits she was teasing us with earlier."

He stalks over with those predatory eyes and lifts her shirt and sucks her other breast in his mouth. "So fucking good."

"Do you want to taste her, brother? She's dripping for us." I ask.

He nods and falls to his knees, grabs her shorts and drags them down to her ankles. Licking his lips, he takes in the sight of her glistening pussy. Sliding my finger out of her and up her stomach to her other breast, he latches his hands around her thighs and brings his mouth to her.

"Remember not a sound."

She nods, just as her legs buckle, but she doesn't make a fucking sound.

"Such a good girl."

Her hand moves to clamp around Jax's hair as she holds him to her. I can hear the sighs in her throat as she swallows down the moans trying to escape.

Jax lifts her leg and throws it over his shoulder as he eats her out. Savage with ferocity. His tongue spears her deep, driving in.

"Everlee. Are you still down there?" Her mother calls out and we all freeze.

Everlee lets out a whimper, then moans, realizing her mistake. "Fuck."

We hear Donna walking down the stairs, but we all stay frozen in our places.

"Yea, mom. I'm here. What do you need?" She calls out.

"Can you bring me a glass of water when you come up?"

"Yea. I'm on my way now. Was just finishing up."

"Were you?" I whisper. "I don't think Jax felt you come around his tongue."

"Fuck you," she seethes.

I smile at her and put her shirt back down, while Jax stands and draws her pants back up.

"I hope you can't finish tonight in your shower!"

"Love. I'll be thinking about your tight little pussy wrapped around my cock. I'll think about your breasts in my hands and in my mouth. I'll think about the taste of your arousal on my tongue." I grab a glass and fill it with water. "I'm about to come right now, just thinking about you. That's what you do to me. I don't even have to touch myself." I suck in a breath under her ear, then bite her neck. "You're lucky, you have to go because I want to fucking mark you so goddamn bad. Let your mother know who exactly her daughter is and who she belongs to."

"Everlee?" Her mother calls.

"Coming."

"Don't lie to your mother," I call after her and she gives me the middle finger over her shoulder without turning around.

"Circle jerk tonight?" Knox asks, walking over.

"Get the fuck out of here," Jax says, shoving him away.

"Thought I'd offer it up, because fucccckkk."

"I call dibs on the shower," Jax says.

"I got the bathroom," I add.

"I call our bathroom first," Knox says before Emmett can.

"Fine," Emmett drones, accepting his fate as the last to relieve himself.

We all wait a minute, because the raging boners we have right now wouldn't be a good look if we ran into Donna in the hallway.

One door closes, then another.

"Clear."

EVERLEE - UNICORN ORGASM

Fucking hell.

I was so close to coming all over Jax's face, and then my freaking mother. Gahh. Twat blocked by my mother. My pussy is still throbbing coming off its near explosion. It was going to be epic, too. All afternoon and all night, the tension has been building. Admittedly, I - we - got a little carried away at the end of the night. Flippin' Callum called me babe right in front of my mother, but I don't think she heard.

Callum and his fucking rules.

No sounds, Everlee.

Ugh. My fingers tangle in my hair as I pull, and then an evil smile spreads across my lips. Callum, and by extension, Jax, are off limits tonight, but not Emmett or Knox.

Wearing only a bedtime tank top that barely covers my ass, I roll out of bed and pull up the covers, stuffing the pillows in such a way it looks like my body. You can never be too careful. The floor creaks like a siren wailing in the boards as I walk across the room and look down the hall.

Knox's room is right across from my mother's, but Emmett. My dear Emmett.

Yes.

He will do with his big, pierced cock.

I'd invite Knox, but it sounds like he's in the shower, anyway. He always sings, so it's easy to pick him out.

Tiptoeing across the hall, I grab Emmett's handle and twist. The room is dark, but I see his figure lying in bed, his erect cock in hand.

"What are you doing?" he whispers.

Not answering, I step in and close the door behind me, locking it for good measure. "What are you doing?"

The glint of his piercings shines with arousal in the little moonlight that's peeking into the room, causing my pussy to quiver with excitement.

He lays his hands flat on the bed and just stares at me as I walk across the room and climb onto the bed.

"Is this a good idea with your mother right across the hall?"

"She falls asleep quickly, plus we can be quiet."

"Can you?" he snickers, and I punch him in the chest.

"Fine. I can go find someone else." I move to climb off the bed but feel a hand wrap around my wrist and pull me back.

"Don't you dare fucking leave."

I lay on my side, throwing my leg over his, and circle my fingers around his chest in an infinity symbol, making sure to flick his nipple ring each time. He grabs my leg and pulls me on top of him so his thick, pierced cock is lodged in the middle of my glistening pussy. The gentle brush of his Jacob's ladder on my clit nearly makes me orgasm alone.

"You were close downstairs, weren't you? You're soaking wet." He sits up and lifts my shirt over my head and tosses it to the ground before he cups my breasts and goes between, sucking each one while kneading the other.

My arms wrap around his neck as I press my chest into his face and grind my clit on his cock. "You feel so good," I whisper.

"I want to taste you. Seeing Jax down there eating you made me hot with jealousy. I wanted to taste you, taste his lips. Anything."

"You should have." Visions of Emmett and Jax kissing over my pussy drive me fucking wild with lust. My hips grind hard onto his cock, chasing my orgasm from earlier. It's right there. "I'm going to come on your cock."

"Good, then you can come in my mouth, before you come again with my cock buried so far inside you, you'll be able to taste my come when I explode inside of you."

"Emmett," I whisper out a moan riding his piercings. His words, his cock, his body are a drug that I can't get enough of.

He sucks my breast into his mouth and clamps on my nipple, pain mixing with pleasure as I explode around him. My entire body quivers as I continue to ride, pushing my orgasm further. He drops my breast and takes my mouth in a forceful kiss, swallowing my moans. His tongue presses in, sliding, twirling. I could kiss this man every minute of every day. His mouth is God's gift to this... well, me. Because he's mine.

When I stop moving, he flips us over on the bed and is on top of me in seconds, his body hovering as he plants kisses on my neck, over my breasts and down to my clit, where he licks up my come. He hums in appreciation as his hands work over my breasts.

"You taste like heaven."

"You feel like heaven."

He places my legs over his shoulders, then sits up so my ass is hovering.

"There." He licks from the bottom of my pussy to the top, where he sucks on my clit. He does it again, but this time starts lower. Like loooower. He tickles my asshole with his beard and my legs clamp around his head.

"Where's your tongue going there, good buddy?"

"Just your pussy, tonight."

Tonight.

"But... I do have plans for our friend."

"Plans? Been thinking of them long?" I tease.

"All goddamn day." He huffs before pressing back in without an ounce of humor in his voice. His hands are moving around the bed and a second later, I hear a click.

"You just happened to have lube on your bed?"

He sucks, pulling my clit out before he answers, "I was going to use it on myself when someone came in."

"What were you thinking about?"

"This." He presses his lubed finger into my ass, and I nearly buck off his shoulders. "How much I love your ass." He pulls his finger out, then slowly presses it back in, working it open. "If I didn't want to press my cock inside of your pussy so bad, I'd take your ass. But the idea of having my come inside of you tomorrow," he moans out, "Fuck. I can't think about it or I'll explode before I even get the chance."

"Look who's moaning now?"

"It wasn't very loud." He licks up my pussy while his finger continues to work my ass. "You may want to grab a pillow to put over your face."

The pillow was a good call. A few minutes later, I'm shattering into a thousand pieces, biting my bottom lip and holding the pillow so tight to my face I almost black out.

He's slipping my legs off his shoulders and my ass hits his bed with a thump, before he's crawling over my body and pressing his cock inside of me. He holds it still for a minute before he pulls out and presses in again.

"Goddamn you feel so fucking good. It's still pulsing."

Needing to see his face, I throw the pillow to the side and take him in. He's gorgeous. His tattoos, his piercings, the way his jaw clenches with each thrust. The rings on his cock feel like ridges inside of me, nearly vibrating and hitting every spot.

"I need more," he whimpers, slamming into me.

He grabs my legs and runs them up his chest, wrapping his arms around them as he unleashes deep inside of me. Pumping faster and faster and faster.

The bed is rocking with a steady thump, thump, thump and I know I'm fucked. Both literally and figuratively.

If mother is awake, there's no way she's not hearing this. I only hope that she's exhausted from the walk to the dolphins and the fact it is super early in the morning.

But I can't stop it. I don't want to.

Fuck it!

I'm taking control.

My impending orgasm smacks me back to the present. He's so far inside of me and grinding his hips that he has to be hitting my cervix. But fucking hell, it feels amazing. I want to ride and buck and fuck him back, but he's in complete control.

"Emmett," I pant out. I feel it. The tidal wave that's going to consume us all. "E."

He doesn't let up.

"Oh my God. Oh my God." A tightness starts at my hips, then travels to my stomach, then washes over my entire body. I think I'm going to blackout. "Oh. E...E... E... so much. Too much."

He presses in one last time and stills, while my body crashes in wave after delicious wave around him.

"Stars. I'm seeing stars E. Holy... shit." I'm trying to catch my breath, trying to form words, but my body is still rippling in after shock. "Stars. If I pass out... fuck... I don't know."

My legs flop to the bed as he pulls out and lies beside me, cradling me in his arms.

I roll over so I'm facing him.

"I think you hit my cervix. I think it made me orgasm."

"Cervical orgasm, the unicorn." He smiles.

"E." I know E is usually the name reserved for Jax, but words are hard to form and I have to use my syllables sparingly.

He kisses my forehead. "Go wash up and come back in here and lie with me."

"I can't." I cringe. Not even two seconds ago, I was saying I was going to take charge and now I'm chickening out. "Screw it. I'll come back."

"I'll set an alarm, just in case."

Happy, but still a little woozy, I roll out of bed and feel like a fish out of water. When I open the door, Knox is on the other side, walking in frenzied circles.

"What are you doing?"

He stops, his brow furrowing. "I wasn't listening," he snaps.

Walking over to him, I wrap my arms around his neck. "You could have joined."

"I know, but he hasn't gotten a chance to spend a lot of time with you because he's been cooking and stuff."

"And stuff?"

Knox shrugs.

"I love you, Knoxxy baby."

He smiles, his eyes beaming. "Evy baby."

His lips feel like velvet under my soft kiss. "Good night, love."

"Great night, Everlee."

He walks back through his door and climbs into bed. I wash up in the bathroom and a few minutes later, I'm crawling back into bed with Emmett. He wraps his arms around me and pulls me in tight. "I love you, Everlee McKinley."

"I love you, Emmett Monroe."

His body is warm and inviting, and I feel myself spiraling into the darkness of sleep minutes later.

EVERLEE – TWILIGHT ZONE

NERVES COURSE THROUGH MY body like a live wire, ready to shoot out and zap someone as I walk down the stairs. By the time I hit the bottom stair, I hear my mother's voice filtering from the kitchen. She's laughing about something, and then I hear Emmett, followed by Lizzy's cackle. Tingles shoot up my spine because a cackling Lizzy means there was likely a joke told at my expense, and after last night with Emmett... I can only imagine.

I remember falling asleep in his arms, but when I woke up, I was cradling my makeshift pillow body in my bed. He must have carried me over in the early morning.

"Good morning darling," mother sings from the kitchen, pouring some milk into a bowl. "Emmett and I are going to whip up some waffles. To learn from *the* Emmett Monroe." She shimmies her shoulders.

"You flatter me," Emmett coos, squeezing her shoulder.

What the fuck is happening? I discreetly try to pinch my leg to see if I'm awake or still dreaming. Moments ago, I was fairly certain I was awake... but... this feels like some sort of alternate reality, or maybe I'm in the Twilight Zone.

"Good morning," Lizzy says, although the infliction in her words makes it sound more like a question than a statement.

"Good morning, Lizzy."

"Apparently, Callum rented us some kayaks. They were just delivered."

"Last time I was in a boat with Callum, we flipped over." I laugh. "Don't know if I want to do that again."

"I was just saying the same thing!" Mother chimes.

"All the more reason to go with me today, so I can make it up to you," he says, striding into the room with his arms open wide. He's wearing a pair of black bathing suit bottoms that make his legs look even more tan with his tattoos he has trickling down from his thigh, and a white button-down collared shirt that has the top two buttons unhooked. I nearly choke on the air surrounding me.

"You ok, Everlee?" my mother asks.

"Yea. All good."

Callum tosses a wink at me. "Good morning, Everlee," he says, smirking.

Ok well, everyone has a shit-eating grin on their face except my mother, who is chipper as fuck. If the rest of the house heard us, then she would have had to... right?

Beckett and Will are cuddled on the couch, watching an episode of Ted Lasso, and start laughing hysterically. It looks like one I haven't seen yet. I've been putting off the last season because I don't want it to end, and I don't want to watch now, but their laughter and the red strings on the television pull me in.

"I'm crying," Beckett says, wiping tears from his eyes.

"What's with the red string?"

Will starts to speak, but Beckett places his hand over his mouth. "We can't tell her. She needs to experience it from the beginning."

Beckett flips off the tv and turns to look at me. "Morning sis."

"Why the fuck does everyone keep wishing me a good morning?"

He clutches his chest and looks at me. "Because it's the polite morning greeting, when someone over sleeps the rest of the house, and is the last one down."

He wasn't being a smartass. "Sorry. I just thought..." I plop on the couch beside him, putting my head on his shoulder.

"Thought I was giving you a hard time about fucking one of the men so goddamn loudly last night. It woke me up from my slumber."

My face flushes ten shades of red. "Fuck. You think mom heard?"

"Well, she's getting older, but she's not deaf. The house was damn near shaking Ev. What were you thinking?"

"I wasn't?"

"No shit."

"Why is she in such a good mood, then?"

"Probably because she's panicking on the inside wondering what kind of hussy she raised."

"You aren't helping."

"I'm not trying to. I have to use this instance of your fuck up to my advantage, so when I do something bad, she will be like... well, it wasn't as bad as that one time Everlee fucked a guy right beside my room."

"It was diagonal."

"Close enough."

"Maybe she thinks it was Lizzy."

"Who's ready to eat?" Mother chimes carrying over a platter of waffles.

"That's what she said," Beckett whispers.

I roll my eyes and shove him on the couch. "That doesn't even make sense."

JAX - MAN OVERBOARD

AFTER BREAKFAST, WE ALL head to the beach to enjoy the nice day. It's hot, without a cloud in the sky, but at least there's a nice constant breeze coming off the ocean. Knox, as usual, set up the chairs and umbrellas for the ladies after his beach run, so Donna coos and sings his praises.

The little turd, of course, eats it up.

I'm not jealous that she seems to have formed a connection with Emmett and Knox. I can't compete with a chef or the golden retriever that is Knox.

Through the course of the morning, we play bocce ball, toss the football around and take a walk to the dolphins while Beckett and Will head out on the kayak first.

When we get back, Beckett and Will are laying on the sand under the tents.

"Everything ok?" Ev asks, nudging her brother with her foot.

Beckett moans.

"That good?" Knox asks, shaking Beckett's leg with his foot.

"That was hard."

"Yea. I don't know if I can do that." Everlee looks at us.

"It's fine once you get past the beach. That was exhausting. The waves kept crashing and sending us sideways, and at one point, we flipped over. Fortunately, we were still on the beach, so we just pushed up and tried again."

Ev looks at Callum, then me, back to Callum. "You're sure you want to do this?"

"Yea, but if you don't want to, we don't have to. I thought it could be fun."

She sighs, rolling her shoulders, "Fine."

"Well don't make me force you." Callum laughs.

"Everlee is as stubborn as a mule," Donna chimes in.

"I'm not stubborn. I'm determined. Much like Lizzy. She isn't bossy, she's just aggressively helpful."

I let out a low hum, and both Everlee and Lizzy snap their heads in my direction. Lizzy has a shocked look on her face. "Jax! I thought we were making a genuine connection."

I don't respond, because no matter what I say, it will elicit another response and I just want to sit in a chair for a little and soak up the sun. In quiet.

"Just be careful out there. It was getting a little choppier, which is why we came back in. We ended up further down the beach and had to walk the kayak back up."

"Thanks," Callum says.

"Also, I'd recommend have one of the guys push you out past the beach. That took us a lot of time since you were all gone."

"I'll push you," I volunteer.

"Our hero," Everlee says, placing her hand on my bare chest.

I clasp my hand over hers and lean down to kiss her, then stop, realizing her mom is here and watching, so I pat her hand, then remove it. "You're welcome."

"Let's go!" She chirps, shifting her life jacket down. "I hate these things. They always ride up my crack and push up on my chin."

"You're wearing it," I say sternly, adjusting it on her.

She huffs.

"I'll have lunch ready in the house when you get back," Emmett calls after them.

I'm glad he got to spend some one-on-one time with Everlee last night. But I'm a little upset I wasn't there with them. Not jealous of them being together without me, just... I don't know. I don't know what any of these feelings mean that I've been having lately. I know I'm not gay because I don't look at other men and want to do with them the things I want to do with Emmett.

It's just Emmett.

It's always been just Emmett.

Well, Emmett and Everlee. She is everything to me. It's like she brings out these feelings. The way she looks at Emmett and me is... I don't know. It's like she wants to see us together, like it turns her on. And I want to do that for her, but selfishly, I want to do it for myself. The few times I've taken Emmett, while he's taken her, are... magical. I want to do it the next time we're together. Feel his ass wrapped around my cock.

"You ok there?" Ev asks, looking at my cock.

Fuck!

"Yea," I snap without meaning to as I stand to walk them over to the edge of the beach.

"What are you thinking about?" she presses.

"Sinking my cock in that ass."

Her eyes flare with excitement, and she stops and looks at me. "Whose?"

The one word causes a tingle to move up my spine. The fact she didn't automatically assume it was hers was both electrifying and terrifying at the same time. It also confirms she wants to see me with Emmett as much as my cock wants to take Emmett. "Does it matter?"

She smiles, hands clasped under her chin. "It really doesn't because I love you no matter." She gives me a quick kiss on the cheek and runs to meet Callum at the kayak.

After a moment, I continue to move towards them, ignoring the nagging feeling to turn around and search out Emmett to see if he saw our little interaction. He, of course, would be too far away to hear anything, but would he know? He's always been able to read me like an open book which has been equal parts frustrating and nice.

Ev and Callum climb into the kayak, aim the tip towards the ocean, and start to push forward. Looking over my shoulder, I see we're far enough away from the group that they can't make out what we're doing, so I lean down and kiss Everlee on her cheek. She turns to look at me and brings her hand up to my chin and kisses me on the lips. "I love you," she mumbles against my lips.

"I love you," I whisper back. And I do. With everything in me. For some reason, the words feel... more. Like I need her to know how much I love her, so she doesn't doubt it because of my feelings for Emmett.

She studies my face like she can hear my thoughts and feelings, then grabs Callum's shoulder. "Let's go hot stuff before I change my mind."

He grabs her hand and pulls it over his shoulder and kisses her knuckles.

"When the next wave comes, I need you both to paddle hard," I say, crouching into position.

It takes several attempts, but they get pushed off, clear the waves and get out to the ocean. Ev looks back at me and smiles.

A strange feeling tingles under my skin as I watch them paddle further and further out. Worry? I trust Callum with our girl, but that doesn't change the fact that something could happen to them, to her. The waves are definitely getting choppier and the wind has picked up.

Shaking my head, trying to get rid of all the bad thoughts, I walk back over to the seats and take the one Everlee had been in beside her mother.

"I'm surprised you got her to wear the life jacket. She's always hated them."

"I wouldn't have given her a choice," I huff.

Donna smiles at me. "Hey Jax," she says casually.

"Hey Donna." I look over at her and smile, feeling like a prying question is about to be asked.

"Tell me a little about yourself. Callum is your brother, yes?"

"He is."

"You two, I seem to know the least about. Very tall, dark, and mysterious. And handsome. Obviously. It must be something in Ms. Mary Mae's water."

"There isn't much to know about the brood," Lizzy chimes in, and I cut my eyes at her, causing her to laugh.

"I have picked up on this," she says, pointing between Lizzy and me. "This love hate relationship between you two."

"He hates he loves me!" Lizzy cackles, and I don't correct her. My words are the gas to her flame.

"Oh Lizzy, it's hard not to love you," Donna says.

Lizzy looks at me and shrugs her shoulders before turning back to her conversation with Tony and Emmett.

Donna's eyes are focused on me, like she's still waiting for me to speak, but I don't know what to say. I'm not the one for casual chitchat. I speak with purpose.

"I don't really know what to say that you don't know." My eyes stay focused on Everlee and Callum out in the water. They are getting further out, but are still in front of us for the most part, although it looks like they are fighting for that position. Why did he want to go out there today? The wooden edge of the handle bites against my clenched grip.

"You seem to care about her," Donna says, pulling my focus.

She's looking at my hands with a death grip around the handle of the chair, so I release my grip, rubbing my hands on my knees and admit, "Yes. I do. She's an amazing woman."

"She is. Her ex..." she shakes her head. "I thought he was going to be the one, but..." her words fall off.

"He wasn't the one for her."

"You know Rich?"

"I know enough about him not to like him."

Donna chuckles, but doesn't say anything for a minute. "Yea, he did a real number on her. Took away the shine she once had, but... I've seen it come back in recent months, and

I wonder who I have to thank for that." She tilts her chin up like she's expecting me to jump at the chance to claim that title. Unfortunately for her, I'm not the braggadocios type.

"You know," she continues, "I just worry about her. Marriage and kids. She's not getting any younger."

"Is that what she wants? Marriage and kids?" I can't stop myself from asking the questions before my lips are moving and the words are tumbling out of my mouth.

She smiles at me. "She says no, but that seems to be a newer thing. She's always talked about her wedding day and starting a family. She was over the moon about it when she was with Rich. But lately, she's said it's not really in her cards and I can't figure out why."

Because of us, my subconscious chimes and the words sting.

"Could you imagine, little Everlee's running around?"

The image of little toddlers wobbling around runs through my head, causing me to smile.

"Or little Lizzy's?" Lizzy butts back in. It takes me a moment, but I realize she's trying to run interference between Donna's questions and me.

"I would rather have a dozen little Everlees than even one little Lizzy," I laugh.

"You better tell Ev that!" Lizzy chuckles.

"Uh-oh," Donna says, standing up, eyes focused on the ocean.

"What?" I ask, following her gaze and see Callum and Ev have flipped over.

A wave crashes on top of her, pushing her head under water. Callum is there, fighting the waves, calling out to her, but she can't hear him. Another wave crashes and her head disappears under the surf while pushing Callum further from the kayak and Everlee.

"Shit!" I shout out, tearing across the beach.

Panic grips my heart like a vise.

Fuck!

The sand is like weights on my legs, slowing me down and preventing me from getting to her.

Her head falls under again, like she's fighting with an invisible monster.

"Everlee!" I shout out.

Why did they have to go out there today? The wind was picking up when Beckett got back and even said it was getting rougher!

The water hits my feet and splashes around me as I run deeper.

Another wave crashes.

Her head disappears from view.

Fuck!

"Everlee! I'm coming!"

I hear the faint screams of the girls behind me, but I don't turn around. I need to stay focused on Everlee. She's my priority.

After the next wave crashes, I dive over it and into the water and swim towards her. Peeking up quickly, I still don't see her, but I'm laser focused on where she was. Another wave is coming and I dive under just as it crashes. This water is murkier than shit, but it's not my first time in dark water. Flashbacks of my times with the SEALs come back, but I push them out of the way.

Breaking the surface of the water, I take in a gulp of air. Callum is pushed further to the right of the kayak, still trying to paddle back to where Everlee is.

"Jax!" He yells, "I can't get to her. The fucking current."

"I got her! Go to shore!"

Diving under the water again, I push through and see her looking at me, gasping for air. Her eyes look tired and panicked.

I'm coming for you, Squirt. Keep fighting.

My muscles strain against the waves and the current trying to push me away from her. But nothing can stop me. Nothing *will* stop me.

In the distance, I see her body floating above the water, but she's face down.

Fuck!

Pushing forward and paddling with all the strength I have, I don't break my eye contact with her, scared that if I do, she'll disappear.

Her arm feels like a limp noodle under my rough grasp, but I flip her onto her back, then slap her face a little, but she doesn't come to.

Goddamn it, Everlee. You better wake up. I'm not fucking losing you.

Looping my arm around her, I swim parallel to the shore. I need to get her back, but we're in the middle of a rip current and need to get out of it first. In the distance, Knox is pulling Callum out of the water, and pointing further down the shore, so I follow. He sees it and is guiding me away.

He dives into the water and starts swimming straight out, giving me a point to meet him.

"Come on, Squirt. Don't leave us." I glance down at her and her head is still lolling from side to side and my stomach is twisting into vicious knots. Damn it! Why can't I swim any faster? I'm a fucking SEAL. Swim, you piece of shit!

Let's go tadpole! You're nothing more than a piece of shit. Swim. You think because you grew up without a mommy and a daddy that makes you special? Makes you different? Let's go! Instructor Bradford's voice echoes in my head on repeat.

Shifting Everlee in my arms, I paddle harder, ignoring the waves crashing around us with my sights set on Knox up ahead and waiting.

Push.

Kick.

Paddle.

Kick.

"Come on, baby."

After a few more minutes, Knox is swimming over to us and grabs her from me. "I got her." His eyes are intense and focused as I let her go.

Everything inside of me is telling me to fight to keep her, but I know she's better off with him right now. I swam us through the current and my body is tired and screaming at me.

We have her on the beach within a minute and Knox is already pulling the life vest off her. He tilts her head back and blows two breaths into her mouth, while I grab her hand and squeeze.

"Come on, babe. Breathe." I kiss her knuckles, urging her to suck in air.

Knox blows into her mouth two more times, her chest raising and she starts to choke on the water, so he rolls her onto her side and she spits it out, coughing and gagging.

She takes a few deep breaths, then her eyes find me. "Jax?"

"Hey Squirt." I kiss her forehead before helping her sit-up.

"I helped too," Knox whines and she looks over at him and grabs his hand, kissing his knuckles.

Emmett and Callum are around us a moment later, crouched around her.

"I'm fine. I'm fine," she says, pressing her palms into the sand, still taking a few deep breaths.

"Ev!" Beckett yells, followed by Will.

"I'm fine."

"Let him look over you darling," Donna says with her arm wrapped around Lizzy's.

"I'm fine."

"Everlee," Callum and I both say in a commanding voice and her eyes snap to attention.

"Fine," she huffs.

She has all the sass she usually does and her color looks good, but I'll feel better after Beckett and Will look her over.

Emotion rocks me deep within, as the adrenaline from the moment tapers off, causing me to fall back onto my butt and grab my knees, but my eyes are still focused on her. Every rise of her chest, every pulse in her neck, and every sigh and eye roll she's giving Beckett.

"She looks good, but I'd still take her to the hospital to have a doctor evaluate her."

"You've got to be kidding."

"Everlee," I bark louder than intended. "We almost lost you. Knox and I carried your near lifeless body back to shore. You're going to the goddamn hospital to get checked out."

Her eyes are wide, and tears form on the rims.

Fuck. Shit. No. No. No.

"I'm sorry," she says, crawling onto my lap. "I don't want to scare you. I didn't mean to. It's just that those waves kept crashing on my face and the current or something was pulling against me. I couldn't get away."

Brushing the hair off her face, I rest my forehead on hers. "It's ok. We've got you now. You're safe, but we would all feel better if a doctor gave you the green light. Do this for us? You scared us."

"Ok."

Lizzy clears her throat and we all look up at her, then Donna.

Fuck.

She's staring down at us with a look of confusion and understanding.

Well, we're fucked. There's no way she didn't see through all that. We're damn near hovering over her, protecting her like she's ours. Which she is, but we're excluding the rest of her family. When Beckett gave his two cents, then backed away, the four of us closed in that gap.

"I'll go get the car," Emmett offers, pushing off the sand.

"Let's go."

"I'll stay here," Lizzy says.

My tired muscles shake when I stand with Everlee in my arms. "Donna? Do you want to go with us?"

She tilts her chin up. "I think..." she stares at Everlee, "I think you all have it handled, but I'd ask you call to give me updates?"

"Of course, ma'am."

She nods slightly, still trying to process and piece together what she witnessed. Questions clearly weighing on her mind. Hopefully, she just saves them until we're back instead of unloading them on Lizzy. This conversation should probably be handled delicately, and Lizzy... well... is a raging bull in a china shop.

"Evy," Lizzy calls out. "You've always been the dramatic one. If you didn't want to cook breakfast for dinner with me tonight, you could have simply said that instead of doing all this to get attention." Her words are joking, but the quiver in her voice gives away her emotion. She's scared.

"I love you."

"I love you." She wipes a tear from her face with the back of her hand.

EVERLEE - TRUTH BE TOLD

A BEACH HOUSE HAS never looked as good as it does right now. The weird pinkish hue the setting sun shines on it makes it almost glow. Or it could be the tint on the windows. I was instructed not to touch the door, because Callum insisted he open it. The boys have been babying me since my near drowning accident. I told them on the beach I was fine, but they insisted I go to the hospital, so we all waited there for a couple of hours before the doctor gave me the thumbs up. And when I say all waited there... we all five waited in a tiny ass triage room. The room itself wasn't tiny, but to have four oversized men in the room with the doctor and the nurses, it was tiny. I noticed several of the nurses doing laps and staring into the room.

Yes. My men are hot and it didn't help they weren't wearing a shirt, since they came straight from the beach. At one point, the doctor had to come in and tell them they needed to go to the gift shop to buy a shirt since they were distracting his team. The guys, of course, had to rock, paper, scissors to figure out who had to leave.

Knox lost.

And had the boys been concerned with that fact, instead of me, they would have realized what a bad idea it was sending Knox to get shirts for everyone. He came back with the most flamboyant and colorful Hawaiian print shirts he could find. He said there wasn't a lot to pick from, but I don't believe him. Seeing them all, Jax and Callum, especially, in Hawaiian print shirts, made me laugh to the point of crying.

When the car door opens, Knox moves to lift me into his arms, but I hold out my arm. "While I love being in your arms, I can walk this short distance."

"Just because you can, doesn't mean you should."

"Knox," I scold.

He grimaces, causing me to chuckle.

We walk through the door and Lizzy comes barreling around the corner, arms wide open and screaming like a crazy lady. "Boo boooo!!"

"Lizzy," Jax says sternly, stepping in between us, holding his arm out.

Placing my hand gently on his arm, I push him out of the way. "It's ok Jax."

Lizzy waits a beat then gobbles me in her arms. "Don't you do that to me again!" she yells, then whispers, "You need to talk to your mom. She was asking questions, though she would never come out and just ask *the* question about you and the guys." She pushes me away and looks over at me. "What did the doctor say?" Then pulls me back in for another hug and whispers, "Asking about the men, if they're good to you, if you're happy." She pushes me away again and I'm beginning to get dizzy.

"Lizzy." I mouth thank you and give her a little wink. "I'm all good. Just sucked in a little too much water. The doctor said near drownings can happen even with life jackets if you keep getting water splashed in your face. Between the current and waves..."

"So you're saying you couldn't keep your mouth closed?"

"Seems like that would be your problem instead of mine." I laugh and she shrugs. "Doctor just said I need to be watched throughout the night, but should be ok."

Lizzy's eyes grow wide because she knows what that means and also knows the men are going to want to be with me the entire night.

Over Lizzy's shoulder, I see my mom walk into the room and look at all of us, followed by Beckett and Will.

"Sissy!" Beckett throws his arms wide and runs over dramatically, mocking Lizzy. "Are you ok, my love?" He pulls me in tight, then whispers, "Please on your love of cock, talk to mom. She's putting pieces together about the men."

"Yes, I'm ok," I say, pushing him off me.

Will walks over and gives me a hug. "Thank God you're home. Becks has been a nervous wreck. Glad you're ok."

"Thank you."

"Can mom get a hug?" she asks meekly.

"Of course. Hugs for everyone!"

She smiles and walks over. "I'm glad you're ok."

She turns to the boys, "Thank you all for taking care of my girl."

"Of course ma'am."

"May I?" she asks holding her arms out wide in their direction.

"Come here!" Knox says, stepping up and opening his arms for a hug.

She moves around, wrapping each of them in her arms, her eyes filling with tears more and more. She ends with Jax and reaches up to grab his cheeks, just staring at him with tears running down her face. "Thank you. You didn't even hesitate." She brings him in for another hug.

I take a few deep breaths, psyching myself up for the conversation I thought I'd never have. Part of me is glad this happened, though... so it forces me to have it. The boys have given me more confidence in both the bedroom and my personal life, but I need to continue it in all aspects of my life. I need to take control and take what is mine. Images of Sammie float through my head, as do her words of commanding strength.

Nerves course through me as my pulse races. "Mom? Can I talk to you?"

Lizzy is walking back into the kitchen, but leans back and does a full one eighty, looking at me in surprise with her eyes wide open. They dart from side to side like an animal trapped in a cage, then she holds up both hands, fingers crossed and blows me a kiss.

Beckett stands beside her, eyes equally as wide with a slow motion 'oh shit' puckered on his lips.

"Sure, honey."

"We'll go outside."

Lizzy and Beckett quickly scramble into the kitchen, pushing after each other.

"Dinner will be ready in about thirty minutes. I've got two quiches in the oven and other stuff and stuff... and fruit and stuff," Lizzy mumbles.

Leading mother across the dining room to the back of the house, my pulse grows louder and louder in my ears, thumping like a steady drum. A fast beat, but steady.

The air is a few degrees cooler than earlier, but still muggy with more clouds in the sky. Maybe that's a good sign? No rain means I'm not about to blow up my entire family for the men I love?

Taking a deep breath, I let the air fill my lungs and just hold it, letting it slow down my heartbeat. We pause on the deck, the air thick around us. Over my shoulder, I see Beckett and Lizzy peeking behind the curtain in the corner, like little children looking for Santa's sleigh outside.

"Let's go to the beach. It's a little cooler down there." And away from prying ears. I need to do this, but do it without the added stress of others listening to every word.

"Sure, honey." Her voice is shaky.

She is nervous too.

We walk across the boardwalk and place our shoes near the stairs and step onto the soft sand, being sure to avoid the scattered pieces of broken seashells former vacation goers had likely left. I hadn't noticed them before, but it's baffling how acutely aware of your surroundings you become when you have potentially unsettling news to share. It's like your mind focuses on any and everything else, but what you *need* to say.

Someone had brought the kayak back up and tucked it against the dune right in front of the house, along with our chairs and umbrellas. I toyed with the idea of setting them out, but I felt this news was better delivered standing up. So *you can run if you need*, my subconscious chimes.

I take a deep breath, psyching myself up to speak, then blow out the breath.

We walk down the beach and I do this a couple more times, each time no closer than the last to actually speaking.

Mother grabs my hand, and we stop walking for a moment. "I know there is something you need to tell me, and I want you to know that no matter what it is, that will not change the way I feel about you. You are my daughter, and will always be my daughter, and I love you."

A knot the size of Kansas is stuck in my throat as I try to hold back the tears.

We start walking again.

"Mom."

One word.

Progress.

Now add another.

"Mom, I..."

My stomach is churning, my hands are clammy, my heart-beat is racing and I swear my vision is pulsing.

"Mom. I'm in a polyamorous relationship with Callum, Jax, Emmett, and Knox."

She nods her head, but doesn't speak.

I continue, filling the space with words and thoughts that fly out of my mouth like vomit. "They are fantastic. Amazing. And so wonderful." Tears start streaming down my face, but my voice doesn't crack. "They treat me with so much respect and love and..." I sigh. "They have given me so much confidence. I feel like the woman I was meant to be with them. They love me so much and I love them. I've been so excited to share them with you and dad but I've been so scared... so scared you would disown me. Not understand-"

"Everlee." She grabs my arm and we stop walking. "Breathe."

She stares at me, her eyes searching my face, and I search hers back for any hint of what she's thinking, feeling, or about to say.

She cocks her head to the side.

This isn't good.

No good can come from a head side tilt.

That's the look you give someone when you need to deliver bad news, but you want to come across as more sincere. Like the pain of the words is too much for your head to hold, so it falls to the side.

A warm resolve passes through me, and I close my eyes. This is it. So long family dinners and holidays. Hello bullet train to hell.

Oh God. What if she kidnaps me and tries to convert me back to... well, monoamory. I know that's not a word, but I can't think of what the correct word would be that's not polyamory. Why would polyamory mean multiple lovers but monoamory can't mean one lover?

She'd never kidnap me and try to convert me. Everlee. Take a beat.

"Well, I suspected something most of the week." She walks again, and I follow. "Not really sure what I expected, though. Couldn't wrap my head around you with all of them, but I could see it, you know. The way they are with you and you with them. Hell, even Beckett and Lizzy. You all just sort of fit. I assume they both know?"

"Yes."

"The way they watch after you, care for you. I see it. I do. They love you. Earlier today, watching Jax run after you without a thought for his own life to rescue you." Her voice cracks as tears pour down her face. "My God Everlee, if that's not love, then I don't know what is."

Her words do little to calm the worry jolting through my body, because I feel like we're only climbing up a hill for the cliff to appear and swallow us up.

"I don't know much about polyamory. Have you been... this... for long?"

Her confusion around the politically correctness makes me chuckle. "It's not really a thing I am. I'm in a relationship with four men."

"I can hardly keep your father happy, and here you are with four," she huffs, trying to smile.

"But to answer your question, no. They are the first and will be the last. I've never felt anything like this before."

"It's new." Her words don't come across as harsh, but just a fact.

I bobble my head from side to side. "It's been since February."

"What? So Easter was planned?"

"God, no." How could I tell her I signed an NDA and a sexual contract, only giving me two good fucks... without saying all those words? "We met in February and things were going great, really great... and I got scared and left them. When they showed up at Easter, it was a complete surprise for all of us. We had no idea either was going to be there and we sort of reconnected. I was miserable during that time without them and the same for them. It was then I realized I wanted to give this thing a go, because I couldn't imagine spending one second without them."

"Your new place... is their house?"

"Not really, but technically. They wanted me out of my apartment, and they had a place... beside their house, they weren't using. So they gave it to me." I hold my hands up to clarify. "Let me stay in it. I pay them rent. Plus, it's closer to Lizzy and in a better part of town, and Rich doesn't know where I am."

"Is he still a problem?"

"I don't think so. We had a talk when he showed up at my place after Easter. I told him I forgave him for cheating on me and being a complete douche, and told him we would never be a thing. I think he finally got the message."

"Does he know about your poly... I forgot what you call it."

"No. He doesn't. Although it would probably help." I laugh.

We walk an unknown distance before she speaks again. "So... why didn't you think you could tell me?" Her voice cracks, like the pain of me not being able to tell her weighs on her more than my news.

When I turn to look at her, she doesn't look back. Worry is etched into the lines of her face.

"I didn't want you and dad to disown me or hate me or..."

"Everlee. We would never do any of those things. We may not understand your choices, but we will always love you. You obviously know the struggles we had initially with Beckett when he first came out to us. We had to talk to Pastor John for a while, not because we didn't love Beckett or wanted to change him, but because we were scared of where his choices may lead him. We know that's not the case anymore, which has put our heart at ease and when we go to talk to him about you, we will come out the same."

"Pastor John has his hands full with us."

"He always has." She smiles and rubs my cheek. "It's probably time for dinner, so we should start heading home. Plus, it's getting dark."

"Are you mad?"

"Mad? No, Everlee. Not mad. I know you see your father and I as closed off to the changes of the world, but we're trying to be educated. You know... we went to a pride event with Beckett last month. That was so much fun. Now seeing everyone kissing everywhere that was a lot, but not because they were gay. I've just always found public kissing and grabbing and other things they were doing, not my cup of tea."

"Yea..."

"Would you go to those? Are you part of the LGBTQIA+ now? Where does poly... you know... fit?"

"It's hard to say... some say yes, others say no."

"I will not pretend like this will be an easy adjustment for your father and I, but we will try. We will love you and will support you no matter what."

Relief pours through me as I empty my lungs of all the air I had, blowing out and relaxing my shoulders.

"I'd love to meet your boyfriends? Is that what I call them?"

"I guess. I've never really thought about it, but I guess that fits, even though they feel like so much more."

"What do Lizzy and Beckett call them?"

"My harem."

Her head falls back in laughter. "I'm not there yet, so I'll stick with boyfriends."

"Sounds good."

She grabs my hand and pulls me into a hug. "I love you, Everlee. There's not a lot you can do to make your father and I turn our backs on you, and having four very attractive men who worship you is not one of them. I want you to be able to come to us with anything."

All the worry and stress from the entire day unleashes and I breakdown in her arms and start crying.

"Oh Ev, it's ok baby," she says, rubbing the back of my hair. "I think you're just tired. You've had a very long and eventful day... and night."

She looks at me when I push off her shoulders to look at her.

"Really? Right across the hall. You could have tried a little harder to be quiet."

"Oh my God."

"Those were baby making moans if I ever heard any. At least that's the way I sounded when I got pregnant with you and Beckett."

"Mom!"

"What? I had to listen to you, so guess what... the rest of the walk back to the house you can hear about your father and I. I think it's only fair."

"Mom."

She is true to her word and finally stops talking about the night Beckett was conceived when we're walking up on the boardwalk. Callum is on a call but ends it when he sees us. His brow is furrowed, like he's stressed about something, but smiles when he sees me smiling.

"I'm going to go inside and let you two talk for a minute." She rubs my back as she steps inside, and I hear Lizzy call her name for help in the kitchen.

"Well? How did it go?"

Needing to feel his arms wrapped around me, I throw myself at his chest and he lets out a puff of a breath before he wraps his arms around me.

A low chuckle shakes in his chest as his arms hold me and he kisses the top of my head. "She loves me and sees the love you all have for me and can't be mad at that. I think it will take some time for her and dad to adjust, but she didn't shun me, so that's a good thing. Is everything ok with you?" I lift my head, pressing my chin on his chest, not wanting to pull away yet, but wanting to see his face.

"Nothing we can't handle. We just need more support at Allure. I don't think anyone realized how big of a part Sammie played in the day-to-day operations to make it run smoothly."

"Me."

"You, what?"

A smile crosses over my lips as I take in a deep breath and push away from him. "I want to manage it. I want to quit my job and work at Allure full time."

"Are you serious? Are you sure?"

"Yes, to both. I've been thinking about it for a while. I'm so done with the monotony of my corporate job. I work every day to make someone else money. I want to be in charge of making us money. The fight. The zest. Sex clubs have always been for men. I want to make them for women too. I want to help give women the confidence y'all have given me, that Sammie has given me. I want to create a safe space for people to learn and explore their kinks. I have so many ideas."

He brushes the hair behind my ears. "You don't need to convince me. I love it and I love you."

"Then kiss me."

"Really?"

"Yes."

He cups my cheeks and presses his lips to mine and I nearly melt. His kiss is powerful, wanting. His tongue glides in, claiming me. He pulls away a second later, placing his forehead on mine, leaving me breathless. "I love you, Everlee."

"I love you, Callum. Now, do you want to go meet my mom?"

"I'd love to."

My body feels like it's walking on clouds because I'm so happy. I just all but essentially quit my job to work at a sex club, moments after coming out to my mom about the guys. My life has basically flipped on itself in the matter of a few minutes and I couldn't be more excited.

When we walk in, Lizzy and Tony are standing in the kitchen, Beckett and Will are on the couch, and my mother and the rest of my guys are standing around the dining room table watching Callum and I walk in.

Lizzy looks like a wildcat who's been cooped up in a cage for too long. Eyes wide, soaking up every detail, every move, hands twitching and waiting for answers.

"Mom," I say, and what little noise was in the house stops. Even the air conditioner cuts off at the same time. "I'd like to introduce you to Callum, Jax, Emmett, and Knox. My... boyfriends."

My eyes flitter to Lizzy, who looks like a soda bottle ready to explode. She's shaking from side to side with so much happiness it's about to burst out of her little body.

"Boys. It's a pleasure to finally meet you." She smiles.

"You'll learn this soon enough, but when she was naming everyone, she saved the best for last," Knox chirps, walking over to give my mom a hug.

She laughs, patting him on the chest. "I'm sure she did."

"Thank God you know! It was killing me!" Beckett moans from the couch.

"I'm sure it was darling," Mother says sarcastically. She looks around with a sly grin and says, "Well, you know what this means?"

"No," I say nervously.

There is a clicking noise to my left and when I turn, Lizzy is snapping pictures of us with her phone, capturing this perfect moment. She throws a wink out at me and my stomach tightens. This is it.

This is that perfect moment you see in movies.

Mother chuckles, bringing me back to earth. "This only increases the chances of me having a grandchild by four times! How can I not be happy about that?"

"Oh lord," Beckett and I groan at the same time.

"Yes! Mama McKinley with the priorities!" Lizzy cheers from across the room, sending pancake batter smack onto Tony's face. "Shit. Sorry. I got carried away. I'm just so excited!"

Looking around the room, I notice the boys aren't cringing, rather laughing, and part of me takes it as a sign that *maybe* kids aren't off the table?

CALLUM - HAPPINESS

IT FEELS LIKE A weight has been lifted off Everlee and this house. Her mother knows, and soon so will her father. Donna said she'll discuss this with him when he gets back from his trip on Sunday. Speaking with Everlee after dinner, she said her mother had already suspected something was up, even though she wasn't quite sure what *it* was. She said at the end of the day, Donna wants her children to be happy, even if that means their lives take a different path than she had originally planned, which I think, speaks volumes to the people they are.

After dinner, we all talk about Everlee and Beckett growing up and, of course, a handful of embarrassing stories, mostly at Everlee's expense. Between the guys' eagerness to learn everything we can about her, and Donna, Lizzy, and Beckett eager to embarrass her, it was a win-win for everyone... but Everlee. But we'll make it up to her. And even though she was oohing and ahhing and grumbling the entire time, she was also laughing a lot.

When I walk back over with a bowl of popcorn to sit on the couch, Donna stands. "I'm going to head to bed. It's been a long day and I'm beat, plus, there was this racket last night that kept banging and kept me up."

In typical Lizzy fashion, she makes some sort of bow-chic-ka-bow-wow sound, garnering a laugh from half the room, which is all the encouragement she needs.

Donna walks upstairs and as soon as her door shuts, Lizzy and Beckett fly across the couch, ignoring me and the bowl of popcorn on my lap, causing me to nearly spill it.

"Spill the tea," Lizzy and Beckett say in unison.

"I'm going to let you all talk." I stand up, then look back at Everlee. "I'm going to go outside and fill the boys in on the call with Sammie." I look at Everlee and she pumps her eyebrows with a smirk because she knows that also means about her coming to Allure full time.

The guys and I walk outside and take the left side of the deck, where the two oval couches are. Knox tries to steal my popcorn, but I shove him off and he trips, nearly falling into the pool.

"Not cool, bro."

"Don't come after a man's freshly popped popcorn," I warn.

"Sharing is caring," Knox volleys back.

I reluctantly hold the bowl out. "Take a handful, not the bucket."

"Stingy!"

"Watch it, or next time you will end up in the pool on purpose."

"So what did you need to talk to us about?" Jax asks, pulling the conversation away from Knox and popcorn.

"So you know the problem we knew we were going to have with the management at Allure once Sammie pulls away?"

"Yea," they all nod in unison.

"We have a solve."

"Well?"

"Everlee."

"What about her?" Jax asks.

"She's going to quit her job and work at Allure full-time. She wants to really take ownership and manage it with Knox. She already has a lot of great ideas to bring into the business."

"Has she managed something before?" Jax asks, only mildly concerned.

"I don't think so, but neither did we until we did. I know she can handle it-"

"I wasn't meaning she can't do it. With the learning curve, I just want us to be aware so we can make sure we're support-ing her."

"Does anyone else love how she's really stepped into her own?" Emmett asks. "She's like a completely different woman than the one we first saw in our club with that red satin get-up on with those wings."

"We should have her wear them again. You know we still have them at the house," Knox says.

"You never gave them back?" Jax asks.

"No. I couldn't. I took them and hid them in my closet. I was hoping they'd be like the magical princess slipper that brings her back to us."

"Bring what where?" she asks, walking outside with the rest of the crew.

"You," I say.

She walks over and climbs onto my lap and wraps her arms around my neck.

"How do you feel?" I ask, planting a kiss on her head.

"Good. Fantastic. I don't think we're out of the woods yet with my parents, but I don't think they're going to turn their backs on me anymore. It may just be awkward for a bit."

Beckett chimes in, "She's always been a daddy's girl, so this will be hard for him at first, but I think he will see how... natural it seems and it will be ok." He gives his sister an encouraging smile.

This is it. The moment in your life where everything slots into place. Like a ball that's been bouncing around for a while trying to find the one hole. Everything feels... right. The week started out great, then got a little tense and awkward when her mom showed up, but is now ending even better than the week started.

Tomorrow is our last day here, before our early morning flight on Saturday. I'm not looking forward to leaving, but this is also the most days I've ever taken off consecutively in... forever. I wasn't too keen on taking the week, but I also wanted to give Everlee this. I, we, would do anything for her.

Her head tilts up to look at me, almost like she can hear my thoughts.

"Want to go for a swim?" I ask.

"Now?" A smile slowly spreads across her face.

"Sure."

"Last one in is a rotten egg!" she shouts, leaping from the chair and jumping into the pool. I jump in after her, followed by Knox, and then I lose track. It's just a flurry of arms and legs jumping in.

Jax swims over to her and grabs her. "You aren't going underwater, though. Just in case."

She presses her lips to his. "I love you, too!"

KNOX - HOME IS WHERE THE PUSSY IS

LAST NIGHT WAS A lot to process. Between Everlee almost drowning, her mom finding out about us, and Everlee quitting her job to work with me at Allure... it was a lot. We stayed in the pool swimming with everyone until sometime after two. We went to bed and a few minutes later, my door was squeaking open and a little figure was tip-toeing in, flapping their arms like wings.

She's such a goof and I love her all the more for it.

She falls into my bed and curls into me and falls asleep in under a minute. So fast, in fact, I'm not one hundred percent sure she didn't sleepwalk into my room.

"Good morning," her sweet, sleepy morning voice says, and I sit my book down on the nightstand. "What are you reading?"

"Nothing fun," I frown. "Jax wants me to read these management books."

"I guess I'll need to read those, too." She smiles, then adjusts in the bed, so her chin is resting on my chest. "Are you ok with me quitting my job? Technically, I haven't done it yet, so if you feel like I'm stepping on your toes, then we can pretend like I never said anything."

"Everlee," I flip over so I'm straddling her in the bed. "I'm thrilled and excited you are going to work at Allure with me." I run my finger up her stomach splitting her button-down top open.

"Knox," she sighs, "my mom is across the hall."

"Is she?" I ask, leaning over to fall between her legs, planting kisses on her stomach.

"Knox," she warns, but her hands slide into my hair.

"Tell me to stop and I will." My lips continue to kiss up her stomach until I reach her breast. Her perky little nipples are already pebbling with anticipation before I swirl my tongue around the first one.

A small moan echoes from her chest as I move to the other breast. It fills my mouth so perfectly, as I suck it in, letting my teeth gently clamp on her nipple. Her legs are writhing underneath me as her hands continue to rub and grab my scalp.

Moving off her breast, I slowly work my way back down her stomach. "Tell me to stop Everlee." My fingers loop around the top of her underwear as I pull them down and plant kisses on her hipbones. "One word from you..." I say, pulling her underwear down a little further, exposing the top of her beautiful pussy.

Pausing only for a second, I look up and see her eyes wild and filled with lust, staring back at me. Her teeth are clamped on her bottom lip and her chest is heaving.

Smiling, I slip my tongue down her center, and her hips slowly buck up, serving her pussy to me and a moan escapes. A hint of her arousal hits the tip of my tongue and it's like something broke inside of me, releasing the beast. Her underwear flies across the room as I scoop her ass up in my hands. "Last chance," I say, only for the look she's giving me now. The hunger in her eyes begging me to fuck her with my tongue.

"Eat me, Knox."

My cock twitches and I dive in, hungrily swiping my tongue from the bottom to the top, licking up all her arousal. "So fucking good."

Her legs make there way over my shoulder as her hands plant firmly in my hair, pressing me to her, her back arching off the bed.

Her moans are muffled, and when I look up, I see a pillow over her face and can't help but smile. Sliding my hands up her back, I lift, so her whole body comes off the bed, and she's now sitting on my shoulders with my face buried in her pussy. I pull away for just a second, only to say, "I don't want your moans muffled."

"But..."

"She's on the beach for an early morning walk."

"How do you know?"

"Do you trust me?"

She nods and I slip my fingers up between us and curve them inside of her pussy. To prevent her from falling, I crash backwards so she's on top of me now.

"Sorry," she whimpers, after I add another finger.

"You want to ride my face?"

"I want to ride your cock."

"After you come on my face. I want to taste you Everlee. I want to feel you pulse around my tongue."

"Knox," she pants and begins rocking her hips, fucking my fingers while my tongue works her clit, sucking and licking.

She's rocking faster, so I know she's getting closer. Pulling my fingers out, I press my tongue in as far as it can go, and begin to work her clit with my finger. That's all she needs. A little nudge. Her legs clamp around my head as her movements get slower, but deeper and she presses against my face, riding out her orgasm.

She waits a beat, then quickly shifts down my body and sinks onto my cock without hesitation. "Knox," she moans out.

My hands grip into her hips as the feeling of her tight, wet pussy around my cock causes tingles to move down my spine. Tightening my core, I thrust my hips off the bed and slam into her, causing her to grunt out.

"Did that hurt?"

She presses the palm of her hands to my chest and continues to ride, tossing her hair behind her. "No."

She's slowing her rocking, so I wrap my legs around her and flip us over, with my hips pressed into hers and my forearms holding me off the bed. "You want it hard and fast, or do you want me to take my time?"

"Fuck me hard Knox."

"As you wish." Wanting more leverage, I grab her right leg and hoist it up, opening her pussy up to me so I can rock into her.

"Knox. Knox," she puffs out between thrusts. "Harder."

"Damn Ev. We still have the whole day ahead of us."

She lets out a muffled chuckle that sounds like a rainforest bird cackling. I flip her over so she's hands and knees on the bed. My fingers grip into her hips and I thrust hard, my ass clenches as tingles race down my spine. She feels so fucking amazing as she clenches around me.

"Yes!" Her head falls lazily to the bed.

The sound of wet slaps and feeling her shudder around me causes my balls to tighten and I explode inside of her.

"Everlee," I breathe out in ecstasy, as I collapse onto her back. After a few breaths, I press a kiss to her neck and taste the salt from our combined sweat on her skin.

Her arms buckle and we both fall to the bed with my cock still inside of her. I wish we didn't have anywhere to be right now, because I could fall asleep right now with my cock like this. It's my favorite place for it to be. When I fell asleep inside of her last time, I swear it was the best sleep I've ever had. I felt safe. At home.

She is my home.

EVERLEE - NO GOLDEN SHOWERS

THE HOT LEATHER BALL smacks hard against my hands and I take off running, feet digging into the warm, hard sand.

"Go! Go!" Knox yells.

Looking to my right, I see Jax running alongside of me to block Beckett before he tosses me a quick wink. A second later, Emmett is tackling Jax and they fall to the ground. A taunt is exchanged between them, but I don't see who started it, only hear the howls of laughter that come as soon as I cross our makeshift goal line.

A moment later, Jax, Knox and Callum are running over, picking me up.

"Guess your tackling me didn't help," Jax pokes at Emmett.

"There's always next time," Emmett sends back, lightly punching at Jax's shoulder.

"If you can catch me." He pumps his eyebrows.

"Let's go!" Beckett claps. "Team! We're down by two, but that's ok. Emmett, you take Jax."

"Gladly," he smirks.

"Tony, you take Knox, I'll take Callum, and Lizzy, you do you, girl."

"Come on baby," I say, bending my knees and pressing my hand onto the ground, coming face to face with Lizzy.

She tries to lurch forward and kiss me, but Beckett's already asking for the snap. "Next time, boo."

She tosses the ball to Beckett and moves to my right. Trying to stop her, I move to my right, but she spins out of my grasp and takes off down the beach and I run after her. The three extra inches she has on me serves her well. She slowly pulls away from me, hands in the air, ready to grab the ball from Beckett.

The ball is released and soaring through the air, so I sprint faster, but not fast enough. She leaps into the air and catches it, lands and continues to run.

Fucking track star, I grumble, slowing to a jog as she crosses their goal line.

Track or running, in general, is not my thing. It's like my legs are allergic to it and they forget how to work and cross each other, sending me flailing in an epic fashion onto the ground. The guys crowd around her, cheering while a pair of arms wrap around me, picking me up into the air.

"What was that, Ali? You just give up?"

Knox.

"Yea, these legs weren't going to reach her. She has those model long legs and was a track star in high school."

"Maybe we picked wrong then," he teases, and I flail wildly in his arms, trying to get free. His lips press to my ear, "Just kidding, love. We could never choose wrong with you. I'd rather lose one hundred games of beach football than lose you." He lets me down, spinning me in his arms, pulling me to his chest.

"You had me worried."

He kisses my forehead.

"Everlee!" Lizzy shouts at me, pulling my attention.

"What?" I ask, turning around.

"Is this what it feels like to be you? In your harem?" She's holding her arms around to the men around her.

"Still missing one." I scrunch my nose playfully at her.

"Girl... too much!"

Will runs over to the group. He's been sitting under the tent with my mom, keeping her company this morning. "Becks."

"What's up, babe?" he asks, slipping his arm around him.

"Are you still wanting to leave after dinner tonight?"

"Yea, why?"

"Cap called and asked if I could come in tomorrow morning?"

Beckett grimaces.

"I can say no, if you want me to."

"If you want to, you can. Sucks for you because I'll be sleeping in the whole day."

"He says he only wants me there to help run a community event in the morning, so I'll be home in the afternoon and then I'll go in for my shift the next morning."

"I'm good with it. Do you want me to help you?"

"Come to my house? Don't know what the others would say about an outsider coming in. Plus, they already got rid of you once."

"Shut it!" Beckett jumps on Will and they wrestle, laughing.

Mother told us this morning she's going to head home after dinner, and Beckett and Will said they'd leave with her to make her feel more comfortable. She swore it had nothing to do with the news from yesterday and I believe her. She wants to get home and clean the house, do laundry, and get all the groceries before dad gets home. It's a habit that started when Becks and I were young that she's stuck to, even though it doesn't make as much sense anymore. The house was clean before she left, she's only doing the laundry for the days she's been here, and the groceries... well, that makes sense.

"Is our game done?" Knox asks on deaf ears, as his arms wrap over my shoulders.

The boys have been moderately more affectionate in front of my mother, but have still been respectful, which I can appreciate, as I'm sure she does. This morning she was chatting up a storm with Emmett in the kitchen, planning out where she wants him. HIM, not me, to take her when she comes to visit in a few months. She wants to definitely eat at Bo's for dinner and then have him show her other fine cuisine restaurants. She about lost it when she found out we knew Sophie Lorenz.

"I guess so," Jax says, then jabs Emmett. "Better luck next time."

Emmett lowers his shoulder and rams into Jax, and they fall. Then Knox jumps in, followed by everyone else. One giant wrestle match on the beach because everyone is just... happy.

Once the crowd naturally settles to a stop, we all run into the ocean to wash the sand out of our hair and off our body.

"What was that?" Lizzy yells.

"Not me!" Tony returns.

"No, seriously. What the fuck is that?" She asks, swimming beside me.

"Don't bring whatever it is over here!" I shout, trying to swim away from her, then scream out. "Fuck! Ow! Ow! Fuck!"

"What's wrong?"

"My legs are burning!"

"Get her out!" Callum commands. "There's jellyfish."

"Ow!!" Lizzy screams. "Ass wipe! Shit!"

A minute later, Lizzy and I are crawling onto the beach, still crying.

"Pee on us!" Lizzy screams.

"What?" I bark, clenching in pain. "I've gotten kinkier, but golden showers still haven't made it onto the list yet." I scream out again as another wave of pain passes.

"No, you sick fuck. To neutralize the sting."

"That doesn't work!" I yell back.

"Peeeee on meeee Tony!"

"I wouldn't do that," Jax says, scooping me up. "She needs a hot shower."

Tony looks from us to Lizzy. "No pee for you, Liz." He walks over and scoops her up, then groans. "Jax made it look so easy."

"It's ok babe. I've got a bigger ass than Ev that weighs me down," she says, grabbing his muscles.

"Thanks babe, for trying to make me feel better."

"Anytime," she groans out. "Now give me a hot shower or your pee. I'm in so much pain, I'm about to pee on myself!"

"Please, not in my arms. That's a hard no on my kink list."

"What about you Everlee McKinkley?"

"Still crackin' jokes," Jax moans.

"You know. I'm disappointed in myself that it took me this long to come up with it," she says, looking at us upside down from Tony's arms.

"What happened?" mother asks, standing up from her chair.

"Jellyfish sting near the hoo-ha Mama McKinley."

"Oh dear. Both of you?"

"Yea," I moan.

"Everlee. The lord is telling you to stay out of that ocean. You better listen."

"He's telling me something." My head falls back into Jax's arms as he sways from side to side. The sting is coming in slower pulses now, with a few second reprieve, but then feels like fire again.

When we get upstairs, Jax calls to Tony. "Hot shower, but not scalding, enough to take the burn away. Probably twenty minutes."

"No kinky fuckery in there, you two," Lizzy scolds, pointing her finger at me.

EVERLEE - WHAT'S FOR LUNCH?

JAX WALKS ME INTO the bathroom and sits me on the counter while he adjusts the temperature for the shower. The way his muscles move and tighten on his back when he leans into the shower causes my stomach to tighten. Damn, he is one sexy man.

"You know, I can take care of myself."

"I know," he says simply, offering nothing else.

He walks over to me and slowly reaches his hands around my neck and unties my top, letting it fall to the sink. "How does it feel?"

"Right now?" I pant out like a horny school girl.

He smiles, understanding the statement behind the question. Sliding his hands under my armpits, he lifts me off the counter and stands me up. He slowly drops to his knees, planting a kiss along the long red streak that starts above my left hip and angles down to my right leg as he pulls my bottoms off.

My fingers lock into his hair, offering me balance as I step out of my bathing suit.

"Do you need help in the shower?"

"Hmm," I drag out, bringing my finger to my chin flirtatiously as I climb into the shower.

The hot water hitting my jellyfish sting makes my legs buckle as I let out a groan.

Jax rushes in and grabs me, hoisting me back up. "I was only kidding about needing help, but now I think you may actually need it."

"I'm ok. It just caught me off guard."

"So you don't need my help?" he asks, standing in the shower with his bathing suit still on.

I stare at him for a second, because the water droplets running down his face, then dripping on his shirt does things to me. Almost makes me forget I have lava coursing over my vagina and not in the good way. "I definitely need help." I latch my fingers onto the top of his shorts and give them a gentle tug. He takes over, sliding them the rest of the way down.

"No sexy time, though. You're injured."

"Are you serious?"

He lets out a puff of air.

"I may need to get someone else to help me, then. I heard orgasms help the sting go away faster."

"Is it the same place Lizzy heard that peeing on a sting helps?"

"Possibly."

"Well, we should at least try one of those. For scientific purposes only."

"Of course." I thrust my fist in the air. "Go science!"

"Dork," he winks. He runs his finger over my sting and an ache radiates through my body, but not as bad as before. "Here." He grabs me by the shoulders and positions me under the showerhead. "Let's wash your hair."

He works his fingers through, massaging my scalp, then adds in the shampoo, working it into a thick lather.

"Conditioner, lots of conditioner."

He works the conditioner into my hair and lets it sit while he grabs the loofa, squeezes soap on it, then works it over my body. "How's the sting?"

"Not too bad."

He drops to his knees, so his muscular tattooed frame is sitting in front of me, looking up at me with those dark eyes. He runs the loofa slowly up my leg, brushing it over my pussy before he moves it down the other leg.

"You know, the shower seems to be our favorite place to have sex."

"Who says we're having sex? You're injured."

My eyes shoot open, like a child who was promised ice cream, but it just got ripped away.

He chuckles. "We only talked about orgasms, and *that* you will have." He leans his head down and feathers his tongue up to my clit.

"Jax," I whisper out. "I can handle it."

"You may be able to, but we won't find out right now." His words are final. His hands tighten on my ass as he brings me closer to his face. The bite of the sting only burning for a second, before his tongue expertly works my clit, making my head spin and my pain fade away. His tongue presses in, swirling, lapping.

"Yummy," he says, running his fingers up my leg and threading them inside of me. He curves them just right as he continues to pump them in and out while he sucks on my clit. He moves with precision that is no match for me.

My hands fist his hair as I rock against his face and onto his fingers, pumping my hips in rhythm.

"Jax," I whimper out, pressing my head onto the tiled wall.

He continues to suck on my clit as he plunges his fingers inside of me again.

"Shit. Fuck. Mother damn."

He's working me faster and faster, then reaches up and pinches my nipple between his thumb and forefinger, sending pulses of pleasure straight to my needy little cunt. I was trying to hold out, to savor this moment, to convince him we needed to have sex, but he's skillfully working me, making it impossible. He knows which buttons of mine to push and he is pushing them all at the same fucking time.

"Jax, I'm about to come."

The door opens and I freeze, but my body doesn't. My orgasm crashes around me as my eyes lock with Emmett. A smile curls his lips as he watches me come undone on Jax's face.

When my moans stop and Jax stands up, we both look at Emmett who's still watching, drinking us both in.

He clears his throat. "Your mother wanted me to give you this."

"I'd invite you over here, but Jax says no sex for me right now because of the sting, which barely hurts anymore."

"Guess the orgasm worked," he says, cutting the water off behind me and walking over to Emmett. "It was that or peeing on her." He leans around him, his arm brushing Emmett's and grabs a towel.

What is Jax doing? Flirting? Taunting?

Emmett's eyes rake over Jax's sculpted perfection and land on his hard cock, then look back at me. My breath stops and my pussy quivers again. Please let this be the moment. Please.

I want them, us, together. So bad.

Emmett's lips quirk and he nods at the hydrocortisone on the counter. "Put that on when you're dry." He turns and walks out and I feel crushed. He wanted to. Jax's cock was right there for the taking.

Jax looks up and I swear I see a hint of frustration or longing. Maybe I'm projecting my feelings on him.

FAAACKK!

Ever since I saw Roy Kent on the freaking TV, my fucks have turned to facks! I'm not even a Brit!

I slip some loose clothes on and rub hydrocortisone on the less angry red mark stretching across my abdomen to my leg.

"Ready for some lunch?" I ask.

"I just ate."

"Har har."

He kisses my forehead. "See, I can be funny, too."

"A man with many masks."

EMMETT - DON'T RUIN PERFECTION

Escaping into the bedroom, I press my back against the door. What in the hell was that? The brush of his arm? The way I looked at him... like him him, like cock him. Everlee drinking up every drop. I can see it in her eyes how badly she wants this, but I don't know if Jax does. If he doesn't, then we risk blowing apart our perfect little family, and that's what it is right now. Everything is abso-fucking-lutely perfect. Her friends know, her family knows, she's quitting her job to work at Allure. She's embedded herself into each of us.

Perfection.

Not wanting to be seen, I head downstairs to where everyone is scavenging through the fridge to reheat any leftovers and eat the rest of the deli meat. Tonight's menu is operation clean out the house of all the food.

After lunch, we all decide we've had enough of the beach and especially the ocean for the week, so we stay at the pool and on the deck, soaking up the last rays of sunshine. Because of the late lunch and the threat of a pop-up shower this evening, Beckett, Will and Donna decide to take off around five. Beckett volunteers to drive their mother back while Will takes their car. Donna tries to pretend she doesn't want to be a hassle, but everyone can see she's relieved.

Donna gives all the other guys hugs first, then walks over to me last. "You and me have a date in a few months."

"Yes ma'am. I look forward to it."

She gives me a hug and whispers, "Ev has never been as happy as she is with you all. Continue to take care of her and just love her. I worry about her."

"You have my word, Donna."

"Call me mom."

Something about her words cause my insides to clench with happiness.

Acceptance.

That's what she offers Everlee and Beckett, and now us. Acceptance. She may not understand or agree with our relationship, but she loves without condition.

We see them off, all standing outside for a little while longer. A somber feeling sets around each of us. This week has been fun, relaxing, stressful, eventful, and nearly every other emotion in between, but it all ends tonight. Tomorrow we will go back home and our vacation is over. We have to go back to work and figure out what we're going to do in this next phase of our life. A phase where there aren't secrets from family, where we can be open, try new things...

Try new things.

Be open.

These words feel different, because this week, thoughts and feelings about Jax have surfaced and I don't know if it's because of Everlee, or something else... but...

Emotions and confusion swell inside of me, and when I glance at Jax and see him and Everlee looking at me, butterflies erupt in my stomach and my cock jerks to life.

Shit.

Fearing I'm two seconds from losing control and fucking everything up, I walk inside.

Space.

Space is good.

Even though I feel like it's just kicking the proverbial can down the road. Ever since the beginning of the week, when he was touching my cock. Like *touching* it, I haven't been able to get him out of my mind.

Fuck!

I try not to slam the front door because I don't want to draw attention to myself. I just need to talk with Everlee and tell her what's going on. She has to see this can't be a thing.

A few moments later, I'm walking into my room and crashing on the bed.

EVERLEE - PENIS SNAKES

STANDING OUTSIDE EMMETT'S DOOR, I take a deep breath before I knock. When he walked inside a moment ago, he looked frustrated about something. Trying to give him space, I waited five minutes, which doesn't sound like a lot, but for me it's a record.

"Come in."

Slowly pushing the door open, I peek my head in and see him lying on the bed.

"Hey, Love."

"You ok?" I push the door closed and pad softly across the room and climb onto the bed, curling into his warm body.

"I am."

"You left."

His hand brushes through my hair as my leg crosses over his and my hand finds a place on his chest. "I just needed some space."

"Do you want me to leave?"

"Never," he says, pulling me on top of him.

"Do you want to talk about it?"

He lets out a low hum. "I just want to lie here with you for a bit."

"Ok." My hands fall to his side as I find my comfy place on his chest. He's going to get hot wearing me like a blanket, but cuddling with him is one of my favorite things.

Run!

The woods of Infernus are whipping by in a flash as sticks and twigs break under my feet.

No. Not under my feet, behind me.

They're getting closer.

Chancing a glance over my shoulder, I see her floating towards me like she's the snakes on her head.

Medusa.

My eyes quickly dart away, but it's too late. My legs slowly get heavier, like I'm running with dried cement on my feet. Looking down, panic tears through me.

Stone.

I'm slowly turning to stone. I can't move. My pulse continues to beat faster and faster, knowing this is it.

The end.

I've felt her stalking me, eager to catch me off guard, and she finally has.

Push.

Run faster.

My legs continue to move forward, but I can feel the weight crawling up my legs, past my knees. The soft earth swallows me up as I fall. The dirt and grass etch deep into my fingernails as I push and scrape to escape, but she continues stalking towards me with an evil smile on her face.

The stone continues to spread up my body slowly, like lava hardening over the ground.

"Where do you think you're going?" Her hands fall to either side of my hips as her body slides over me. Her warm breath blows across my face as the snakes on her head dance and sway with her words.

"Leave m-" The words get stuck in my throat as her finger brushes over my lips.

"Shh," the snakes all hiss, elongating the s.

Medusa slowly bends down and brushes her lips over my breast, as the snakes on her head turn into small penii. Dozens of them, moving and wiggling like snakes, but clearly not snakes.

What in the hell is happening?

Her lips trail down my stomach as her fingers latch around my underwear and she drags them down, exposing my pussy.

Her fingers have the magic touch, reversing the stone wherever she touches. They rub along the tops of my thighs and up the center of my pussy, and I can feel my arousal seeping out of me.

No!

This is not right.

This should not be happening.

The fake moon hangs high in the sky, staring at me. Judging me while my body betrays me. It's eager to feel her mouth on my clit and her hands on my breasts.

Her tongue swipes up the center and the sensation of it makes me feel like I'm about to explode. Tingles shoot up my arms and back as I arch it off the ground. My hands want to move to her head to hold her in place, but the mini penis snakes are still there, so my fingers dig into the ground.

"So wet," her voice deepens as she continues.

Fuck. She's an expert. My orgasm is knocking on the door. My stomach tightens and moans are escaping as my body wiggles and writhes on the soft ground.

Her tongue slips in while the penis snakes run up my body, two of them clamping over my breasts and sucking simultaneously. Another... several... snake around and I can feel them slide into me.

Fuck!

This is so inappropriate, but fucking hell, is it magical.

I moan out as my eyes pinch closed.

"Come on, baby." Her voice is even deeper and sounds like Emmett.

Emmett.

My guys.

I'm betraying them. Where are they?

The door on the other side of the woods opens. I can feel them, their presence, getting closer. I want to reach out to them. Call out. But I can't. I'm chasing my orgasm.

She continues to suck on my clit as the penis snakes continue to pulse inside of me. My orgasm crashes around me, sending my mind spiraling. My back lifts off the ground as I hug her face to my pussy and ride it.

"Good girl."

My eyes fly open and I'm back in the bedroom with Emmett between my legs as I'm chasing my orgasm. The orgasm he gave me, not Medusa.

"Emmett," I breathe out, relief pouring through me.

He chuckles, pulling away from me for a second. "Who did you think I was?"

"Medusa..."

He lets out a low hum and looks across the room at Jax, who's standing at the door, watching. His dark eyes are focused on Emmett, tucked between my legs.

"Where are the others?"

"Tony and Lizzy are still out on their walk and Knox and Callum went to the shopping center just off the island to pick up some dinner for everyone."

"Oh." Why is my heart pounding out of my chest? I mean, sure, it's coming down from one of the strangest orgasms I've ever had, but this is different. It's the three of us... again.

"Oh," Jax repeats, stepping further into the room, his dark hooded gaze falls on my face.

"Did you watch Emmett eat me out while I was asleep?"

A wicked smile flashes across Jax's face. "I did. Although to be fair, with as much as you were moving, I thought you were pretending to be asleep."

"No. I was having some fucked up dream about Medusa and penis snakes."

"Is that why you were moaning so much?"

"Fuck you, Jax! I was making her moan, not her dreams." Emmett rocks back on his hind legs, with his shirt off and his cock hard and pressing at the seam of his pants.

The cool glance Jax tosses Emmett would have made my panties melt if I was still wearing any.

Holy fuckballs!

Jax's gaze turns to me as he continues to move slowly to the bed, like a cat stalking its prey. "What should we do? It's our last night here, and the house is empty."

My stomach clenches and a heat races across my body. "Jax," I whisper out.

"We can do... *anything.*"

My excited gaze flits from Jax to Emmett, who heard the same unspoken words I did. Is this happening? Finally? I'm like a kid in the candy store wanting to flit to all the candy all around me, but indecision keeps me planted in one spot.

"What do you want to do, Everlee?" his voice is low and sultry. He pulls his shirt off and lets it fall to the floor and messes with the waistband of his pants.

A smile curls on the corner of his lips and I know it's because I'm moaning. He usually points it out, but I'm moaning for him, for us, for what could happen.

"Tell us what you want, love," Jax says, giving me control. Is this his way of giving me what I want because he wants it too, but is still too scared to take it? To sample it?

"Anything off limits?" I ask, eyes fixed on Jax.

He shakes his head from side to side slowly and my chest swells with air.

"Use your words, Jax."

He smirks, no doubt finding the reversal of our roles humorous. "No. Nothing is off limits."

"Emmett?"

"No," he says quickly, but not over eagerly.

"Good. Now, both of you take your pants off and climb onto the bed while I grab the lube." Hesitation, or maybe concern, is etched across Jax's face. The same look is on Emmett's, but I imagine it's for different reasons. "Don't worry guys. Safety first." I wink and climb off the bed, sprinting to the bathroom Emmett shares with Knox and grab the lube.

When I walk back into the room, both of the men are naked and laying on their sides facing one another with their heads propped up on one hand.

"Now... who to please first..." I climb onto the bed and plant myself in the small space between them, looking at each of them.

I have to navigate this situation delicately because even though I think Jax wants it as much as Emmett and I do, he's still scared to admit it. Problem is, I'm a bull in a fucking china shop sometimes, so...here goes nothing.

My hand wraps around Jax's cock, while I lean over and press my lips to Emmett's tip. He's already still so hard from earlier and wet with hints of arousal on his tip. Wrapping my hand around the base of his cock, I suck him fully into my mouth until he hits the back of my throat.

"Fuck," he sighs, rotating his hips up, pressing himself into my mouth again.

Not wanting to push him too far, I suck him a few more times, then back off his cock and turn to Jax. "Do you want to taste Emmett on my lips?" My hand is gliding up and down Jax's cock as I inch my face closer to his, but stop just above him. Waiting.

A second later, I have my answer. He wraps his hand around the back of my head and pulls me down into a kiss, his tongue invading my mouth like a pirate searching for lost treasure. My insides clench as I fight not to give in and take what I want right now. This time is about us getting to explore each other, but damn it... I don't know if I can hold out.

"Easy, Jax," Emmett warns, his finger swiping up my center. "She's fit to be fucked and dripping down her leg."

He stops kissing me and pushes me away with his chin, giving me a quick peck before he moves his hand off the back of my neck.

Sitting up, head in a daze, I swallow and steady my focus. "Well, then," I mumble.

Jax pushes off the bed. "Then I say we give her what she wants." He grabs my arm and spins me around, pressing me to the bed beside Emmett. We lock eyes for a brief second, trying to figure out what's going on. "Do you think I don't see the glances you two share?" Jax says, sliding down my body. "See the way you look at me?" Jax flicks his eyes to Emmett as he leans down and presses his mouth on my pussy and swipes his tongue up the center. "Fuck, you taste so good." He plants kisses along my stomach and takes my left breast in his mouth, letting his hard cock slide between my wet pussy. "Emmett." He points to my right breast and Emmett takes it in his mouth without hesitation.

Their hips are grinding their cocks against my leg, so I reach my hands down and grab both their cocks and let them fuck my hands. Slurps and moans fill the air around us, as they nearly send me to another orgasm by sucking on my nipples.

"Wait," I pant out. "I was supposed to be in charge."

"Then take charge," Jax commands with a mischievous grin.

Our eyes lock for a second, like he's giving me his power through our stare. Taking a deep breath, I mumble out, "I want you two to kiss." When they both stare at me, I hurriedly continue. "It's been one of the kinks I want to try on. I see other guys doing it at the club and I find it hot... like really hot. And well, both of you... you're mine, and already super hot... so if you were kissing... then I may damn near explode." I hate I sound so unsure. Where is Sammie when you need her? She'd probably be like kiss now minions in a deep voice then crack a whip in the air, because that's what badasses do.

But I'm not a domme, nor am I a domme in training. Perhaps I can be one day, though?

I'm still laying on the bed with both guys on their knees beside me facing each other. Jax looks from me to Emmett, then slowly moves in. My heart is pulsing and my legs are wiggling with excitement as my pussy pulses.

Emmett leans in some, cautious, slow. Jax closes the distance and their lips touch softly right in front of me. Both are scared, timid, but they don't stop. Jax shifts his weight on his knees and brings his hand up and places it on Emmett's cheek and Emmett mirrors him on the other side.

I take the opportunity to squirt just a little lube in my hands and grab each of their cocks and slowly glide my hand up and down their hard shafts. Their eager moans are music to my ears.

Their kiss deepens and Jax thrusts his hips, rocking his cock into my hand harder and faster. He's moaning louder and moves his hand to behind Emmett's head as he inches closer to him. Their tongues are pulsing in and out, like they have to taste each other now or they'll never get the chance again.

Jax is moving and pumping and thrusting so fast and erratically, like his body is about to explode with... passion and he can't control it. After a few moments, I realize I've stopped moving my hand and I'm just watching them, so I scoot back in the bed to see how far they will go on their own. Within seconds of me moving from between them, their bodies crash together as their cocks feverishly seek each other out.

Holy fucking hell, this is so hot.

My fingers slide down my body, finding my needy little cunt. I'm so wet and slick my fingers glide effortlessly around my clit and pussy.

Jax pushes Emmett back onto the bed as their kiss deepens, like it's been years in the making. Years of pent-up desire and lust that have been pushed down and have now found a crack to escape from. Their cocks glide along one another, seeking friction, pressing and rubbing.

A moan escapes my lips as my fingers thrust inside of me, imagining it's their cocks. My fingers can't move fast enough, as tingles shoot inside of me like fireworks. My other hand slides up my body to my breast and I pinch my nipple hard, imagining it's Jax. He's always so rough with me and knows just how I like it.

My orgasm crashes into me without warning and I buck off the bed as my finger finds my clit and continues to push it along.

"Shit," I hear mumbled.

Opening my eyes from my blissed out state, I find both of the boys staring at me with a love drunk stare. "What? What's wrong?"

"We're completely ignoring you," Jax says, with guilt weighing on every word.

"Please," I scoff. "I don't always need you touching me to get me off," I wink. "Watching you both was plenty."

Jax chortles and pushes himself off Emmett and stalks across the bed to me. "You don't need me touching you?" His eyes darken and a ball lodges itself in my throat. "You don't need my hands on you?" His fingers trace themselves up my leg, brushing beside my pussy, just enough to tease it and make me groan out in frustration. "You don't need my lips on you?" He bends down, his warm breath dances just above my nipple, making it impossibly hard.

Is it possible for a nipple to explode from being too hard?

He glides up my body, his dripping cock brushing against the outside of my thigh while his lips float just above my neck. My body is a wriggling, writhing mess of need.

Emmett moves across the bed and settles between my legs and I almost shout out in glee, but then Jax looks at him slowly from over his shoulder. "No."

"No?" I whimper out, like a puppy whose mother's teat has just been pulled away.

"No. I want his delicious mouth wrapped around my cock while you sit on my face."

"Fuck me," I pant. My head literally just pulsed with excitement, like I could feel my entire body clench and release. My sight went blurry for a second, then refocused.

Jax smiles. "We plan to, Squirt." He tosses a glance at Emmett who is nearly salivating at the mouth.

"I get to watch him, though."

"I'd expect nothing less, love," Jax coos.

Jax lies on the bed as I crawl up to hover above his face and Emmett takes his place between Jax's legs.

"Take care of our girl, Jax."

All of my dreams are coming true.

Jax pulls me down on top of him and moans out as his tongue swipes up my middle. Emmett and I lock eyes as his hand grips around Jax's cock. He sinks slowly onto it and the room freezes.

Time.

The world.

Everything stops moving except for us.

Watching Emmett take Jax's gigantic cock in his mouth sets my body on fire. Jax's tongue stops moving for a second, but his hands grip tighter onto my thighs. I'd bet my entire paycheck, if I were to look at Jax right now, his eyes would be in the back of his head.

Emmett slowly drags his tongue and lips back up and looks at me. The look is... hard to describe. It's like pure fucking magic. My body wants to ride Jax's face until I squirt down his throat, but the other part of me wants to take this slowly. Savor every second of this.

Emmett goes back down again, and I slowly grind on Jax, letting his tongue spear me.

JAX - ANYTHING

HOLY FUCKING SHIT.

Holy fucking shit.

His mouth.

His goddamn perfect mouth is wrapped around my cock.

Holy shit.

It's perfect.

I'm going to fucking blow my load down his throat in like two seconds, which would be super fucking embarrassing, but goddamn.

Fucking Everlee. She did this. I love her so much, but I don't know if I should be mad or happy. Mad because I can't see any other way in the future besides this. Mad because it took me so long. Mad because I love it so fucking much. Or happy. Happy this is finally happening. Happy that she loves us and we love her more than anything in the world and are able to explore this side of ourselves without fear.

Oh goddamn, he just went down again.

So slow.

So painfully slow.

I want to thrust my hips and fuck his mouth, but I know the second I do, I'm done for. He sucks cock so good. Fuck me, why did I wait so long? We'd toyed around with girls before and he would let me take him in the ass, but we didn't do it all the time. And that was on me. I liked it too much and didn't want to give in to those feelings.

Shit. Shit. Shit. He just took me to the hilt and the back of his throat just tensed around my cock. Everlee is grinding on my face, because I'm a selfish piece of shit who can't focus on her right now when I should be. No. Instead, she's having to get herself off.

Again.

No.

Fuck that.

My hands grip tightly around her thighs so I can pull her down and drive my tongue into her. She lets out a moan of appreciation as my tongue spears her. She's so wet she's nearly sliding off my face. I knew she wanted this. Wanted us. She's perfect. So fucking perfect. She was made for us and I'm not- we're not - letting her go anywhere. I will give her anything she wants. Marriage? Kids? I will find a way to make it happen for her. She is my everything. Our everything.

My head spins and I feel drunk. Drunk from love.

"Damn," Everlee moans out, riding my face harder. "Emmett..." she sighs, "watching you is about to make me come down Jax's throat."

He lifts his head up. "Drown him, Trouble." His hand tightens on my cock and the second his lips move over it, her legs tighten around my head and she's squirting into my mouth. I hurriedly swallow down, ignoring the feeling of being waterboarded because I love it.

"Oh, fuck!" She screams out, trying to lift off my face, but my hands tighten around her legs, holding her to me. My tongue swirls around as I suck her clit. I want her to feel all the pleasure she's given me.

"I've... never..." she pants as she convulses on my face and then collapses down. "That was intense."

With the space between her pussy and my lips open, I suck in a large gulp of air.

She pops her head up and looks at Emmett. "Will you fuck me? I want to feel your pierced cock inside of me."

He pulls off my dick and looks at her. "Trouble. You never need to ask if I will fuck you. The answer will always be a resounding hell yes."

"Will you fuck me... while Jax fucks you?" She leans to the side and turns her head to look at me, along with Emmett.

"Yes."

She squeals in excitement and I can't help but laugh. "You're a dork."

She bites my inner thigh near my cock, causing me to gasp out. "Say it again," she threatens.

"Dork."

She bites me again, so I grab her hips and pull her pussy back to my face and bite her on the inside of her thigh.

"Ouch, asshole," she yells affectionately, climbing off me.

Sitting up, I grab her arm and pull her over to me, her face inches from mine. "I love you so goddamn much, Everlee. I will give you any and everything you could ever want in this world. Anything." I lower my head and her eyes grow wide, like she knows what I'm saying.

"Jax," she whispers, and I press my finger over her lips.

A tear forms in her eye, melting every hard edge of me. I may have just royally fucked up, but I don't care. I mean it. I will give her whatever she wants.

My lips crash to hers as she crawls onto my lap, pressing our bodies together. I catch E's gaze over her shoulder, but I can't read his expression.

She pulls away and reaches over to grab the lube off the bed. "Let's get our fuck on, boys."

I choke out a laugh.

Her humor is her defense mechanism, and I let her have it. She's scared I will change my mind, but I won't. We just have to figure out how to get the others on board.

Two minutes later, she's bending over the edge of the bed with her ass up in the air, with Emmett behind her. His hands are smoothing over her ass just before his hands clamp onto her hips.

"Take me, E." She tosses a wild glance over her shoulder at us.

EMMETT – PEACHES AND CREAM

THIS WOMAN.

This perfect fucking woman.

Her ass is as smooth as silk under my calloused hands and here she stands, bent over the bed, waiting for me.

For us.

Moments ago, I had Jax's cock in my mouth and my god, it was a treat. For years, I've seen it and wondered what it would taste like. Would feel like. He was so hard and the taste of his arousal that was leaking out of his cock for me... perfection. My heart is so full I feel like it could burst right now into a thousand pieces, and it's all because of this woman.

Grabbing my cock by the base, I drag it up her dripping wet pussy. So slick. It takes everything I have not to press in and let it swallow my cock.

My chest presses to her back as my lips fall beside her ear. "I love you and I'm going to show you how much. You're going to be calling our names as you come so fucking hard around my cock. I want you to feel Jax fucking me into you."

She turns her head to the side with a small grin. "I'm about to come just from your words."

Lining up my cock, I press it into her hard and fast. She juts forward on the bed and lets out a sigh of pleasure. Rotating my hips, I make sure to hit every part of her before I slowly pull out. I angle my hips and press in again, and then again, and then again. She presses back into me and I pause when I feel Jax's hand slide from around my back, up my chest, to my nipple ring.

"Are you done playing around now?" Jax toys.

My cock twitches inside of Everlee and my stomach clenches.

Jax slides his other hand up my back to between my shoulder blades and presses me down on Everlee. The cap of the lube clicks behind me as anticipation pulses through me. It's been a while since Jax has taken me like this. He's only done it a few times, then stopped. We never talked about it, rather just let it fade away.

But now. Now I'm so fucking ready to have him take my ass. His finger swipes over my hole and I let out a sigh, burying my face between Everlee's shoulder blades.

"Do you want to take my cock, E?" he asks as his lubed finger presses in slightly.

A strangled moan escapes as my tongue forgets how to make words.

"I need to hear your words, E. You know the rules."

Fucking yes, daddy. That's what I want to shout, but nothing comes out. His finger is pulsing in my ass and I'm about to fucking explode inside of Everlee's tight, wet pussy.

"Yes." My lips close around Everlee's skin as I give her a kiss.

Jax continues to work my hole with his finger, prepping me for his girth. One finger, then two, and lastly three. Within minutes, I'm a moaning mess of need. Everlee's pussy is quivering around my cock, not helping the situation at all. I'd like to get at least one pump before I come inside of her.

Jax pulls his fingers out and the cap of the lube closes.

This is it.

His hands find my hips as he presses the tip of his cock at my entrance. He slowly pushes in and my world lights up like the Fourth of July. Sparks are shooting all over my skin as he sinks in deeper.

"E. I love the way your ass takes my cock." He presses in a little further, letting the muscle stretch around him.

I'm biting at Everlee's skin and sucking. Anything I can do, because the feeling is driving me wild.

He slowly pulls out to the tip, then pushes in again, this time a little faster. My back arches up and my cock drives deeper into Everlee as she lets out a moan. I can't take it anymore.

I piston my hips back and forth, pressing my ass back onto Jax and pushing into Everlee. Moans and wet slaps take over, and then a second later, Jax is taking control again and pushing into me. Fast. Meeting his rhythm, I push into Everlee.

She pushes off the bed, changing the angle of the entrance so her finger can work her clit.

"It's like I can feel you fucking Emmett into me, Jax." Her words are short and quick.

"I'm fucking both of you, baby." With his words, he unleashes, driving into me faster and faster.

"I'm about to come," I moan out.

"Not until she does, E."

"Fuck me," I say through clenched teeth.

"No, I've had... I don't know how many orgasms. You go."

"No," Jax says firmly.

She cuts her eyes over her shoulder at Jax, who just chuckles as he repositions his hand on my back. When I look over my shoulder, I find his eyes focused on where we're connected. He's watching his cock play hide and seek with my ass and it's so fucking erotic. My stomach clenches and a tingle shoots up my spine as my balls begin to tighten. Oh fuck! Fuck! I can't come before Ev.

I wrap my hand around her waist and find her beautiful wet pussy and focus in on her clit. She can get off with our cocks inside of her, but clitoral stimulation is the sure way to get her. Circling my finger feverishly, I lean over and plant soft kisses up her spine, then lock onto her neck and suck. I've seen the marks that Jax leaves and know she likes it. Something about this moment. I want to claim her like Jax is claiming all of me.

"E!" she shouts, then buries her head on the bed, hands squeezing onto the comforter.

I bite and suck harder as my finger presses and circles. She pushes back on my cock, taking control, and now I'm being fucked both ways. In some ways, I feel like the conduit between Jax and Everlee fucking, with the way they're both riding me.

"You need to hurry E. I'm too fucking close to exploding inside of you."

"Do it!" she grunts out.

"Fuck!" Electricity shoots through me like a wildfire, and I can't control it. Jax may have better orgasm control than I do, but damn... he's not currently being fucked both ways right now.

A guttural moan purges itself from my body as I explode inside of her. I think this is the most powerful orgasm I've had in my entire life because it feels like a fire truck hose letting loose. My knees buckle and with it, Jax's cock. He grabs me up, pausing for a moment, letting me regain my strength before he continues.

I pull out of Everlee and flip her around on the bed and bury my face in her pussy. Her arousal is mixed with my come, but I don't care. Focusing on her clit, I suck and roll my tongue as I push three fingers inside of her. Jax is close, but I know he won't come until she does, so I aim for all her sweet spots that I've learned. Where she likes it. How she likes it. The pressure.

Curling my fingers, I press as I continue to suck and lick.

"Emmett." she moans, fisting the comforter, digging her head in looking at the wall behind her. She's close, but this isn't her first couple of orgasms, so it's fighting.

"Watch us, baby girl. Watch Jax take me. Do you enjoy watching him?"

Her head curls back around and her eyes lock on me, then swing up to Jax, who has slowed down for a second.

"This is what you wanted? Do you want me to tell you how it feels to have him so deep inside of me?"

"E," she pants, scraping her teeth over her bottom lip.

She does. My words are helping push her orgasm to the edge.

"How rock hard he feels? How every thrust is like fireworks exploding inside of my body?"

Jax clears his throat. "You have to stop talking, E, or I'm going to come so fucking hard in your ass."

"Do it. It's yours. Fuck me, Jax. Claim me."

Everlee moans out, grabbing her breasts.

"Your ass takes my cock so good. Do you like it?"

"I fucking love it," I cry as he pushes in.

My mouth falls back onto Everlee's clit and my fingers pulse faster. Snatching the lube off the bed, I quickly put some on my fingers and press one at her hole. God, I wish I could press my cock in her ass right now and take her like Jax is taking me. Maybe next time.

She's close.

Her hands lock onto the side of my head, as her body hurls itself off the bed and her legs squeeze around my head as she rides my face.

I press my finger all the way in and she shudders, screaming out our names with a whole other line of jumbled words. A second later, Jax is groaning and his thrusts come in staccato'd juts. When he's done, he slowly pulls out and we both fall onto the bed beside Everlee.

"Well, that was unexpected," she mumbles, curling her head into my chest, with her back pressing against Jax's.

"Was it though?" I ask playfully.

She puts her finger over my lips. "Shh."

"Are you going to sleep on us, Squirt?"

"No," she mumbles with closed eyes.

"Why don't I believe you?"

"Orgasms... take a lot of... energy out of me. And I just had, like, fifty twenty."

"That many?" Jax retorts and I smack his arm. Our eyes lock and there's something there. Something that wasn't there before.

A connection.

A wanting.

His eyes squint at me, then he reaches over Everlee and lets his hand fall across my back. I do the same, reaching over Everlee and holding him as well. This is perfect. We are perfect.

I don't know what this means, but I can't wait to find out.

Jax is finally letting down his walls with me, and I couldn't be more excited. And it's all thanks to Everlee.

"I love you," I whisper against her skin before I give her a kiss. She doesn't hear me because she's passed out. Her breath is deep and heavy and she looks like a beautiful angel.

EVERLEE - WHAT A WEEK

THE SHAKING OF THE bed wakes me up sometime later. I really tried not to fall asleep, but damn it. Orgasms are like my melatonin. Take more than four and out you go.

When I roll over, the bed is empty, but still warm, and I hear the shower running in the bathroom.

When I push the door open, Emmett and Jax are in the shower and my heart swells.

"Come on Ev," Emmett encourages.

"I don't think there's enough room." There really wasn't. It was a standard size shower and those two men were taking up nearly every inch.

"There is always room for you, love." Jax tosses out his arm and gives me a nod, encouraging me to come over.

"I'm looking at us and looking at the shower. There is no room. It's ok though."

Jax rinses the shampoo out of his hair and steps out of the shower. "I'm done."

"Jax." I frown.

"I am. Promise. But I will stay and watch you two." He pumps his eyebrows at us. He plants a quick peck on Emmett's lips before he steps out of the shower, then walks over to me and cups both of my cheeks in his hands and places his forehead against mine. "I love you."

His words feel like there is more weight to them than just the usual I love you. I didn't want to push so soon, but I feel like what happened earlier is the beginning of something new. A new chapter in our lives. The fact they were in here taking a shower together when I walked in is a testament to that.

Fifteen minutes later, the three of us are walking down the stairs at the same time Lizzy and Tony are walking in from the beach. Her hair is a mess and there's sand all in it.

"Pleasant walk?" I nod and pull at my hair.

"Fuck me," Lizzy groans. "I was attacked by privates."

"Do you mean pirates?"

"That's what I said."

"You said privates."

"Well, that too." She winks and bats her hand over her shoulder as she walks upstairs.

"Hurry up, Captain Hooker!"

"Why do I have to be the hooker?" Tony whines, following her like a love drunk puppy.

"Have you seen yourself? Clearly, if one of us was going to hooker and one was going to pimp... I would be the natural pimp." Their door closes and a second later Lizzy is screaming and laughing.

"Well, then. It's our last night here." I frown, looking around.

"Did you have a wonderful vacation?" Emmett asks, sliding his arms around me and resting his chin on my shoulder.

"I did. Definitely didn't go as expected with my mom showing up, but in some ways I'm glad she did. She got a chance to meet all of you and then... *meet* all of you. Hopefully, once she tells dad, she'll still be cool with it."

"I'm glad your parents know about us. I know that was hard for you," Emmett says, spinning me in his arms and pushing my hair behind my face. He stares at me, his eyes holding mine like there's so much he wants to say but doesn't know where to start.

I don't know what's going to happen between him and Jax or, if anything, will. Jax has always been so guarded, but hopefully after this week. After today. He can let down some of his walls and let us in.

Him and Emmett have always had a unique relationship than the others, so who knows what the future will hold.

The front door opens behind us, and Callum and Knox are walking in holding several large pizza boxes. "Oh looky loo, who's up from their nap," Knox chimes across the foyer.

"Good naps?" Callum asks, his eyes raking up and down me, leaving my stomach clenching. How is it possible that I can get so turned on with his glance after just having sex? It's not like I was left unfulfilled, because I was very fulfilled. Over and over again, both physically and literally, and even emotionally.

Not right now, but soon, I need to talk to Jax. He's grown so much in the last month alone and I want him to know I see that. It's important he knows I see it and that I love him even more for it.

"Do I smell pizza?" Lizzy shouts, opening her door with her hair wrapped up in a towel.

"Yes, darling," Knox coos. "Delightful walk?"

"The best ever!"

Emmett and I stay standing in the middle of the floor while everyone moves around us. Almost like one of those scenes in the movie where they show the couple standing there in bliss watching the world move around them in a blur... only it's not a blur. This is my life. These are my people.

Somehow, I managed to find four guys I'm obsessed with and who are equally as obsessed with me, who love me un-conditionally. My best friend knows, and now my family. On Monday, I'm handing in my resignation and will work full time at Allure. A sex club I partially own.

Some people looking at my life from the outside could say I'm moving way too fast, but I don't agree. I'm moving at the pace that makes sense for us all. It's like we were all meant for one another and were just waiting to find each other. Most of my life, and especially with Richard, I felt like I was swimming upstream. Finally, for once, I'm cruising down the stream in a unicorn floaty sipping an Old Fashioned and life couldn't be better.

Emmett scoops me up and slings me over his shoulder, and I let out a squeal of laughter.

"Dinner on the back porch for our last night," Callum commands. "We can watch the moon dance on the waves."

Knox takes the stack of paper plates in his hand and smacks them against my ass.

"Careful, Knox, or you may end up in the pool."

"I'd like to see you try."

"I'll gladly toss your ass in," Jax chimes, walking up behind us.

"This is an Everlee and me situation."

"Hate it for you. But I come with Everlee."

"Really?" Lizzy asks, clearly wanting to poke the bear. "She always says you come after her."

"Lizzy!" I smack and kick at Emmett so he will put me down.

"I don't think that's a good idea right now. I'm hungry and I'm fairly certain if I let you down, all of us will somehow end up in the pool."

Jax tilts my chin up and presses his lips to mine. "I got you, boo." He winks. "Hey Knox. Come here for a second. I want to show you something."

"Bullshit," he says, finding a chair and hugging the pizza boxes like they're his lifeline. "Jax. I don't trust you. In fact, I don't trust any of you. Maybe Tony. He seems like a good dude."

"Thanks man," Tony says, walking outside, pulling his shirt down. He looked freshly washed and wet, just out of the shower.

A few minutes later, we're all sitting around the pool, listening to the waves crash in the distance and enjoying the last hours of our beach vacation. What a week it's been!

Bloopers

<u>COCK THAT I'LL DO</u>

"Let's play a little game." She's thinking, clearly a game she's making up on the fly and then she smiles. "I shall call the game... Cock-that-I'll-do... kind of like cock-a-doodle-do."

"Yes, yes, go on," Knox says, rubbing his chin like a nerdy professor who's deep in thought.

"You will all lay on the bed with blindfolds on, in a circle. I will be in the middle, and I will suck your cocks in a circle and the last one to... moan, twitch, or move in any way, will get to fuck me first.

What's coming next?

As mentioned in the other books, Halloween will be the next holiday. This one will be a little different. Think about the shows you watch and how they sometimes do "In another world" around Halloween. Maybe I'm making it up, but that's what I will be doing. The Halloween holidate book will be our fave five meeting again, but in a paranormal world. What do you think they will be? Vampire? Shifter? Troll? This book will be a "standalone" if you will... someone who hasn't read the holidate series, or only reads paranormal, will be able to pick up this book and read it without being lost. But never fret faithful followers. You will see Easter eggs throughout the book and perhaps hints and clues that have been dropped and planted throughout the series will be revealed. MUUUHAHAHAHAHA!

I will likely have a human progress report at the end of the book checking in to see where our fave five are. Probably a chapter or three ;)

About the Author

Hi friends! Follow me below for all the updates, behind the scenes and bonus content!

You can always email me at authorsnmoor [at] gmail.com or message me below. I do rely more on facebook, Insta and TT for most of my communication.

Website
Etsy Shop AuthorSNMoor
Tiktok@authorsnmoor
Instagramsn_moor
FacebookSN Moor Author — Author SN Moor Fan Group
GoodreadsS.N. Moor
Amazon